THE MURDER LEDGER

P. L. HANDLEY

For Sarah, Ellis and Morgan

CHAPTER 1

Everything must balance.

Alun Hughes could hear his late father's words as if they were being drummed into the base of his skull. It was a motto he applied to every aspect of his life: cooking, cleaning, work — even his long term relationship. Balance was everything.

Alun Hughes Senior, a lifelong accountant and the proud founder of *Hughes & Son Accountancy Services*, had always taken great pride in being a man of *balance*. After all, a balanced ledger was a happy ledger.

Bookkeeping was about order, and without order, there was chaos. On the morning of June twentieth, the life of Alun Hughes *Junior* was as orderly as it had always been. That was... until Megan called.

Megan had known Alun since they were in college. She was, as the accountant liked to call it, his "debit to his credit". Although these were terms normally associated with the increase and decrease of accounting ledgers, Alun had always found the notion of debits and credits to be quite romantic.

When it came to double-entry bookkeeping, you could never have one without the other.

Megan, on the other hand, did not care for debits and credits. She had also struggled to see the romantic side of her boyfriend's theory, especially when the two words were neatly written out on the inside of her annual Valentine's Day card.

Her personal call to the office that morning had been highly irregular. The hours of nine until twelve were normally dedicated to the completion of quarterly VAT returns, a section of the day that Alun had come to cherish. You always knew where you stood with VAT returns: no small talk, no mixed feelings. Everything was laid out in pure black and white.

Phone conversations, however, were an absolute minefield. It was the opening line of Megan's phone call that should have been the first sign of trouble.

"We really need to talk..."

But it wasn't until the final blow of the last sentence that things really started to look bleak.

"I'm so sorry, Alun."

Megan's decision had come as quite the surprise. Alun was adamant he had done everything in exactly the correct manner; he'd remembered all of the birthdays and all of the Valentine's Day cards; he'd maintained a spotless apartment with everything in its proper place; he'd done all the shopping and planned all of the meals (his colour-coded spreadsheet for the local supermarket run had proven invaluable over the years). He had even scheduled in a time for casual conversation (something he had secretly loathed).

Despite the meticulous planning to ensure everything in his relationship was perfectly balanced, his long-term girlfriend of nine years had just broken up with him.

When he came off the call, the room fell silent, and the VAT returns remained unfinished. He spent a good ten minutes staring at the piles of empty columns, desperately pondering on the best course of action.

Did he finish the returns? Did he cheer himself up with some extra filing? Or, did he open up the bottle of 1972 Highlander that was still sitting in the cupboard?

The taste of malt whiskey against his dry lips came as a welcome relief. He didn't normally drink alcohol at ten in the morning and had been saving the bottle until the end of another financial year (a time of great joy and celebration). Toasting the culmination of twelve months of work had been a tradition introduced by his late father. It wasn't easy running a local accounting firm single-handedly, but the Hughes family had done so for two generations. Having no staff had meant a lot more work, but it had also provided a lot less room for error. *Hughes & Son* were not an accountancy firm that made mistakes.

After a few more sips of whiskey, the figures on Alun's desk were soon dancing around him like a plague of insects. He had never been much of a drinker (a clear head and a cup of camomile tea was always more productive).

That day's impromptu bout of careless indulgence had eventually found him rummaging around in his father's meagre collection of CDs. By the time his bottle was half-empty, he had decided that a spot of music would be a good idea. The old disk player in the back cupboard had not seen the light of day for over ten years. Alun had always preferred to work in silence. Any form of distraction had been strictly avoided, but now he craved all the distractions in the world. The onset of negative emotions were already starting to cloud his judgement – even more than the whiskey. He needed to free his mind, and his father's old copy of *Shania Twain's Greatest Hits* would have to do.

The choice of music had started off on quite an upbeat note, with the lyrics of "That don't impress me much" having prompted the accountant into a careless dance routine around the office. But it was the flurry of slow songs like "From this moment on" and "You're still the one" that had resulted in the breakdown. By track eight, he was lying in a pile of scattered invoices, balling his eyes out at the memory of his long-term girlfriend. He was crying so much that he didn't even hear the doorbell.

It was only after the loud music had started to die down, at the end of yet another cruel love song, that he caught the end of a giant banging noise against his front door. Using his last ounce of willpower and determination, he picked himself up off the whiskey-stained paperwork and stumbled over to the hallway. It had been a while since he last stood up, and the reality of his intoxicated body was soon made clear by an accidental trip across his own foot. The stumble was so unexpected that it sent him straight into the glass of a framed accounting qualification.

"Is everything alright in there?" asked a female voice.

Alun jolted upwards like an intrigued meerkat. The voice from outside had sobered him up for a moment.

Was it Megan?

He buttoned up his crumpled shirt and frantically tried to address the state of his ruffled hair.

Had she come round to apologise? Had it all been a huge mistake?

The front door swung open to reveal a young woman in smart clothes and a concerned face. It wasn't Megan, but the person was very familiar, nonetheless.

"*Alun*?"

The accountant slouched against the doorframe to keep himself upright, his bloodshot eyes studying her like an unexpected tax bill.

"*Rhiannon*?"

For a moment, he saw the resemblance of a girl he had known in school, a girl he had obsessed over for six straight years, until the inevitable disappointment of their graduation party. Standing there before him was a woman in her early thirties. She had aged well – a lot better than he had, at least, and she still possessed the same good looks and wild spirit that she had conveyed to him all those years ago.

"Is this a bad time?" she asked, as they both gazed down at the dark stain across his white shirt.

"Uh, no!" Alun blurted out.

If he had thought walking had become hard, stringing a coherent sentence together was proving downright impossible.

The woman in smart office attire squinted, as she recognised the Shania Twain song blasting out from inside.

"Honestly," she said, "I can come back later."

Alun straightened himself up in a hopeless attempt to look professional. "Have you made an appointment?"

"Do I need one?"

"Well, yes... all clients need an appointment."

Rhiannon made no attempt to hide her disgust.

"Wow, thanks a lot, Alun. It's only been, what – ten years?"

He tilted his head to the side for a quick calculation. "Fourteen years, to be precise. And three months..."

She rolled her eyes. "Well, I guess *you're* the accountant."

Alun watched her pulling out a pack of cigarettes from her handbag. He tried not to judge.

"I haven't come here to get my books done," she continued.

"Oh, okay." The cloud of smoke caused him to choke. He thought about reaching for his inhaler. "Then why *are* you here?"

Another puff of smoke.

"Well, luckily, it's not for this delightful catch-up we're having. How are you by the way? I'm doing just fine. Thanks." She looked down at the whiskey stain again and tried not to judge.

The question was far too much for Alun's drunken mind to

even process. He pulled out his glasses in the hope that they would clear his distorted vision. They did nothing.

"I'm really good. Very good, actually." The words did not come out without a struggle. But they did come out, somehow. He pointed up at the sign above their heads with the words: *Hughes & Son – Chartered Accountants*. "As you can see — I'm a partner now."

He waited for the look of sheer admiration. It never came.

"Oh, wow... so you are." Rhiannon finished her cigarette with a new degree of urgency. "Now, do you mind if I come in?"

Alun squirmed in the doorway, not knowing quite where to turn, as he chose his next words very carefully.

"Uh, well, if it's not my accounting services you require, then... how exactly can I help you?"

Rhiannon sighed and chucked away her cigarette butt. It landed in a nearby plant pot and Alun tried his very best not to protest (he could always remove it later).

"I need to see your ledgers."

The accountant almost choked on his own breath. It was surely the fantasy of any lonely financial advisor to have an attractive young woman appear on his doorstep, asking to see his ledgers. And yet, still, it made him uncomfortable.

"Sorry, excuse me," said Alun with a cough. " You want to see my —"

"That is what you call them, isn't it?" Rhiannon asked. "Ledgers — books — whatever technical term you number crunchers like to use. I need to look through them."

The man standing in her way looked around. He was perplexed and confused. "I'm afraid all of our paperwork is highly confidential..."

He was about to descend into a long-winded explanation of *GDPR* regulation, when the young woman shoved him aside with little hesitation.

"Don't you worry, *Special Agent Hughes*," she reassured him. "Your secrets are safe with me."

It was not the first time Rhiannon had forced her way inside a property without permission. Door-stopping, as they liked to call it in her line of work, had always come easy to her. If the information she needed was only a brick wall away, she would always find a way through in the end. She certainly wasn't about to let Alun Hughes from River Bran Secondary School stand in her way.

Unlike Alun, Rhiannon had very little memory of the boy she vaguely remembered throwing chewing gum on during GCSE Chemistry. Academically, she had performed very poorly during her last years of school. When it came to popularity and athleticism, however, she had thrived. Being captain of the girl's netball team had been far more important back then. Her circle of friends had not included pupils who were top of the class in maths or those strange individuals who graced the stuffy practice room of the school orchestra — and they certainly had not included Alun Hughes, who had also found himself on the far outskirts of her wide but selective social circle.

There were times when Rhiannon wished that her popularity at school could have served her better in the next stages of her life. Unfortunately, it had done very little.

Alun found his intruding guest admiring the recent carnage of his unplanned whisky binge. She tried to ignore the Shania Twain video streaming on his laptop (she had seen a lot worse) and began rummaging through a line of filing cabinets.

"You won't find anything you're looking for in *there*," Alun assured.

She flicked through a series of names, many of them locals that she vaguely remembered from her youth. The name she was looking for didn't come up, and she slammed the first drawer closed in a flash of anger (she had never been patient).

"You don't even know what I'm looking for," she said.

"Then why don't you care to enlighten me," Alun countered. "After all, this is *my* office you're looking through."

Rhiannon stopped searching and turned to face him. His confrontational tone had surprised her. She had already summed him up as a doormat with no backbone. His newfound assertiveness hardly made him Clint Eastwood, but he had a lot more nerve than she gave him credit for.

Nobody was more surprised at his angry comments than Alun himself. The alcohol had given him a Dutch courage that he already disliked. He prepared himself for the worst. This woman standing in front of him, who looked like she could eat him alive, let out a deep sigh and folded her arms.

"Alright," she said. "I'm looking for the accounts of a woman named Mari Doyle."

The name sobered the accountant up again for a moment. For he knew the name well.

"*Mari Millionaire*, you mean?" he asked her.

"That's what you call her, is it?"

"That's what *everyone* calls her."

It was true: Mari had won the National Lottery only a year or so ago. She had been the talk of the town for weeks. It wasn't everyday that someone you knew won the lottery, and Mari Doyle knew everyone.

"So you know the story, then," Rhiannon continued. "Sweet old lady wins big — barely spends a penny of it — and then carries on working at her local flower shop."

"What makes you think she hasn't spent any of the money?"

His question intrigued her, as he knew it would.

"You tell me," she said. "You *were* her accountant."

It was now Alun's turn to be surprised. He could barely ask the question: "What do you mean — *were*?"

Rhiannon's confidence evaporated. She had not intended to let this next particular piece of information slip.

"I don't mean *anything*," she said. The atmosphere in the room had moved from playful to serious very quickly.

Serious conversations had always made the young journalist uncomfortable. She would have hated being a doctor — to be confronted with the horror of delivering bad news to a patient, a person she didn't even really know in the first place. This is why she had always felt it best to keep people fully at arm's length. Personal connections were a waste of time. There were times when she had questioned the impact of this philosophy on her turbulent love life. But those concerns were for another time.

"I'm investigating the woman's disappearance," Rhiannon announced, her chest puffed up and her face smug. "At this point, I'd be surprised if Mari Doyle is even still alive."

CHAPTER 2

"Are you a police officer?" asked Alun.

Rhiannon let out a patronising laugh.

The accountant was surprised how a person could find amusement during such a conversation.

"Police officers need search warrants," Rhiannon said. "I'm a journalist. All we need is a good hammer."

"Which newspaper do you work for?"

Rhiannon shuddered. It was a question she had dreaded. "*The Merioneth Press.*"

A small smirk emerged from Alun's lips. He was hoping for something a little more exciting — a household name, perhaps, such as *The Times*, or, dare he say it, even the *Daily Mail*. Instead, the mention of his town's local newspaper had come as a great disappointment.

"I did used to work for the *Mirror*," she quickly added.

"But not anymore?"

She gritted her teeth. "No. Not anymore."

It hurt her to utter these words; it was still too soon.

"That must have been a big move for you," Alun said, eventually. The look of fury in the woman's eyes implied that he was beginning to tread on delicate ground. "Moving back here to Pengower, I mean. Didn't you move to London after we finished school?"

"Yes, I did. I *used* to live in London. Now I live here."

That was all she was prepared to say on the matter. She was not about to divulge the details of her personal life with a drunken accountant.

"Mari's accounts," she said, firmly. "I need to see them."

Alun saw the desperation in her face. Client confidentiality was a golden rule, especially in a town as small as Pengower. The reality of other people's finances was a responsibility he took very seriously. On the other hand, the suspicious disappearance of Mari Doyle had also made him rather curious. He sensed there would be a lot more to this story. If disclosing a few ledgers would lead to more details, then he was more than willing to oblige. Besides, he already knew there would be nothing of interest.

"They're filed under the letter B, for Blodwen," he said. The journalist's face lit up. "Her maiden name?"

"The name of her limited company."

Rhiannon nodded. She could picture the sign: *Blodwen's Flowers*. The shop had been around for as long as she could remember; that horrible font, those sickly colours. She had never cared for the flowers that much, either.

"Well it's a much nicer name than *Doyle*," she said with a shudder.

Even Rhiannon had recognised that surname when the news came through of Mari's disappearance. She had known a few Doyles at school, and they were not a family to be trifled with. If you messed with one Doyle, you messed with them all. It was certainly not a family she had expected to be associated with that shy woman from the flower shop.

"You remember Ceri Doyle, from school?" Alun asked her. "Mari is her mother."

Yes, Rhiannon *did* remember Ceri Doyle. They had been in the same year and were far from friends (you were only friends with Ceri Doyle if an act of social suicide was on the cards).

"*Scary Ceri*, you mean?" Rhiannon asked, with a smirk. Alun was taken aback by her childish comment. Teenagers could be very cruel — and so could adults, it seemed.

"Sorry..." she said, suddenly. "Old habit."

She was genuinely embarrassed at the accidental throwback to her old, teenage self — the same person who would have quite happily teased another girl to tears if it meant boosting her own position at the top of the adolescent food chain. She could still feel the shame, even after all these years.

Alun and Rhiannon said nothing to each other, whilst the financial records of Mari Doyle were laid out across the floor. Years of expenses and receipts were placed in date order, everything from regular pension payments to weekly shopping bills.

"Hardly anything's changed," Rhiannon said. She chucked away a copy of the woman's most recent bank statement and knelt backwards to view the piles of paper. "She won the lottery only a year ago, but her spending has stayed exactly the same."

"I told you there was nothing exciting," said Alun. "Mari was a highly predictable client. Always has been."

Rhiannon shook her head, almost disgusted. "Are you telling me that she won eighteen million pounds and never actually spent anything? Not even a little splurge?"

Alun smiled. He had been aware of Mari's conservative spending for quite some time and had admired her for it. Many of his clients would often complain of their plummeting bank balances and, yet, would be quite happy to max out their credit cards on a new subscription that they didn't really need. He would have liked to believe that, had *he* won the lottery, he would have acted in the same, exact way.

"Mari is a creature of habit," he said. "She has all her shopping lists and outgoing expenses memorised in her head. She never bought anything she didn't need."

Rhiannon gave him a dismissive frown.

"You almost sound impressed," she said.

Alun shrugged. "I admire her self control."

"Well, I for one could do with a decent handbag and some new boots."

She felt like grabbing hold of the receipts and chucking them into the air. She would have quite happily torched the whole lot had it not been for her manners (it was quite rude to set fire to another person's carpet).

Rhiannon had hoped for at least a tiny morsel of useful information. It wouldn't be long before the police would come sniffing around that same paper trail, and she wanted to be far enough ahead. Surely there was *something* that would lead her to the woman's whereabouts.

Alun watched her rummage through the paperwork for a second time.

"I suppose there was *one* change she made," he said.

The journalist perked up. "And what was that?"

"Shortly after her lottery win, she started renting a house in the middle of town."

"Oh, whoopty-doo..." Rhiannon muttered. Her glimmer of hope had been flattened in an instant. "Who chooses to rent a house when you can buy half the street? Talk about the last of the big spenders."

Alun shrugged. "It would have been a big adjustment for her, I would imagine. She'd previously spent her whole life living out on the family farm. Mari used to cycle four miles to work and back. Never used a car."

"This woman's sounding crazier by the second. No wonder she's gone missing."

Rhiannon looked back down at the paperwork. Even the mere sight of it gave her a headache.

"What makes you so sure Mari's disappeared?" Alun asked her.

"Because it was reported to the police. The tip-off came in yesterday morning, and I heard it from the horse's mouth that afternoon. She has a grandson who cuts her grass every week and does a bit of cleaning. They seem close."

"You've already spoken to her grandson?"

Alun received an annoyed glance in exchange for his seemingly stupid question.

The woman's thoughts raged inside of her: Did he think she was some kind of amateur? *Of course* she had spoken to him. She knew there would be more to this story than a missing person case. *Please* let there be more, she prayed.

"He was more than willing to cooperate," she said. "Anything to spread the awareness of his grandmother's disappearance."

"It would have been very strange if he hadn't," said Alun.

The room went quiet.

"Are you suggesting Jack Doyle murdered his own grandmother?" Rhiannon asked, knowing full well that the blunt question would make him uncomfortable.

"Uh, well no..." The accountant squirmed in his tight shirt and loosened his collar. "I never said anything about *murder*."

"Well Jack seems to think *someone's* murdered her."

"Did he say that?"

"He didn't have to. I read between the lines." Rhiannon stood up. "He's not the brightest lad. In fact, I think he might have some learning difficulties. He might even be autistic."

"That doesn't make him unintelligent. It can be quite the opposite, especially if it's high-functioning."

The reporter turned to him in surprise.

"You're an expert on autism now, are you?" she asked. Alun dodged her eye contact, as he often did with people. He had never been officially tested for autism, or any other mental conditions for that matter, but he *had* been accused of being on the spectrum.

"I'm just saying people shouldn't be underestimated," he said.

Rhiannon sighed. "Well, if Mari Doyle *has* been murdered, the suspect list goes way beyond her grandson. There are plenty of people much higher up the family tree who stand to benefit from the death of *this* old millionaire. Jack seemed pretty concerned, to say the least, and I know a liar when I see one." She picked up the empty CD case on Alun's desk. "Really? *Shania Twain*?"

The accountant blushed.

"My office assistant must have left it behind."

Rhiannon shook her head and gathered up her belongings. "I guess I'm all done here."

Alun followed her back to the front door. He could smell the perfume trailing behind her, like a rope pulling him along. It reminded him of Megan.

"Sorry I couldn't be of more help," he said.

She turned around and, for the first time, he caught the shade of blue in her eyes.

"Sorry I interrupted..." She took one last look around the office. "Whatever it was you were doing."

Alun's mind honed in on the Shania. Had she heard it playing from outside? Surely not.

Rhiannon caught him blushing again. He was a lot better looking than she remembered — not that she remembered very much about dorky, little Alun Hughes (apart from the chewing gum). She normally hated accountants, but this one didn't seem too bad, she supposed.

"Let me know if you think of anything else I might have missed," she added, slipping him a business card. "And yes, before you get any ideas, that is very much my *work* number."

She was quite used to men expecting more than just a phone call. Why they could never accept that she had a job to do — that it wasn't all about *them* and *their* needs — she could never understand.

Alun accepted the card with a blast of disappointment. He had hoped that his meticulous filing system had impressed her enough to meet again, on a more personal basis. Having the most popular girl in school needing his help would have been a teenage dream come true. It seemed that his life hadn't turned out so bad after all.

A minute later, and he was back in the emptiness of his own company. He walked over to the pile of scattered papers on the office floor and thought about Mari Doyle. He had always been fond of her. Clients didn't always bring along cake with them when dropping off their receipts.

The thought of her disappearance continued to niggle him. The thought of *any* unsolved mystery or puzzle was enough to make him sweat. He had once spent an entire night agonising over the disappearance of a missing debit entry on one of his books. Fortunately, he had managed to locate it by the time morning had broken.

"Every bubble will always rise to the surface in the end," his father had always said.

Alun had certainly come across one whopper of a bubble this time, and it appeared it was now time for a strong cup of coffee and a chocolate penguin.

The records of Mari Doyle's finances dated back at least five years. News of the woman's lottery win had created quite the wave of excitement in the office of *Hughes & Son*. The initial thrill, however, had been very short lived.

It had turned out that National Lottery winners were provided with their very own financial advisor. Going from a weekly wage to an eighteen-million-pound deposit was a big shock for anyone, and Mari had been very well looked after. Alun had not even had the chance to even *see* the enormous cheque. Before anyone knew it, the money was safely tucked away in its own private bank account.

Weeks later, and it had been business as usual on the Mari Doyle ledgers. He had presumed that any further excitement was long gone. But he had presumed wrong.

The accountant knelt down amongst the piles of paperwork, as Rhiannon had done not that long before him. His eyes squinted at the various numbers clogging up the pages, his eyelids like mechanical apertures scanning across the narrow columns. Each ledger became a single branch on an ever-growing tree. The reporter's previous rummage would never compare to his own well-trained eyes, which had grown more than accustomed to fishing out small anomalies.

After scouring the details of Mari Doyle's personal bank statements, he moved on to the accounts of her limited company. *Blodwen's Flowers Ltd.* had always boasted a full bill of health when it came to its profit and loss statements. It had produced rather a modest income for a small business, but it was still an income, all the same. Mari was the sole owner, and (with only one additional part-time employee) the shop had served as a stable form of income since the day it first opened. Flowers did not last forever, and her satisfied customers had always come back for more.

No matter what the industry or trade, a company's true DNA could be found deep at the heart of its accounting system. Each ledger was like a web of interconnecting arteries, all flowing with lines of daily transactions. Alun had often likened it to a Jenga tower — remove just one piece of information and the whole balance sheet would fall apart.

Like everything else in his small world, it all came back to *balance*.

The numbers on the floor jumped out at him in a frenzy that many would find highly disorientating. Numbers were prone to do this from time to time, and it was often a good sign that he was closing in on an unwanted irregularity.

Although there were no errors to be found on this occasion, what he *did* stumble on was far more interesting.

Alun stared down at the set of accounts and let out a wide, satisfied smile. It seemed there was indeed a lot more to Mari Doyle's story than her sudden disappearance, and the accountant had found his first clue.

CHAPTER 3

The town of Pengower was nestled deep in the historic county of Merionethshire, North Wales. A sparsely populated and highly mountainous region of the country, the surrounding area boasted its fair share of castles, lakes and tight-knit communities that had all been around for thousands of years.

These days, Pengower was known more for its bustling weekly market and delightful selection of local Welsh cakes. In a town where most people knew each other and secrets were very hard to keep, Saturday mornings had become a popular time for catching up on local gossip.

Alun Hughes had found himself strolling down the busy high street on the warmest morning of the year so far. He generally avoided market day, and the arduous task of navigating his way through the various crowds of people reminded him of why. It had always been strange to see his quiet, little town become swarmed by hordes of excited visitors, all looking for a good bargain and a bite to eat.

Unlike the keen out-of-towners, Alun's focus was not on the range of artisan goods, but on a lonely looking flower shop that appeared to be closed. Standing beside a market stall covered in a range of fragrant soaps, he gazed over at the large sign poking up above the shoppers: *Blodwen's Flowers.*

On the opposite side of the road he saw the name of another shop: *Jones Family Butchers.*

He thought about the discovery he had made the night before. If even just one of his many theories turned out to be correct, the plot was soon about to thicken.

MORWENNA WILLIAMS ANSWERED her door with a pleasantly surprised look on her face.

"Alun..." she said.

"Good morning, Mrs Williams," said the accountant.

The woman in her early-sixties was dressed in a bright pink dressing gown with a mug of tea in her hand.

"What a surprise," she replied. Her face let out a flirtatious grin, and she flicked back her long hair. This was a woman who took very good care of herself, and she wasn't afraid to let other people know it.

"Is Rhiannon in?" asked Alun. They were words his teenage self would have been more than happy to utter. Back then, however, he was not so fortunate.

The older woman seemed disappointed by the mention of her daughter's name.

"Oh, well, yes," she said, taking another quick glance at the young man's slender waist. She had always admired good dress sense in a man, especially one as smart as Alun. Luckily for her, he never left the house unless his shirt was meticulously ironed.

"*Rhiannon*!!"

Her scream carried throughout the house, whilst her playful stare caused the accountant to squirm on the edge of her doorstep. To his great relief, Rhiannon emerged into the hallway in no time at all.

"Alun?" the younger woman asked, even more surprised than her mother. "What are you doing here?"

"Don't be so rude, love," said Morwenna. "He's a good man, this one. Did our books for us last year, didn't you, hun?"

"Uh, yes," Alun replied. "I'd almost forgotten, actually."

"Oh, I haven't forgotten," said Morwenna, her dressing gown now drooping down below her shoulders. "You were such a lovely lad."

Rhiannon caught sight of her mother's wink and wished for the expensive tiles beneath her feet to swallow her whole. "Mum! Can you — *please*?"

Morwenna acknowledged the deathly stare and bid them a reluctant farewell.

Alun let out a sigh of relief and had almost started to relax. Then he saw the furious face staring back at him.

"I told you to call me," Rhiannon snapped. "How did you even know I was here?"

"John-fruit-and-veg told me you'd moved back in with your parents."

"How did *he* know?!"

Alun shrugged. "That man knows everything."

Rhiannon winced in disgust. "God, I hate this town." She looked behind her to make sure nobody was in earshot. "Besides, I've not *moved back in*. I'm staying here until I find my own place."

The accountant nodded as if he believed her.

"Not that properties are flying up on the market everyday," she continued. "Does anyone around here *ever* move house? Just once in their life?" Her eyes caught sight of the folder underneath the man's arm. "What you got in there?"

Alun smiled. He thought she would never ask.

"I did some further analysis after you left," he said. He was determined to enjoy this moment as much as he could and had rehearsed what he was about to say many times over.

"*Analysis*?" asked Rhiannon. This was exactly why she hated accountants. They couldn't just talk like normal people, as if what they did was far more complicated than it was. Now the man thinks he's a doctor, she thought.

"Mari Doyle's accounts..." Alun cleared his throat. The word analysis had been a good choice, after all. "It turns out there is more going on in those ledgers than you might have realised."

She tapped her foot. "In a nutshell, please..."

Her words had thrown him. He had hoped to be invited in, or even be offered to discuss his findings over a nice meal.

"Well," he said, "Your search was more focused on her personal bank statements..."

Rhiannon sighed. Of course it was all *her* fault. "So what *should* I have been looking at?"

The accountant pulled out the folder and began riffling through the papers. He paused for a moment and looked around. The small cul-de-sac was lined with red-bricked houses, all identical to each other. It had been built quite recently, and, if Alun remembered rightly, its properties had not been cheap. It seemed Rhiannon's parents had done alright for themselves.

"Actually..." Alun muttered, giving the quiet neighbourhood another glance. "These records are bit too confidential to be shown out here in the open..."

He watched the pair of blue eyes roll. She had taken the hint.

"Alright, fine," she said. "Come on in, then."

She left him fumbling with his papers and disappeared inside.

When Alun saw her again he was sitting on a luxurious, white sofa in the middle of a living room after his own heart. He loved the minimalist style of modern homes and clearly so did

Mr and Mrs Williams. Their carpet was spotless, and the enormous windows were blinding him with daylight.

"Tea? Coffee?" Rhiannon asked him the questions as if she had been held at gunpoint.

"I'll have an Earl Grey, please, if you have it."

The request was met with great disapproval, and he was soon left to his own devices. He took the opportunity to walk around and admire the tasteful woodwork above the impressive fireplace.

As he went on to run his fingers along the engraved pattern on the enormous oak table, he spotted a cluster of framed photographs with a familiar face. There she was: the teenage girl he remembered from school. Her hair was darker than he had first recalled, and it occurred to him, suddenly, that he was no longer a sixteen-year-old boy. Both of them were rapidly approaching their late thirties and had already lived a sizable chunk of their adult lives, yet here they were, shooting the breeze in her mum and dad's front room. Where had all the time gone?

Just as he began pondering over the shortness of life, he caught a glimpse of someone standing there behind him. In the reflection of the large mirror was a small figure with a pair of curious, wide eyes. Its full head of hair reminded him of a small dog he had seen on his way through the market.

"Oh," he said, struggling to find something else to say. "Hello there..."

His words were met with a high-pitched giggle. Standing in front of him was a small boy in a superhero costume.

Alun looked around the room. Unfortunately for him, he was the only other adult present. One of his greatest fears had come to pass: he was alone with a child.

"What's your name?" he added, slightly annoyed that his greeting wasn't reciprocated. He looked down at the flamboyant red cape. "I suppose I should probably know which superhero you are..."

He tried thinking of names. *Which one was it?* There were far too many superheroes to keep track of these days, anyway. Superman had been more than enough for him. Back in *his* day, *The Avengers* had been nothing more than a dated sixties programme your father still liked to watch.

He decided to take a guess: "Super... *boy*?"

"My name is Thor!" came the angry response.

"Oh. Yes. Of course it is." The accountant couldn't help but question the choice of name. Wasn't Thor a pagan God? It didn't matter, he supposed.

"I see you've met my little Hercules..."

Alun looked over to the doorway to see a proud Rhiannon clutching a tray of hot drinks.

"Actually, the name is *Thor*," he corrected her.

His comment was ignored and the teas were placed down on a coffee table that Alun had been considering for his own home.

"Gwyl, did you want to help Nana in the garden?"

The boy nodded and began flying his way out of the room with his arms held high.

"He seems... nice," Alun said.

"He's always been a trooper," said Rhiannon. "Gwyl's had to put up with a lot of changes recently. Good job he's a strong one."

"Well, he is a pagan God."

Alun's attempt at a joke was met with silence. Perhaps it wasn't the right choice of moment. He could work on that.

"So, let's have it then," she said, looking down at the folder still clutched in Alun's hand. He had always been a clutcher. "Show me this mind-blowing discovery of yours."

The accountant became giddy again. He was more than happy to put the focus back on accounting. It was an area of conversation he felt much safer in, much more than the awkwardness of small talk. He thought about stretching out his finger joints but decided it would probably be too much.

"Mari Doyle's personal finances might not have changed in the last couple of years," he said, "but her *business* accounts tell a different story. It's actually very interesting."

Rhiannon very much doubted it, but she decided to hear him out.

"Her profits and capital have remained exactly the same since before she won the lottery," he continued. "No change there. What's different is her balance sheet." He lifted up a report that might as well have been written in Cantonese as far as Rhiannon was concerned. "You see, a company's net profits can remain unchanged, but the asset and liability amounts can still go up and down — provided they both do."

"And how is this relevant?" asked Rhiannon. "In English, please."

"Well, since the beginning of last year, the company has seen an additional source of monthly revenue. As well as that, it has also seen the exact same increase in expenses."

"What's so interesting about that?"

"Why would a longstanding company suddenly increase its spending, only to receive the same, exact income? It doesn't make any sense. You would just break even." He lifted up an invoice. "Then I discovered that the new outgoing amounts were all going to one supplier."

The reporter peered down at the invoice and saw the company name: *Jones Family Butchers*.

"Dai Jones? The butcher?"

"Exactly," said Alun. His smug grin practically shouted out the words: "Ta-da!"

"Why would a flower shop be paying such large amounts to a butcher?"

The accountant would have happily stood up and taken a bow. He would have also settled for a pat on the head.

Rhiannon looked at one of the bank statements. “Wait, are you telling me that little Mari Doyle has been laundering her own money — all with the help of Dai Jones? Why on earth would she do that?”

Alun shrugged. “Numbers can say a lot, but they can’t tell me everything. There might be one person who will know for sure, though.”

They stared at each other, both knowing full well what the other was thinking. Rhiannon was glad she wasn’t a vegetarian.

CHAPTER 4

"I need you to watch him for me."

The words still haunted Alun, as he found himself standing in the middle of the children's playground. It had not been the outcome he had hoped for, especially after spending the best part of his evening combing through a year's worth of accounts. There had been no "Well done!" or "Alun, you're a genius!".

Rhiannon had been keen to make good use of his new finding, but she also needed someone to look after her only son. Fishing out as much information as she could from a suspicious butcher would have been quite hard with a three-year-old by her side. This is where Alun came in.

The reporter's parents, Mr and Mrs Williams, had chosen the perfect time to embark on a visit to the shops, and the woman had an incredible gift for getting what she wanted when necessary.

The playground had been Rhiannon's suggestion. "You'll barely have to do anything," she had said. What she had failed to include was the strong possibility of having to squat down on the smallest seesaw Alun had ever seen. She also hadn't mentioned the need to accompany someone on a slide so narrow, his backside had become fully lodged. It had been hard to endure an onslaught of amused heckles from an audience younger than his own coat.

He had never been a fan of the playground. Even at the age of three, he had been known to *tutt* in disapproval at the rowdy behaviour of fellow children.

Saturday mornings appeared to be a popular time, and the accountant had already managed to fill his shoes with sand that he suspected to contain more than its fair share of human excrement.

"You're not pushing fast enough," said the small boy on a brightly-coloured roundabout. As a bored Gwyl folded up his arms, a dizzy Alun was beginning to feel like a confused bobsledder on a never-ending track. He had already got the edges of his coat stuck twice, and he would have liked to see the smug person dressed as Thor do any better.

By the time he had released the rotating steel structure for the last time, the world was spinning as it had been during his whiskey binge the day before.

Straight ahead, he could make out an amused mother sitting beside the sandpit.

"Is that you, Alun?" the voice asked.

Although Alun's vision was heavily distorted, he could still make out that familiar face with an unmistakable amount of red hair on top.

"Oh, hey, Gwen," he said, still struggling to walk straight.

The confused woman glanced at the boy spinning around behind him.

"Since when —" She didn't need to finish her sentence. There was no doubt she was referring to the small child, who might as well have been conjured up by a cruel witch as far as Alun was concerned.

"Oh, no," he said, quickly, "He's not mine. In fact, I've only just met him."

His answer only confused the situation further.

"So you just like hanging out in children's play parks, do you?"

Gwen's question caused the man's eyes to widen.

"No, no!" he said. "It's nothing like that!"

The woman couldn't help but laugh at his sudden discomfort. "Alright, I'll believe you. Even if you are dressed for a court hearing." She looked down at his expensive shoes. "Those will never be the same again."

A disgruntled Alun wiped away some more mud.

"I'm, uh... babysitting for someone," he added.

"So am I, actually. My sister's gone to Wrexham. Looks like we've both been lumbered."

She pointed to two unruly boys fighting over their turn on the zip line. Suddenly Gwyl didn't seem like such hard work.

"We certainly have," Alun agreed.

Now that the world had stopped spinning, he took his first proper look at the woman. Gwen had been two years below him in school, but the years that followed had melted away any age gap. He was quite certain she had played in the same local brass band, right before Megan had grown sick of the loud wailing every night (trumpets were hard to practise quietly). If he had told Gwen that he was actually looking after the child of Rhiannon Williams, the most popular girl in school, she would never have believed it.

"Have you heard the news, then?" asked Gwen. "About Mari Millionaire?"

Alun was stumped. He had no idea that the old woman's disappearance had become public knowledge.

"You know about her disappearance?" he asked back.

Gwen scoffed. "Disappearance? Yeah, right... Everyone knows a rich person like her doesn't just disappear, especially with a family like *hers*."

Once again, Alun was almost lost for words.

"Who told you she'd disappeared?"

"I heard it from my brother's kids. They're mates with that girl who works at her shop on weekends. Got a right mouth on her, she has. Been telling everyone."

He knew exactly who she was referring to. Ruby was Mari's granddaughter and the only other employee at *Blodwen's Flowers*. Her customer service skills left a lot to be desired, if he recalled, but Mari never had the heart to let her go.

"So which one of them do you think did it, then?"

Alun's face jolted to look at her. "Excuse me?"

"You know — that weird family of hers," Gwen said. "They're all as mad as a bag of frogs. One of them had to have done it. I'd put my money on the whole lot. Do you reckon they all planned it together?"

"It's quite unlikely," said Alun, hoping he was right. "I'm sure she's probably sunning it up on the Costa-Del-Sol as we speak."

Gwen let out a cheeky grin. "Come on... which one? The older son? He's always seemed dodgy. Then there's the quiet one. She's definitely a psycho."

Alun checked his surroundings. It had suddenly become apparent that they were discussing the possibility of cold-blooded murder amongst a rabble of energetic children.

"We probably shouldn't... you know..." he muttered, coughing a few times whilst pointing at the sea of small ears.

"You're not around kids very often, are you?" she asked. "They don't care what we've got to say."

They swapped their polite conversation for a moment of

awkward silence. Alun would have preferred that option from the start. Before he could appreciate being relieved of any further small talk, Gwen leant forward and squinted towards the climbing frame.

"Wait, isn't that one yours?" she asked him. "Seems a bit young for the monkey bars."

Alun looked over to see Gwyl dwarfed by the enormous structure, whilst he prepared to attempt what appeared to be a death-defying jump into the unknown.

"Oh, dear God... No!!"

Gwen watched Alun go charging off in a burst of panic. She did a poor job of holding back her amusement.

Jones Family Butchers, like many of the local businesses in Pengower, had sat on the high street for generations. It was one of two meat specialists in the town, the other being owned by two brothers who were on the verge of retirement.

Dai Jones, although he was no spring chicken, was adamant that he had many more years left in him yet and had already loaded up five whole pigs into his fridge by nine o'clock. Carrying an entire pig over your shoulders was no easy feat, and he had seen plenty of young men struggle over the years. It was all in the technique. "Work smarter, not harder," he had always said.

That Saturday morning, the shop was the busiest it had been all week. Most of his regulars had all been and gone. There was: Dilys-two-slices-of-ham, Sammy-sausage-roll, and, of course, old Tex (whose real name was Arthur).

Dai had seen all the usual faces gracing his shop floor, but there was one face he had not expected to see. The woman was young and very good looking. She seemed very out of place, whilst possessing an air about her that screamed out *city-girl*. But as she moved closer to the counter, Dai could see that this was in fact Ioan Williams' daughter.

"Alright, Dai," Rhiannon said, as if she'd lived in this town her entire life.

"Little Rhiannon?" asked the butcher, as he attempted to chop up a line of lamb cutlets whilst speaking with her. "Not so little any more, I see. How's your dad?"

"Avoiding his wife, mostly," she replied.

"I bet he is! She always was a right stunner, your mam. Always did a good job of keeping him on his toes."

The two chuckled. Rhiannon had always liked Dai. Although, observing him now, after all these years, she wouldn't trust the man as far as she could throw him. She was no longer the naïve little girl who enjoyed watching him slice up ham.

"What brings a city slicker like you into my shop after all these years?" Dai asked, his cleaver chomping at the joint of lamb with a series of loud *clanks*!

"Mari Doyle."

The clanking noise stopped. Dai looked up at her in surprise, the warmth in his face draining away.

"I beg your pardon?" asked the butcher.

It had been the exact reaction Rhiannon had been hoping for. When it came to interviewing suspicious characters, she had learnt to go straight for the jugular — get straight to the point and assess their first reaction. And Dai's reaction was a corker.

"Know her, do you?"

Rhiannon's confident smile made the man even more uncomfortable. This was no longer that little girl he had remembered. Instead, she had been replaced by a cold, ruthless journalist.

Dai looked around his shop to see if anyone was listening.

Fortunately, many of the customers were all gormlessly waiting in line, and the others were mostly hard of hearing.

"Is there something you want to ask me, Rhiannon?" asked Dai, a little flustered.

"I don't know," she replied. "Is there something you want to tell me, Big Dai?"

The butcher dropped his cleaver and signalled to the back room. "This really isn't a good time, young lady."

Oh, so this is was how it was going to be, Rhiannon thought. *Young Lady*... Who did he think he was? She would make him pay for those words.

She marched behind him, as they headed into the back room. Quarters of raw beef hung from a steel rack, and a range of different knives were all laid out across the wooden butcher block. It certainly wasn't the most welcoming sight, Rhiannon thought.

"I don't know what game you're playing or who put you up to this, but —"

The butcher tried to calm himself down. He could feel his blood pressure rising, and the doctor had already warned him about that.

"I'm not here to play games," said Rhiannon. "I just want to ask you some questions."

"What right do you people think you have to go around interrogating people. You're not the coppers!"

"*You people*?"

"Journalists! That's right — your old man told me what you were doing down there in the big smoke. Don't think you can try all that stuff up here! This is a good town!"

The room went silent. Rhiannon sat back and let the man have his rant. It had been easier than she had expected. She had barely asked him anything and already the man was coiling up his own noose.

"I'm sorry, Rhiannon," said Dai, his face buried in his enormous hands. Rhiannon had always wondered why butchers all possessed such big hands. "I'm just a bit stressed at the moment, that's all. I've got a lot going on."

The journalist almost sat back against a tray of liver and thought better of it. Instead, she stood up and crossed her arms.

"So, I assume you're aware of her disappearance?" she asked.

"Isn't everyone?" he asked in return. "People gossip like anything in this town."

"But not everyone has an arrangement with her like *you* have."

Dai looked up from his giant sausage-fingers. He had always worn his heart on his sleeve, and she knew that would be her way in.

"That's right," she continued. "I know all about the payments. It doesn't look good, Dai."

"I don't know what you're talking about."

I see, thought Rhiannon. He had decided to lie to her now. Well, in that case, the gloves were well and truly off.

"I'm sure the police would be quite interested in your little connection."

The butcher stormed over to her, his face bright red. For a moment she thought he was going to strangle her with his own sausages.

"You have no idea what I've been through with that woman!" All of a sudden, the large man was a snivelling wreck. "I loved Mari with all my heart! I always have!"

It was now Rhiannon's turn to look shocked. She had not expected the conversation to head in that direction.

"Our shops have overlooked each other for decades," he continued. "I used to watch her through my window putting out the tulips. We finally had our time together and then *this* happens! She disappears!"

Dai had lost all control of his emotions. It seemed he had been bottling them up for a few days.

Rhiannon tried her best to make sense of the situation. “So... you’re saying that you and her were — are — what, some kind of an item?”

“*An item*?!” cried the butcher. “The woman is my wife!”

CHAPTER 5

Rhiannon stared at the piece of beef hanging from its great hook. The smell of meat hung in the air like a third presence, and she was genuinely considering turning to a plant-based diet again the minute she left the butcher shop.

She handed Dai a tissue from her pocket, as he snivelled in front of her (he didn't need to know that it had already been used). The man seemed to be embracing the opportunity to express his true feelings, as if they had been bottled up for days on end.

"We didn't want anyone else to know," he said, eventually. "We'd been planning to do it for a while. I'd have done it a lot sooner if it were up to me, but Mari was too worried about that rotten family of hers. She knew they'd be thinking it was all my idea — that it was all about the money. That lottery win has been a curse for her ever since those numbers came up."

"Does anyone else know about your marriage?" Rhiannon asked. Her question seemed to evoke another emotion: fear.

"We haven't told a soul," said the butcher. "Mari knows her family too well. She was genuinely concerned for my well-being.

That says all you need to know about her horrible offspring. How on earth such nasty pieces of work could ever come from a woman like Mari is beyond me. She didn't deserve that lot. What she needed was someone to love her properly. Not people that were counting down the days until she popped her clogs. If there was ever anyone in danger, it was my Mari. *Now* look what's happened! I should never have let her out of my sight!"

The reporter paid close attention to every pause and intonation. She had often referred to herself as a human lie detector. It was a gift she accredited to her recently failed marriage. Lies were easy to detect when they were coming at you on a daily basis, especially from a man as dishonest as her ex-husband.

She had no doubt that Mari's disappearance had come as a great shock to the man in front of her. But if he had expected floods of sympathy, he had thought wrong.

"Why aren't you out there looking for her?" she asked.

The butcher jolted up his head, startled by her blunt tone.

"Don't you think I've tried?" he said, his eyes wide and raw from the lack of sleep. "The minute I realised she was missing, I searched everywhere: her shop, her house — I even contacted those awful children of hers. Ended up having to feed them some excuse about a meat delivery. I only came into work today to keep my mind off things for a few hours."

"You could've called the police."

"And tell them what?" The anger in his voice was back. "That I'd married a lottery winner and now she's disappeared? Who do you think the number-one suspect in that case would be? When she turns up —"

"Turns up — *what*?" She knew what he was about to say but preferred to hear it said aloud. The word she was waiting for never came. "What makes you think she hasn't just taken off for a life in the sun? She has the money for it."

"Mari would never leave this place," said Dai. "I tried to

convince her of a honeymoon but she'd have none of that. We had a private ceremony in the end. A bag of chips by the lake was more than enough for her. She was all about the simple pleasures in life. Like flowers..."

The butcher let out a warm smile. Rhiannon was on the verge of being sick and it was not due to the smell of meat.

"Wow, that money really *was* wasted on her," she said, still thinking about that handbag of hers, which still needed replacing. "You can't blame people for getting frustrated."

Dai wiped the sweat off his brow with her overused tissue and descended back into his natural state of self-pity. The young woman was still trying to see what a woman like Mari had ever seen in him. Perhaps it was the big hands, she thought.

"If you must know," said Dai, "I was always going to inform the police myself until someone beat me to it."

"Her grandson, Jack," Rhiannon said. This piece of information piqued the man's interest.

"Is that who it was?"

She could have kicked herself. Giving away more info than she needed was a rookie mistake. Perhaps she deserved her new position at the *Merioneth Press*, after all.

"I think that's enough for now, Dai," the reporter said, before noticing the layer of sawdust beneath her feet. It appeared to be everywhere.

The butcher noticed her confused stare. "It's to keep you from falling on your backside," he said.

Rhiannon did her best to kick off the excess dust from her favourite pair of shoes and headed for the door.

"Oh, before I go..." she said. Dai looked up at her, dreading the final question. The way he perched against the large butcher's block, his body hunched over and his face miserable, made him look quite pathetic. He was like a sulking toddler, and Rhiannon knew exactly what they were like. "You know more than I do about Mari's friends and family; if you had to pick one person who would be quite happy for her to disappear, who would it be?"

The butcher didn't even have to think. He let out a disgusted grunt at the mere thought of the person he had in mind.

"Barry Doyle," he said. "That man is the worst human being I have ever met."

ALUN'S long walk home had felt like a journey back from battle. His body ached every step of the way, and his mind raced faster than a hungry greyhound.

The playground was bad enough, but it had been the horrors of a certain child's bedroom that had truly driven him to madness. Never before had he witnessed such carnage. It was worse than the time he had fallen asleep without doing the dishes. How the boy could fall asleep without ever having seen an inch of his own carpet was beyond him. Someday, that child would forever become lost amongst the piles of endless toys, never to be seen again.

"I'll be back in an hour," Rhiannon had said. Alun knew now that her optimistic timekeeping could never again be trusted.

Her trip to the butchers had at least been eventful. It seemed there was a lot more going on in Mari Doyle's life than they had thought, and she had been a lot more successful in her love life than Alun had ever been. The revelation about her secret marriage had spawned a whole load of unanswered questions (and Alun hated unanswered questions).

One thing he did know for certain was that he would be sleeping well that night. It was amazing how much keeping up with a three-year-old could do for a bout of insomnia. His first night's sleep as a single man had been abysmal. The second one would require a lot less whiskey.

As he approached his quiet street on the outskirts of the town, the appearance of a parked police car had caught him by surprise. Berwyn Street was normally the most boring and non-eventful neighbourhood in Pengower (it was why he had chosen it).

He approached his front door with a feeling of unease, and it wasn't until he slipped in the key that he caught the large shadow drowning out his own.

In a split second, his petrified face was shoved hard against the brass door number, and his arm was twisted in every direction.

"Hold it right there!" cried the voice behind him. "Mr Hughes, I'm arresting you on suspicion of murder. You do not have to say anything, but it may harm your defence when questioned in court..."

Alun yelped out from the sharp pain shooting through his bent hand. The police officer behind him was twice his size and had the strength of a gorilla.

The accountant tried his best to speak, but his words were muffled by the wooden door: "That's enough, Mel! I saw your car parked!"

The police officer released his grip and let out a deep laugh.

"Still wet yourself though, didn't you?" he cried. "That was the best reaction yet! You daft sod!"

His powerful hand slapped the other man hard against his back.

Alun took a moment to readjust his sore joints, as the laughter continued.

"I've been waiting here for ages to do that," said the policeman, as he ripped open a bag of thick crisps and began chomping away with his mouth open.

"Glad my taxes are going to good use," Alun said, before the next wave of excess potato sprayed his face.

"Didn't think a boring bugger like you had anywhere to be," said Mel. "How's your missus? She left you yet?"

A dark cloud began hovering above Alun's face, as he was reminded of his ex-girlfriend.

"Uh, yes," he said. "She has, actually."

Mel began to laugh, until he realised his old friend wasn't joking. "Oh, hey! I was only kidding, bud! You two seriously broken up?"

"Yes. Yes, we have."

"Well that's a crying shame, lad, it really is."

Alun shrivelled up as an enormous arm started reaching around his shoulders.

"I'm sorry to hear that..." Mel added. He tried to think of an appropriate thing to say next. "Hey! You hear about my promotion?"

His friend had not heard about the promotion, nor the new bathroom that he went on to mention. Mel had always been able to swerve the conversation at any given moment. Anyone who didn't know him might have taken offence, but Alun knew he was just being Mel. He had been that way since they were children, only now he was a sergeant instead of a constable. The man was like a six-foot version of the three-year-old that Alun had just been looking after: no empathy, no self-awareness and bundles of energy.

"You'll never guess what my latest case is!" said the new sergeant. Alun had a feeling he was about to find out. "You know that old bid who won the lottery?"

Oh, good, Alun thought to himself; the missing persons case was about to be solved, all thanks to the great Inspector Mel.

The impromptu visit to his home was all starting to make sense now. It was just like the time Mel had copied his friend's homework at school. Now he was coming over to pick the only decent brain he could lay his hands on.

Mel didn't have many friends. There weren't many people who would put up with the policeman's obnoxious behaviour and long rants like Alun could. It was like putting up with an annoying relative that cornered you at every wedding. The accountant was also open to the suggestion of beer, and there weren't many individuals who would share one of those with the man, either.

"Missing persons don't interest me normally," said Mel. "But I got a good feeling about this one."

"This woman does ring a bell," Alun humoured him, "But I don't think I've got much for you."

He was quite certain he would be interested in the tidbit about Dai Jones, but Alun's wrist was still very sore, and, well, Mel could figure that part out for himself.

"Last time she was spotted was..." the policeman pulled out his pink, spotted notebook and began flicking through the pages. Bless him, Alun thought; he's bought a notebook this time. There must have been a sale on at *Smiths*. "Eleven-thirty on Sunday morning."

The man looked quite proud of himself. He had been busy with his questioning and had already managed to narrow down an eye-witness account of her last known whereabouts.

"The Reverend Owen confirmed it for me this morning," said Mel. "Turns out the lady was a devout Christian. She was more regular to that church than my own bowels, she was."

Alun tried not to think about the contents of his friend's toilet and instead turned his focus back to Mari. The fact she had been to church just before she was reported missing didn't strike him as very important.

Or was it? Was the great Inspector Mel actually getting warmer?

"I'm putting my money on the vicar," said the police officer. He saw the surprise in his friend's face. "That's the one I always go for in Cluedo — Reverend Green."

"I thought you said it was a missing persons investigation."

"How many old ladies do you know that suddenly go off the grid?" Mel began applying some imaginary tanning lotion and looked up to the sky. "You reckon Mrs Flower-Shop is out there living it large in the sun? Nah, there's no sun where she's gone."

Alun felt a shudder down his spine. His old friend's blunt choice of words continued to disturb him. He hoped that the man was more sensitive and professional when going about his investigations (if that's what you could call them).

"This town needs a good murder," Mel continued. "Imagine my chief inspector's face when I'm ten steps ahead of those numpties over at CID."

"Ten steps ahead?" asked Alun, who had become good at sounding impressed. He was particularly astounded by the fact the man could actually count to ten after all these years.

"Well, you know me," said Mel, puffing out his large chest. "I'm like a bloodhound."

Alun did know. He also knew the man had been longing to play detective since they were on the school playground. He even remembered one unfortunate instance involving a magnifying glass and a burnt toe, but the less said about that the better.

Unfortunately for Mel, exams had never been the man's forte, and there was no doubt in the accountant's mind that it was this very flaw that had kept him walking the beat for all these years. Then there was the charming personality and flawless people skills...

"Come on, Harry Potter," said Mel. "There must be something you've heard around town that could be a clue?"

Goodness, he used the word *clue*, Alun thought. The man knows all the technical jargon.

"Sounds like you know a lot more than me," he said with a shrug.

Mel hated it when his friend sounded like he was just stroking his ego. But then again, he didn't mind too much, either.

"Well, a fat lot of use you've been today." Mel stretched out his body as if their discussion about the case had been a day of hard labour. "That's enough work for now. Fancy a pint?"

Alun could feel his wounds from the playground again. "Sorry, I can't tonight. I'm busy... very busy."

"Suit yourself." The tall man bid him a farewell with a tight headlock and a quick hair ruffle. "Enjoy your new bachelor life."

Mel's last sentence continued to wound Alun long after he had entered his empty house. He looked around his living room. Nothing had changed since he had left that morning: the white walls, his perfectly hoovered carpet, the purposefully simple furniture layout with few ornaments and no clutter. It was like nobody lived there at all. Everything was in order.

The person who had entered the house, however, was still very much a broken mess. His usual safety blanket of a clean house had done nothing for his aching soul, and the unexciting contents of his bare fridge gave him no further comfort.

As he stared out through the kitchen window, his hands soaking in the warmth of a washing up bowl, the spire of St David's Church poked up in the far distance, as it had always done. Tonight, it seemed more prominent than ever. The man's overactive mind worked its way through the more painful memories of his ex-girlfriend, until it landed on a vision of Mari during her last sighting. The woman had become quite the useful distraction at just the right time.

He wasn't normally partial to an evening stroll around a quiet graveyard, but, tonight, the great church was calling out to him. If he squinted hard enough, he could even make out the orange glow coming from inside. The Reverend Owen appeared to be working late.

CHAPTER 6

The graveyard at St David's Church was normally quiet on a Saturday night. Most of its inhabitants had long left this land of the living, and all that remained was the occasional fox or a small population of field mice.

Alun had found the steep climb towards the church's entrance a great challenge for his expensive shoes and began contemplating the future investment of a pair of wellington boots. He had always enjoyed a good walk but usually tended to avoid one that involved very long grass and a high risk of injury.

His parents had never been very religious, but he had been taken to numerous Christmas services as a child and had spent many hours gazing up at the church's impressive feats of architecture. Wiping off a layer of mud against the wet grass, he had begun to regret his impromptu walk amongst the unsociable gravestones, and it had taken the nostalgic glow of the stained glass windows to almost make the whole thing worthwhile. The halo of moonlight surrounding the building's pointed steeple was mesmerising at such a late hour, and it had distracted the man from the creeping presence not too far behind him.

At the highest point of the graveyard, Alun could almost see the entire town of Pengower. Streetlights glimmered in the distance, and the cold air created a cloud around Alun's pale face. The sound of footsteps caused him to jolt around, but he saw nothing but a line of quiet graves with names that were barely legible.

He had never been a believer in ghosts or the supernatural — apart from the ones responsible for the convenient disappearance of many of his client's VAT receipts. But if there *was* such a thing as a lingering spirit — and if Mari Doyle was *indeed* no longer a fellow member of the land of the living — he would have been quite happy to be offered up a small clue to the mystery of her whereabouts.

Standing in the company of the town's deceased population, it had dawned on the accountant quite how empty his life had become. Did he not have anything better to do on a Saturday night? The answer was not a fact he wanted to think about.

Alun had always liked a good graveyard. It was a glimpse of the past and a snapshot of the future. A person would find it hard to feel too stressed about life when faced with the hard reality of their inevitable, final resting spot. Ultimately, we would all end up in the same place, although, some of us might get there a little quicker.

He had heard the stuttering noise behind him very clearly this time. Whoever was following him, they must have been hiding behind the gravestone just to his right (either that, or it seemed ghosts were very real indeed).

Alun wouldn't have to wait long to find out, and he soon found a pair of wide eyes staring back at him from deep in the shadows. The face showed itself, and the rest of the body followed. A mouthful of saliva slid down the accountant's throat like a great slug. Behind the body was a pointed tail, and it began wagging faster than a furious windscreen wiper.

"I think you've made a new friend," said a man's voice.

Alun turned his attention away from the curious Border Collie and placed it firmly on the amused vicar standing behind him.

"Reverend Owen?" Alun asked, already knowing the answer.

"Good evening, Alun," said the reverend. "It's been a long time."

Alun felt a sudden tingle of guilt, as if he'd failed to visit an elderly relative after so many years.

"Oh, well, I suppose it has," he muttered.

"In fact, I've not seen you at my door since your mother played the organ."

That was true, Alun thought. His mother *had* played the organ all those years ago. She was not a devout Christian but had loved a good singsong. She would have bashed the old ivories for anyone who would listen.

"She had a lot of talent, your mother," the man added.

The reverend was far better looking than Alun had remembered, and he was ageing remarkably well. It must be all that red wine, the accountant thought.

"I'm sorry, I didn't mean to disturb you, Reverend."

"Nonsense! You will always be welcome here, Alun."

Alun felt the man's disarming smile draw him in. The reverend had a way about him that made a person feel safe and welcome whilst in the bubble of his company. It was hard not to like the man, and his optimistic nature quickly became infectious.

"What brings you up here at this time of night?" asked the vicar.

"I don't quite know," Alun replied. It was true: he didn't quite know.

He had hoped that Mari Doyle's last sighting would have offered up a small lead to her current location, but he wasn't prepared to disclose that. Mari's disappearance had made it to the forefront of his overactive mind again; it was all he could think about. "Obsessive" had been a key word over the course of his doomed relationship with Megan. Obsessing over any new problem — big or small — was steeped in the accountant's nature; he just couldn't help it. An unsolved problem could lead to days of sleepless nights. It was a trait he knew would either be his great strength in life or his unfortunate downfall.

"The Lord can find us in the most unlikely of moments," said the reverend.

Alun was tempted to disagree with the idea that he had been lured to the man's church by an act of God, but he soon thought better of it. For all he knew, the man might have been right.

"Would you mind giving an old man a quick hand?" asked the vicar.

Before Alun could answer, the man had disappeared through the main entrance. The accountant could feel the reverend's charming pull, once again, and admired his great confidence that he would soon be followed.

The inside of the church had the same, exact smell as it had done all those years ago. Alun remembered it well: the oak, the dampness, the burning wax. He entered to find the vicar standing at one end of a long bench. To the side of him was a half-painted wall.

"Would you mind helping me lift her?"

Soon, the wooden bench was screeching its way across the tiled floor and away from the faded wall. Alun held up his own end with the face of a struggling Olympic weightlifter. He wished he had mentioned his bad back, but it was too late now — the damage had been done.

The two men lowered the heavy piece of furniture with a shared grunt.

As he took a moment to recover his head from the increased blood flow, Alun noticed the tins of paint beside them.

"You're a good man," said Reverend Owen. His helper was more than happy to take the compliment. If a vicar thought so, then it must have been true, Alun thought. "I really want to get this wall finished by tomorrow. It's been crying out for a new coat."

Alun was more interested in the dog collar. He was fascinated how a person could still wear such an uncomfortable looking neck piece even through a session of decorating.

"This whole building could do with a facelift," the man continued. "But there's hardly any money left for that. A man with your profession will appreciate that, I'm sure."

The accountant raised an eyebrow. He was not aware that his choice of career had been common knowledge within the walls of St David's Church.

"Unfortunately I just *count* the money," Alun said. "I don't make it." He had always enjoyed using that line in such circumstances. It always seemed to lighten the mood with some of his clients. On this occasion it had gone down a storm, and the vicar let out a laugh so loud it echoed around the ceilings.

"I could say the same thing about miracles," he said, waiting for a similar reaction (he never got one).

The two shared a long silence, whilst Alun tried to come up with a reason to leave.

"You've heard the terrible news, I take it," said the reverend.

Suddenly, the urge to leave had evaporated from Alun's mind. He waited for the man to elaborate but had to settle for the sound of paint being slapped across the wall.

"You mean, Mrs Doyle?" he asked.

The reverend nodded without ever taking his eyes off the wet paint.

"All we can do is pray," he said. "She will be found when the time is right."

Alun felt a shiver down his neck. He couldn't tell whether it was from the extreme lack of heating or the vicar's cold tone. His jovial manner had disappeared quicker than the blood in his own toes.

"I heard she was last spotted in this church," Alun said.

The painting stopped. He had the vicar's full attention now.

"Where did you hear that?"

The man turned to look at him.

"Oh, you know... just word of mouth. We all know how the people of this town like to talk."

The reverend almost looked relieved. "They certainly do."

He placed his brush to one side and took a deep sigh.

"Mari had become a good friend," the vicar added. "We people of the cloth are not really in the business of making close friendships. It can be a lonely life being the person who is supposed to have all the answers. But Mari never needed any of those." He took out a handkerchief and began clearing up his glasses. "She was happy to talk about anything: baking, flowers, family. There were often times she'd be giving *me* personal advice."

Alun looked up towards the stained glass windows up above them. The night had darkened their colour, but he could still make out the biblical figures staring back at him.

"Now, don't get me wrong," the reverend said. "Mari was more devoted to God and this here church than anyone I have ever met. She never missed a service, and the flowers on display were always her own donation. But she was far more than just another member of the congregation."

The angelic figures continued to look Alun directly in the eye. It was as if they knew far more than he did about Mari and her strange disappearance.

"Was there anything out of the ordinary during her last visit?" he asked, more abruptly than he intended.

The reverend smiled. "Now you sound like that policeman

who came over yesterday. I'll tell you exactly what I told him: she was as delightful as always. In fact, she even offered to make us a small donation. She was always full of ideas when it came to fundraising."

"How much was the donation?"

The conversation was, yet again, ground to an almighty halt by one of Alun's unusual choice of questions. Reverend Owen stared at him with suspicious eyes.

"Are you sure you were just aimlessly walking up here, Alun?"

The accountant went paler than the new coat of paint. He stuttered his way to a response: "I, uh, I was just —"

An arm wrapped around his shoulder. The reverend appeared to find his awkward response amusing. "Relax, my dear boy. We all care about Mari's wellbeing. I'm not naïve enough to assume that I'm the only one to have befriended her. She was a kind woman."

Alun tried not to gulp in front of him. He reminded himself that lying was a sin, and that, in all likelihood, the reverend was telling the truth.

"I've distracted you long enough, Reverend," Alun said with a squirm.

"You are very welcome to call me Tom, if you would prefer."

Alun had wanted to avoid a first-name relationship, but he decided to give it a try.

"Thank you, Reverend — I mean Tom!"

The vicar watched Alun head back towards the main door. When he reached the opening, he peered out into the gathering mist outside. The Border Collie he had seen earlier was now waiting for him with its wagging tale.

"I think your dog wants to come inside!" Alun called out.

"He's not my dog!" the reverend called back.

The dog and his new friend, Alun Hughes, were now staring

each other down. The short whimper and pleading eyes were all it took to melt the accountant's heart.

Alun inspected the collar on his new, hairy friend. Two dog collars in one evening, he thought to himself. He patted the animal on the snout, and they both headed home.

CHAPTER 7

Barry Doyle sat behind his desk like a bloated sea lion. He knew the extra sausage with his large chips had been one too many. The early lunch had brought about his afternoon slump even earlier than usual. Next time, he would opt for just the salad. Yes, next time, he promised himself.

The owner of *Doyle's Estate Agents* reached for the bottle of scotch in his drawer and took a swig. He could have sworn there had been over half the bottle left when he arrived that morning. After hauling himself out of the chair with a tired grunt, he circled his cluttered office and took a peek through the blinds of a small window. In the main office, next door, were his team of estate agents, all hovering at their desks like well-behaved worker bees. That's exactly how Barry Doyle liked it. All he cared about was selling houses, and houses did not sell themselves.

The screens of his employees' computers were all faced in the direction of his office window. This was also how he liked it. There would be no browsing through cute, little kitten photos on *his* time. He trusted nobody.

Just as he was about to barge through the door and unleash a tirade of abuse (he felt it was necessary to keep his workers on their toes), he spotted an unfamiliar young woman gazing at the display of new properties. She was smartly-dressed with striking good looks. Just his type, Barry thought, whilst licking his lips and curling his moustache.

Meanwhile, over in the next room, Rhiannon was busy studying the large display of photographs. She had been surprised at all the high figures. Even an old, lonely looking farm house was vastly out of her own price range, and there would have been a time in her life when she would have barely considered it for free. It seemed Pengower had become quite the popular choice for new home buyers. Perhaps she was going to have to consider renting, after all — anything to get out of her parents' house.

"Can I help you, madam?"

She turned to find a strapping young man in a sharp suit. In her mind, he screamed *estate agent*, but she would be lying if she said the attention wasn't nice, especially from a man with such a good haircut.

"Uh, yes," she replied, in her best damsel-in-distress voice. She was quite happy to let him feel the hero, at least for a moment.

Just as the charming man was about to reply, he winced at the sound of a deep voice coming from the other side of the office.

"I'll handle this one, Elgan," called his boss.

Barry Doyle's office door was wide open and the man himself was filling the entire doorway. He smirked as if he'd just won a prize. A disappointed Elgan nodded in defeat and returned to the safety of his desk.

"Perfect," muttered Rhiannon, under her breath. It could not have played out any better. A meeting with her new prime suspect, and she didn't even have to work for it. Although, something told her the real work was about to come.

She did her best "pleased" face and headed over to the man's office. The room stank of fast food, and the carpet was stained from years worth of spilled beverages (at least, she hoped they had been beverages).

Barry Doyle's appearance had matched her expectations. He couldn't have looked more sleazy if he tried, sitting there, slumped behind his desk with his sly grin and mousy facial features. The dark rings beneath his eyes didn't help, either. All those years of heavy smoking and drinking were visible for all to see.

"I've not seen you around here before," he said, his ruined teeth poking out through the never-ending smile.

Oh, great, Rhiannon thought. He knew *all* the chat up lines.

"I'm new to the area," she replied, shaking back her long hair in a manner she'd seen on a shampoo advert. "I thought I'd come to have a browse."

"Buying or renting?"

"Buying, of course," she said, trying not to overdo it.

The two hairy hands rubbed themselves together.

"Why would a lovely girl like you want to move to a simple, little place like this? You strike me as a city girl."

"Too much noise and pollution." Rhiannon shrugged. "I like the fresh air."

Barry was about to pull out one of his favourite cigars and decided against it, at least for now.

"I know what you mean," he said and leaned back in his oversized chair. "So what's your budget?"

"What have you got?"

Barry sniggered. He was enjoying this game.

"How about a detached three-bedroom?" he suggested.

"How about something bigger?"

Another snigger. Damn, she was good, Rhiannon thought to herself.

The hairy hands reached for a brochure. He flicked it open and revealed a beautiful looking cottage with a walled garden.

"How about this little number?" he asked. "I'll be happy to show you around."

The woman opposite him did her best not to vomit from his cheeky wink.

"How about the old farmhouse I saw over near the lake?" she asked.

The room went quiet and the man's face was serious for a moment. The journalist started to worry if she might have gone too far, too quickly.

"*Derwen Farm*?" he asked, in a surprised tone. "You're the first person to bring that place up in a while. I'm considering knocking the place down and selling it as farmland."

The suspicion in his beady eyes only made Rhiannon even more uncomfortable.

"Nothing wrong with a fixer-upper," she said, casually. "It just needs a little bit of love and care. Like we all do sometimes."

Her choice of words worked a treat. The wicked smile emerged, once again, and the man rose to his feet.

"How about I show you a few more options over dinner," he said. "My treat. The choice of good restaurants in this town is abysmal, but the Italian's alright."

Rhiannon studied his confident body language. This was certainly a man who was used to getting his own way, and he was about to get it once again.

"I'd be delighted," she said.

THE HIT of fresh air outside *Doyle's Estate Agents* had been a Godsend.

Rhiannon took in a long, deep breath to rid her memory of Barry's office. The market was still in full swing, and she had long broken her new babysitter's trust. Her mind turned to the promise she had made to Alun about being "back in an hour". Still, between her visit to Dai's butcher shop and Barry Doyle's estate agency, it had felt like a productive morning. She had even gone undercover.

If her plan all worked out, the next meeting with the eldest Doyle sibling would bring her one step closer in solving the mystery of his mother's disappearance. Her story depended on it. She might as well have been reporting on a missing kitten at this rate.

She also couldn't help but feel slightly guilty about leaving her accountant friend to watch her son for so many hours. Gwyl had barely slept the night before and will have eaten the man alive.

She would make it up to him somehow, she thought. Perhaps she could get him a gift — like a new calculator — or whatever else those accountant types were into.

As she went to cross the street, her attention was caught by the sight of a parked police car outside the bakery. Standing beside it was Mel, a man she had known since secondary school. He had always been heavily built, enough to give him a distinct advantage in the under-eighteen's rugby matches. His brawn and good looks, as far as she recalled, were the only features of note. He had the mental capacity of a cucumber and the personality of a chimpanzee.

"Any leads yet, Columbo?" she asked, upon her approach.

The sight of Rhiannon coming towards him was enough to ruin the policeman's sausage roll. He groaned as he chewed on the last mouthful.

"It's all take and no give with you," he said. "You were quite happy to take my tip-off about the missing person, but I've had nothing in return."

He brushed away the crumbs from his police jumper and pulled out a chocolate bar (dessert).

"I've got nothing to tell, that's why," she said. "I've come up with diddly-squat so far."

Mel rolled his eyes. "I'll believe that when I read it in the paper."

Rhiannon watched him climb into his car and stood in the way of the door.

"That's obstruction, that is," said Mel. "You wouldn't be the first person from our year I've arrested."

"What do you know about the Doyle siblings?" Rhiannon asked, not remotely threatened by his warning (and the man knew it).

"They're a bloody weird bunch, I know that much. All of them in different ways."

"Any criminal records?"

Mel smiled at her persistence. "There might be one in there."

"Can I see it?"

The policeman shook his head and fired up his car. "Like I said: taking and no giving."

The reporter stepped away from the closing door and stuck her head in front of the open window.

"Alright — did you know Mari was recently married?" she asked.

"Course I do," he lied. *How on earth did she find that out?*

"Then you'll know Dai the butcher is quaking in his boots right now. Especially if there's no prenup."

"He's a dark horse that Dai Butcher," said Mel.

"Do the Doyles know?"

"If they do, they're keeping it quiet. They don't seem to like police officers very much — particularly that Barry."

Rhiannon smiled. "I'm having dinner with him this week."

Mel sat himself back. He was impressed. "You're having dinner with Barry Doyle?" The young woman nodded. She knew she had his full attention now. "Good luck. You won't get much blood out of that stone."

"But if I do..."

The two stared each other down, a half smile on both lips.

"Jack Doyle," said Mel, revving up the engine.

"Barry's son? What about him?"

"You asked who has a criminal record. The lad's got more convictions than sense."

The police car sped away, leaving an intrigued Rhiannon to ponder about the young man she had questioned only the day before. He had been a quiet lad and did not seem like someone who would get himself into trouble.

It was always the quiet ones, she thought.

CHAPTER 8

The appointment at Henblas Farm had gone on far longer than expected. Mr and Mrs Roberts had experienced a very bad year, and it was up to their accountant, as always, to be the bearer of bad news. Although he was keen to get back home, Alun realised it would have been rather bad form to rush their meeting under such unfortunate circumstances.

After giving the distraught dairy farm owners his last piece of financial advice, he excused himself in the politest way possible and made his move for the 1971 Volkswagen Beetle parked in the yard.

Alun hated upsetting his clients. The customer relations side of his job had always been a weakness; he was more of a numbers man than a people-person. Numbers were straightforward: no emotions, no awkwardness, and certainly never any drama. He likened himself to a doctor being forced to interact with his patients. The problems still existed, whether they were spoken aloud or not. He was just the messenger.

Unfortunately for the Roberts family, there was very little anyone could have done at that point (including the cows).

The accountant's new housemate had been waiting for him in the backseat, her tail wagging and her tongue panting. The Border Collie had made herself quite comfortable in Alun's life since their first encounter at St David's graveyard. Her new master had felt like he had no other choice but to take her home that night, and, after finding his favourite slippers soaked in urine, the man had begun to doubt his decision already.

A pet was not something Alun ever had growing up. His mother was allergic to most animals, and his father detested anything that would lose him control over the cleanliness of the house (a child had been bad enough in that area). Despite the lack of furred friends during his childhood, the accountant was slowly beginning to see the appeal; it had been quite nice having someone waiting for him after finishing work. Not waking up alone was always a bonus (the dog had already claimed her rightful side in Alun's bed).

The old Beetle chugged its way down the winding farm track leading out through a series of closed gates, as well as one rather concerning looking cattle grid. *Henblas Farm* was as remote as they came, and Alun was more than relieved at the sight of a main road. For such an old car, the Volkswagen Beetle could handle a muddy road quite well, but when it came to maintaining a decent speed up a steep hill, it was in a lot of trouble. Unfortunately, the Caradog Moors had hills in abundance. They stretched out for many miles, creating a landscape so vast, it was hard not to be impressed.

There were no other vehicles for as far as the eye could see, and the only pairs of eyes were that of a tired Accountant and a lively Border Collie.

"Sit down, Peg!" Alun cried, but it was to no avail. The canine had sussed her master out from the moment they first met, and was fully aware who the boss was.

The name had been a rushed choice. Alun had always liked

the name Meg for a dog, but when he realised that using a shortened version of his ex-girlfriend's first name was probably the most daft idea in the world, he decided to make a quick adjustment.

Peg was in no mood to sit still and had placed her snout firmly through the gap in the open window. An entire sky of looming black clouds hovered above them, and it wasn't long before the accountant was thinking about the possible implications of a thunderstorm, especially in such a wide open landscape.

The great valley to their right went down all the way to a village called Llanisaf, a place even more local than the town of Pengower. Many of Alun's fellow school pupils had hailed from that small part of the world, and many of them still lived there.

The accountant and his dog were just about to turn a giant bend in the road, when the Beetle let out a noise that made its driver feel sick to the stomach. A few gurgles and screeches later, and the struggling vehicle was pulling over to an empty layby. The engine let out a few more gasps for life until it grumbled to a horrible death.

Raindrops began to fall, and the lonely Beetle was now stranded by the side of the road, helpless and in desperate need of resuscitation.

Alun's attempts to throttle the ignition with as many turns as possible was met with a wheezing groan from the engine. He knew, right at that very moment, that he really should have checked on that strange noise the clutch had been making for all those weeks.

The Beetle had been in the Hughes family since before Alun was born. His father had treated it like a son (only with far more tender love and care).

After begging the vehicle to start, Alun had no choice but to abandon his moment of denial and move swiftly onto the next phase in his emotions: *terror*.

The Caradog Moors were not only unforgiving in their nature, but they also lacked phone signal. Suddenly, the accountant's plans for an evening in front of the telly with a takeaway were fast becoming a pipe dream.

His foresight to bring a pair of wellington boots for his visit to *Henblas Farm* was starting to pay dividends, for he would now need them in his daunting new quest for good reception. The man and his dog set off towards the bleak horizon. Rain came falling down on them, just as the dark clouds had promised — not that it seemed to bother Peg. For her, a trek across the moors was seen as a bonus walk, and she licked the falling beads of water as they landed on her nose.

Alun knew very little about the science behind his mobile phone signal, but he likened it to a small radio in his pocket and assumed that their theory of frequencies was pretty much the same. Either way, he knew his best bet was to head for higher ground.

It had turned out that the wellington boots were not the ideal hill-climbing footwear, after all, as they slipped and slid through the wet grass. When he scaled his third peak, Alun lifted up his phone like an Olympian carrying a torch, praying for the Gods to come down with just a few bars of signal. With the dreaded words "*No Service*" lighting up his phone screen, the burst of frustration distracted the hiker from his next, crucial step. Peg let out a worried bark, as her owner went tumbling down the next slope.

When Alun next opened his eyes, he was looking up at the dark skies and lying in a pool of mud. He gave each limb a gentle twitch, just to make sure they were still working. The fall had been significant, but nothing appeared to be broken. The mud, as unpleasant as it was, had at least softened his landing.

Lying there, in the middle of the moors, he had never felt so alone. Both of his parents had passed away many years ago, and now that Megan had left him, he struggled to think of anyone else who would ever really miss him if he never got up again. He was an only child, and although the people of Pengower would eventually notice his disappearance, the news of his passing would probably die down quite soon afterwards.

"Did you hear about that accountant?" they would say. That's all he ever was to most of them: the accountant. With him gone, a lot of people would be stuck doing their own taxes.

As he contemplated the insignificance of his life, Alun's mind turned to the thought of Mari Doyle. That person's disappearance had caused quite the stir and not just because she was a millionaire. The people of the town had loved Mari, and, from what he had heard, she would be sorely missed if she never came back. It was during these thoughts of Mari's glowing reputation that something occurred to him. "Of course..." he thought to himself. He had approached her disappearance in the wrong way, he now realised.

Just as the new epiphany had struck him, whilst he was practically floating in what was fast becoming a muddy bog, he felt something warm and slimy rubbing against his face. The pink tongue had almost woken him up from a strange dream, and the feeling of fur against his cold cheeks filled him with warmth.

Alun sat straight up and was smothered by more licks. He held the Border Collie in his arms and gave her a grateful smile. She had snapped him straight back into his unfortunate and wet reality. People weren't ready for another disappearance, he had decided, and it was time to push on through.

"Come on, Peg," he said to her.

The rain had not eased off and came pouring down in heavy droplets. Alun tried to gather his bearings, but the moorland wasn't making it easy for him. As he began wading through the thick mud and wet bracken, a sudden thought caused him to panic. He patted himself down in a frazzled search.

Where was it?

After checking every pocket for the third time, it dawned on him that his mobile phone was now missing.

Alun looked back towards the narrow, muddy trail he had made down the steep bank, but he saw nothing that resembled an electronic device anywhere. His phone might as well have vanished into thin air, and the harsh weather conditions were starting to affect his judgement (the great fall hadn't helped much, either).

He searched around the bracken, like a frantic madman, and turned to cursing the skies as if they were a tyrannical God. "Give me a break!" he called out. The only reply was a rumble of thunder, and it was a response that shook the accountant to his very core — he had forgotten about the lightning.

Alun was just about to drop to his knees in defeat, when the sound of a familiar ringtone lifted up his spirits. He went rummaging through the bracken, chasing after that relentless jingle, as it got louder and louder the closer he became. He felt a surge of adrenaline, as his freezing cold hand wrapped around something hard and plastic amongst the overgrowth.

The phone monitor was glowing, as he lifted it up towards the sky; a small moment of victory. Below the precious, single bar of signal that displayed on the blue screen was a name: *Rhiannon*.

"Hello? Alun, are you there?"

He had answered the phone without even speaking, and the sound of her voice warmed his freezing body. Eventually, through the wind and the rain, through the numbness in his face, he answered: "I'm so glad you called."

"You sound like you're outside... Where on earth are you?"

"I've broken down!" He tried to compete with the roaring of

gale force winds, as the line crackled. "I'm just off the A4212 – towards Llanisaf!"

"Why would you want to be out there?"

"Keep following the road until you see a blue *Volkswagen* Beetle." The line went quiet for a moment. He had hoped she'd got the message and hoped even more that she would come. "Rhiannon, are you still there?! If you can still hear me..." He looked down at his soaking wet friend. "Bring dog food."

CHAPTER 9

The occupants of the parked Beetle munched on their food whilst listening to the raindrops scattering across the windscreen. Peg was busy eating her own dinner on the backseat.

"Thanks for the pizza," Alun eventually said.

Rhiannon shrugged. "I hadn't eaten yet, anyway. Plus I thought you might be hungry by now. I don't exactly remember there being a *McDonalds* up here on these moors."

She had driven straight over as soon as she had finished their call. Her son, Gwyl, was tucked up in bed. As much as living with her parents had begun to take its toll on her sanity, it did at least have some benefits. A couple of hours on a hillside had come as a much needed break.

"How long did they say they were going to be?" she asked.

Alun checked his watch. "Another two hours."

"Wow. I think you need to get yourself a better breakdown service." She looked across at the seventies dashboard as if it had escaped from a museum. "Not to mention a new motor."

The accountant looked at her. He was both slightly surprised and slightly offended.

"I'll have you know this car has been very reliable over the years," he said. "They don't make them like this anymore."

Rhiannon squirmed to get comfortable in her seat. "No, they definitely don't."

He spotted her shudder.

"It's alright, you know," said Alun. "You don't have to wait until the breakdown person gets here. Peg and I will be fine now. She just hadn't been fed yet, that's all."

Rhiannon ignored him and gave the dog a stroke.

"Where did this one come from, then?" she asked.

"St David's Church," Alun replied.

The name raised a slight eyebrow. "And what were you doing there? Or dare I ask?"

"I spoke to the Reverend Owen, actually," he said. "I hadn't seen him in years."

"The same reverend who, *supposedly,* last saw Mari Doyle?"

The pause had said it all. She stared at his awkward face and grinned.

"Who told you that?" he asked.

"I have my sources."

He didn't want to know.

"Well?" Rhiannon asked. "Did you get anything from him?"

Alun shook his head. "Nothing of interest."

The reporter sighed. "You couldn't help yourself, could you? That freaky, little mind of yours couldn't stop whirling around at the thought of an unsolved —" She chose her next word very carefully, enough to make Alun turn to look at her. "Disappearance..."

"I just needed a walk, that was all."

"Yeah, right. I know your type. Bet you spend all night stressing over a sudoku puzzle if it's not finished."

Alun was slightly insulted. It was true: there *had* been some occasions where he enjoyed the odd sudoku puzzle. But he had never spent all night doing one (the ones in the local newspaper were far too easy for that).

"Don't feel bad about it," she continued. "You must be a natural-born journalist. It's just the way we operate."

"I wouldn't go that far," Alun said with a blush.

"That's what I was told by my old boss." She began mimicking a stereotypical newspaper editor, cigar and all. "He said to me: *Rhiannon! You, girl, are a natural-born reporter. It's embedded in your DNA, love — it's a part of who you are.* Then he went on to tell me I was stubborn, tenacious and ruthless. And he was right."

"All the lovely qualities," Alun added. He was soon smacked on the shoulder with a pizza box.

"Alright, Mr Gravedigger! Don't you get all sassy with me, all of a sudden. You're hardly a barrel of laughs yourself."

She gave him a cheeky wink. He assumed that she must have been joking, but he could never quite be sure with Rhiannon.

"Come on then," she continued, after swallowing her last slice. "That vicar must have told you at least *something*."

"He did mention that Mari talked about making a donation."

"Well that's pretty vague. Next he'll be telling you she was wearing clothes."

Alun frowned at her last comment. "What else would she be wearing?"

Rhiannon looked at him in disbelief. The man's naivety never failed to amaze her.

"Sounds like I'm better off focusing on her family," she said. "Unfortunately for Mari, her next-of-kin all seem quite unpleasant, and they're all expecting an equally large amount of inheritance."

"Ah, but this is the thing, you see," said Alun. "We've been focusing on the wrong people."

His words sparked a look of confusion from his new passenger.

"I did a lot of thinking when I was out there in the rain," he continued. "The thought came to me when I was lying in that puddle..."

"You were lying in a puddle?"

"There I was, looking up at the sky, thinking about what our lives mean — what my life has meant to other people."

Rhiannon rolled her eyes and groaned. "Oh, don't tell me you had a mid-life crisis up here on these moors. Let me guess: your whole life flashed before your eyes, did it? I imagine there were a lot of spreadsheets involved. Can't have been too exciting."

Alun ignored her. He was far too entranced in the memory of his small revelation to be offended.

"Think about it," he said. "If we put all our focus on Mari's friends and family, then we miss out on learning about the most important person of all — Mari, herself."

"I don't think there's much more to know, is there? She's a woman who owns a flower shop, who also happened to win the lottery."

"But that's not who she really is. A person isn't defined by their profession, age or someone else's opinion. If they were, then every school teacher would be exactly the same. But they're not. What were Mari Doyle's dreams? Her passions? Her fears? What was she really like as a human being? Not just on paper."

The car went silent. Peg had fallen asleep on the backseat and Rhiannon was busy contemplating what she had just heard.

"Blimey," she said. "Are you sure you've not just banged your head too hard? You don't sound like the Alun Hughes I know."

Alun smiled, something the woman had never seen him do before; she felt it suited him.

"That's my point," he replied. "*Who is* Alun Hughes? Am I Alun, the accountant? Or am I Alun, the man who hates potatoes?"

"You hate potatoes?"

"Always have, always will." His smile turned to a smug grin.

"Wow," Rhiannon said, shaking her head. "I never thought I'd hear a bureaucrat like you talk about feelings or personality. That bonk on the head must have been a really hard one." She began making shapes in the steamy windows. "Alright, then. So how do you suggest we get to know a person who isn't even around to talk to?"

Her words were followed by another smile; he had been waiting for that question.

"We take a look at the one place a person feels comfortable writing down their most inner thoughts and feelings: her diary."

"Diary?!" Rhiannon didn't know whether to laugh or cry. She was hoping the man had come up with something much better than finding a woman's *diary*. "How do you know she even kept a diary?"

"I remember her mentioning it once, during one of our appointments." He tried to recall the exact conversation. "It only came to me when I was lying out there in the mud. She had only brought it up briefly, but I remember it coming in useful at the time." He closed his eyes. "We were trying to work out the date of a purchase she had made and didn't have a receipt. She said she'd have a look back through her *diary*."

The reporter sighed from her second dose of disappointment. "So she keeps a calendar. A lot of people do."

"No, this was different," Alun insisted. "I asked her about it, and she said she'd written diaries every single day since she was a little girl. She recommended I did the same. Apparently it's quite therapeutic."

Rhiannon was not convinced. As a journalist, she knew how

tedious keeping a journal could be and couldn't imagine a person writing one just for pleasure. "Most people who start diaries never keep them."

"This woman did. She was adamant that she hand-wrote in it — every single day. It had become a sacred ritual for her. She said she had all of them boxed up somewhere. I remember thinking it was quite impressive at the time. Once we had worked out the date, we never spoke of it again."

"She can't have kept *all* of them! It's impossible — it would fill up a library, surely."

"We're only talking about a page a day." Alun pondered, calculating the figures in his head. "That's less than four-hundred in a year, about the size of a book, and then times that by about fifty years or so."

"Trust you to bother with the maths."

"That's a lot of books, yes, but still possible."

"Who can be bothered to write a diary every single night?" Rhiannon started picturing all those notebooks, all the years of scribbling. "Some people are so strange..."

Alun couldn't help but notice that she had looked at *him* when using the word "strange".

"Surely her most recent diary is in the hands of the police by now," she added. "They will have searched that house of hers from top to bottom."

"I think you're heavily underestimating the police officer assigned to this case," Alun said.

They both looked at each other and tried not to laugh.

"Oh, I see," said Rhiannon. "Still in touch with Big Mel then? I've already had the pleasure of reuniting with our boy in blue. Never had him down as a copper. He's not a bad source of info though; he always did have loose lips."

She couldn't hide her amusement at the choice of words. Alun suddenly remembered that the two had a brief history together. Mel *was* captain of the rugby team, after all. How could anyone resist? He felt a strange feeling of nausea in the pit of his stomach and wondered whether it was jealousy.

"It was Mel who told me about Mari's last sighting at the church," Alun told her.

"Captain big-mouth strikes again!"

"I think he was hoping for some info in return."

Rhiannon scoffed. "I bet he did. The only mystery that guy could solve is where his brain disappeared to. Hope you didn't give him any."

"It's not like we're any closer to solving her disappearance than he is."

"What about this diary of yours?"

Alun turned to her, surprised at the sudden flutter of interest. "I don't think it's something she would have left lying around for anyone to find."

"I'm not *anyone*, though, am I?" She gave him a playful stare and placed a hand on his knee. Her eyes were wide with excitement, and he wasn't sure whether it was the cold making him shake or his nerves. He half-smiled back, but she could sense his tension, like a predator smelling fear. She looked down at her own hand, realised it was disturbing him and pulled it away."

The Beetle suddenly felt very small, and both occupants looked away from each other.

"So... we take a look around her house?"

Rhiannon's suggestion set off a string of alarm bells in Alun's head.

"*We*?" he asked. "If you want to break into someone's property then be my guest. But don't get me involved."

"A woman's life is at stake here, Alun," she said. "And don't tell me you're not as curious as I am, because you're a terrible liar."

"It's out of the question," he said, firmly.

They both willingly sat in silence for the next few minutes. The rain had stopped, but the wind was moaning louder than ever. Struck by a sudden thought, the accountant eventually asked a burning question: "Can I ask exactly why you were ringing me in the first place, earlier?"

Rhiannon shuffled in her chair and tried her best to answer.

"Oh, I don't know," she said. "Thought I'd better thank you for the other day. You know, for looking after Gwyl."

"But you already thanked me for that."

In a burst of frustration, Rhiannon accidentally kicked her foot against the glove compartment.

"Do you really analyse *every* tiny thing in your life?" she snapped. "Why did I call you? I don't know, maybe I felt like talking to someone other than a three-year-old? Or my mum and dad... Is that a crime? It's not like I know anyone else in this stupid town — not anymore! It's driving me nuts not having my London mates around. The fact I'm ringing an accountant for a chat shows how depressing things really are at the moment."

Alun didn't know what to say. He hadn't meant to touch a nerve, but it seemed he had prodded one with a very large stick. The woman was fuming.

"Point taken," he eventually said. "Say no more."

"Good. Thank you very much."

Another uncomfortable silence followed, until the sound of Peg snoring filled the car.

"So... Mari Doyle." Alun's change of subject came as a welcome relief. He couldn't stop thinking about those diaries of hers. Rhiannon had been right: he *was* curious.

"How exactly does a person break into a house without getting noticed?"

His question made Rhiannon smile. She thought he would never ask.

CHAPTER 10

Jack Doyle pushed and shoved until his body gave in. He hated it when they did this.

The two trolleys sat in their small parking bay, almost mocking him at his failed attempt to get them free. They had been as stubborn as he was and were determined to stay jammed together for as long as they could.

The trolley attendant mustered up all his will power, grabbed the nearest by its handle and yanked it towards him with a violent force. He listened to that sweet sound of clashing steel, the same noise that two trolleys made when they came flying apart. They would never win, not whilst he was on duty.

The young man added to his long convoy of supermarket trolleys and began pushing them to their rightful place on the other side of the car park. Unbeknownst to him, two pairs of eyes were watching his every move.

"You would never think it, would you?" Rhiannon told her observant passenger.

Alun watched the young man in the bright yellow jacket who was pushing his trolleys to the front of the supermarket.

"Three spent convictions..." he said, still pondering his new piece of information. "He doesn't seem old enough."

"He's twenty-two," said Rhiannon, still polishing off the last of her breakfast muffin. Alun tried to ignore the falling crumbs and keep calm; it wasn't his car they were in, thankfully. Still, there were a lot of crumbs. "He's the one who reported Mari missing. Him and his grandmother were close from what I hear."

"Sounds about right. Mari talked about him quite a few times. She even managed to convince me to give him a week's work experience when he was in school. Can't believe he's now *twenty-two*."

Rhiannon felt like rubbing her hands together with delight. "So Jack knows you?"

"I don't know how well he remembers me, but we got on okay," Alun said, with a shrug. "He barely knew how to use a calculator, but he was quite happy to clean the office and help me move around some filing cabinets. I don't think accounting was his first choice of career paths, but I must have been a last resort. He seemed like a polite young man. Never gave me trouble, anyway."

"Excellent!" Rhiannon said, whilst reaching for her coat. "That means he'll trust you."

Alun looked at her with grave suspicion. He could tell she had plans to approach the young man, and he didn't like the sound of his involvement. He had suspected that the lift back from the garage would come at a price, but a confrontation in a public car park was worse than he ever imagined.

"You're not really going to speak with him *now*?" he asked (even though he already knew the answer). "The poor man's at work."

Rhiannon double-checked her makeup in the rearview mirror. She had been in a rush to get Gwyl ready for nursery that morning and had slapped most of it on without even looking.

When it came to questioning an interviewee, particularly a passive one like Jack Doyle, she was determined to look professional. The makeup was a shield against her tired eyes and delicate mood. She had one rule: never show them what you're really thinking. She knew that a layer of foundation and a spot of concealer probably did very little to mask a person's emotions, but Rhiannon was willing to try anything. The journalist had learnt the hard way, and at the very start of her career, how far crippling self-doubt and a lack of confidence would get you.

"No time like the present," she said. "I've already tried speaking with Jack before. It didn't go too well."

"What makes you think it's going to go any better this time?"

Rhiannon gave him a playful slap on the shoulder. Alun was surprised how much it hurt.

"This time, I've got *you* with me," she said. "If I'm with someone he knows, I might get more out of him."

"He's not a piece of fruit ready to be juiced."

"Actually, that's exactly what he is. Good analogy."

Alun sighed. She had already told him the plan the night before, whilst they were still stranded on the Caradog Moors. It turned out that the breakdown company's time estimation had been very optimistic.

Jack Doyle was the only known person to have direct access to Mari's house. If he could let them into the property, then they wouldn't even need to break in (not that Alun had ever entertained *that* idea).

Jack had visited his grandmother at least once a week to complete his series of household chores and, according to Rhiannon's local police source, had been devastated by her disappearance.

The unsuspecting trolley attendant was just about to complete another top-up of carts, when he looked up to see a familiar looking woman heading towards him. Her smart clothes and formal manner had instilled the fear of God inside of him on their last encounter, and he immediately began walking in the opposite direction.

"Jack!" cried the voice. "I just need to speak with you!"

Jack quickened his pace and kept his eyes firmly planted on the ground.

"I told you everything!" he called back. "Leave me alone!"

"It won't take long, Jack," Rhiannon assured him. "We need your help."

"I'm not helping anyone else — ever again! You're all liars!"

He reached the next bay to find only three trolleys this time. Two of them were stuck together.

"Who's been lying to you, Jack?" Rhiannon asked with genuine curiosity.

"The police, my family — everyone!" he snapped. "Nobody cares about me or my Nan. They just care about what *they* want."

"And what's that?"

The reporter's question was left unanswered. Jack's response came in the sound of clashing steel, as he tried to separate another two trolleys.

"We're trying to find your Nan, Jack," said a new voice from behind the woman.

Jack looked over to see Alun hovering in the background, shivering in his long coat. The excursion through the wind and rain the night before had left the accountant with a slight cold, although Rhiannon would have sworn the man was on death's door the way he had been complaining.

"Mr Hughes?" asked the surprised trolley attendant. He had fond memories of his short tenure at *Hughes & Son*. It had been the first, and indeed the last, office job he ever had. It had also been the only place where he had been treated like an adult. The accountant had treated him well.

"What are you doing here?" Jack asked, again.

"This woman is my friend," said Alun. "I know she might seem a bit, you know — forward..." Rhiannon gave him a stern look at his choice of words but could say nothing. "But we're both just trying to get to the bottom of your grandmother's disappearance."

Jack nodded. He was disappointed that his favourite, former employer would dare to associate with such an obnoxious journalist.

"If that's true," said Jack, "then it's more than her own family are trying to do."

His sentence caused a flash of intrigue from the two people now standing in his personal space.

"I hear you were quite close to your grandmother, Jack," said Rhiannon. Her first hint of sympathy was proving useful in preventing him from fleeing.

"Someone has to look after her," Jack replied. He could feel the anger inside of him starting to build. "I go round her house every week to do a few jobs."

"Did she pay you?"

"Rhiannon!" Alun snapped. Even he was stunned by the bluntness of the woman's question.

"No she did not!" Jack cried, revealing a very different side to him now. He was no longer the quiet, timid young man he had portrayed so far. "I never cared about no money! Not like *them*!"

Her tactic had worked. The reporter was trying to get a rise out of him, and she had succeeded. People revealed a lot when they were angry (and Rhiannon was very good at making people angry).

"Who's *they*, Jack?" she asked.

"All of them!" came the answer. "Dad, Auntie Lesley, Uncle Danny, Auntie Ceri — all of them!"

"How do you know they're after her money?"

"Cause Nan told me. She said they're all just waiting for the money." He waved his arms around in the heat of the angry rant. His voice had become so raised that passersby were now looking. "Especially *her*!"

"Who's *her*, Jack? Your Auntie Lesley? *Ceri*?"

Alun interjected her questions by stepping in front of her. "I think we need to stop now —"

The journalist swerved around him and began chasing after the distraught trolley assistant.

"We need to get into your grandmother's house, Jack!" she called. "We know you have access!"

"Leave me alone!" Jack cried, as he sensed her presence getting nearer. "My dad says I don't have to talk to anyone!

"Did your work do a criminal record check, Jack?"

"That's enough!" Alun shouted. He couldn't remember the last time he expressed such anger in a public place (or any place for that matter), but Rhiannon was very good at making people angry.

The young man in the reflective jacket froze. His anger turned to fear. He had tried hard to find a job. Had it not been for his friend who worked at the supermarket, he would never have even been considered.

"Please don't tell them," he said, without even turning around.

Rhiannon saw the disgust in Alun's face at her behaviour. She had to admit, the accountant seemed quite attractive when he put his foot down. On the other hand, she also considered the fact that maybe she *had* crossed the line this time, especially if Alun was snapping at her. The sight of Jack's terrified face made her feel even worse.

"We just want to have a look around the house," she said with a sigh. "We think your grandmother might have kept a diary that could help us find her. All we need is your spare key."

"I don't even have the spare key," said Jack. He put his focus back on something that would centre his scattered mind: the trolleys.

Rhiannon was left stranded in the middle of the empty parking bays, abandoned without any of the answers she was looking for. She cursed under her breath and was forced to turn back towards Alun's judgmental stare.

"We leave it in the garden shed," the attendant called out. He walked past them with a brand new convoy of empty trolleys. "It's underneath the tool box. That's where she always kept it."

The light in Rhiannon's eyes sparked back up again. Alun could only clutch his own head in dismay.

"Happy now?" he asked her.

CHAPTER 11

"Hold it steady!" Rhiannon called.

Her accomplice frowned whilst holding up his torch. He couldn't believe what he was doing.

"You know this is still classed as *breaking and entering*?" Alun asked, looking back towards the garden, hoping that nobody had spotted them coming around the side passageway.

"How?" she asked back, almost stumbling over an old lawn mower. "We're borrowing a spare key. We're not *breaking* anything."

"We're still entering a person's property without permission! I think if you left your front door open and you found a stranger rummaging around your bathroom you'd be pretty annoyed."

"I'm not a missing person, though, am I?" Rhiannon flashed her torch around in search of a toolbox. "The days are already ticking by. I think you and I both know there's only one way Mari Doyle is going to turn — *Argh*!"

The torch went flying to the ground and she grabbed hold of Alun. The tight squeeze of her arms around his body released an even louder *yelp* than her own cry.

"A rat!" she cried. "That was a big, hairy rat!"

The furry critter she was referring to had long scuttered off into the night. Alun breathed a sigh of relief. He could get jumpy at the best of times when it came to the dark, but Rhiannon's cry had almost sent him running for the main road.

"I think you'll find it was a mouse," he said, still trapped in her tight grip.

"It was huge!" she shouted. "I hate all of them — those toothy, little monsters!"

When it was clear that the rodent had long gone, she released the accountant and gave him a shove. "You were about to ditch me just then. First sign of trouble and you were off!"

"Well I did say I don't want to be here," said Alun, straightening up his ruffled clothes. "It's not like we both needed to come."

"Good to know we've got each other's back, then!" She picked up the torch and continued her search. "You'd have been sorry if I never came back!"

She was right, Alun thought. He would have felt quite guilty and, perhaps, even a little sad. Although, it was hard to contemplate this truth when he was being ranted at in the middle of a garden shed.

Rhiannon plucked up the courage again and tried to forget about the possibility of unexpected creatures coming out to startle her. She flashed her light across a row of shelves, until it landed on an old toolbox. The key had indeed been tucked underneath. It was sitting there for those trusted enough to be in the know. That night, the responsibility of the key bearer had fallen on the unlikely pairing of a journalist and an accountant.

The two trespassers sneaked across the small lawn, their identities hidden in shadow. A full moon lit up the white patio, as two pairs of feet carefully tiptoed across it. The back garden was overlooked by a row of houses with darkened windows. At such a late hour, on a cold night, most of the quiet neighbourhood had drifted off to sleep.

With the help of their trusted key, Alun and Rhiannon were soon navigating their way around the ground floor of house number eighty-five, Pandy Lane. Without the added help of their man in the moon, the only source of light came from the large torch with its powerful beam. The guiding spotlight led the way, from a minimal kitchen to an immaculate living room.

"Are you sure she lived in this house?" Rhiannon whispered.

"Only for about a year," Alun replied. He followed her every move to avoid any sudden walls. "She moved here after an entire lifetime of living on the family farm."

"Well it doesn't look very lived in." She flashed her light against all four walls. "The place is spotless, like a showroom. There's not one thing out of place."

Alun was struggling to understand what she meant. His own home was very similar to this one. Everything was in its proper place: no clutter, stains or unusual marks; a soothing environment that a person could feel calm in.

"Maybe she just keeps a tidy house," he said, impressed at the arrangement of the cushions on her sofa. Good symmetry, he thought.

Rhiannon scoffed. "I don't know how people can live like this. What's wrong with an empty cup lying around? Or a few piles of washing? A bit of clutter never did anyone any harm."

Alun very much begged to differ. A messy home was his idea of a complete nightmare. A cluttered house was an unhappy house, and Mari Doyle's house was beaming with a smile.

Despite the minimalist style of a public hospital ward, there was one area of the room that contained the smallest hint of a personal touch. Carefully laid out on a carved cupboard was a small collection of framed photographs. They spanned a number of decades, and each image had been professionally taken in front of a similar backdrop. The faces of Mari's family members all stared back with forced smiles and a myriad of dated haircuts.

A curious Rhiannon scanned them all with great disgust. She always hated formal family photos and had sworn to never put her own child through such a terrible ordeal. A photo of a younger Barry Doyle reminded her of the looming dinner appointment coming up the following night and almost made her gag. The photo from the early seventies contained all four of the Doyle children, all smirking towards the camera lens. What a shame how some of them had turned out, Rhiannon thought, wishing there was a way she could warn them.

"There they all are," she said, pointing to a family photo containing Mari and all four of her children standing in a row. "Barry, Lesley, Ceri and Danny."

Alun peered at the photograph lit up by her torch.

"You'd think they were a really happy family," he said.

"Well, we all know that's not true. From what I've seen so far, not one of those four has turned out normal."

Rhiannon passed her light across two more recent photographs.

"There's our Jack, the favourite grandson," she said. "And I'm assuming that's a granddaughter."

They both stared at the teenage girl posing in a local netball shirt.

"That's Ruby," Alun confirmed. "Lesley's daughter. She works weekends at Mari's shop."

Rhiannon inspected the remaining photographs until something unusual caught her attention. Hanging from one of the frames was a small pendant; it bore a symbol unlike anything she had come across before.

"I thought dedicated Christians prefer to wear crosses around their necks," she said, clutching the amulet and inspecting its unusual markings. "This looks more at home on a fortune teller."

Alun couldn't agree more. It certainly wasn't something he had ever seen around Mari's neck. "We could really do with a crystal ball right now."

The two of them jumped at the sound of a door closing.

"It's alright," said Rhiannon. "That was next door."

She pushed on through towards the staircase. Alun followed closely behind, until they reached the main bedroom. The double bed was all made and the curtains were wide open.

Rhiannon let out a short gasp and almost dropped her torch. When she realised that the stranger lurking in the corner was in fact her own reflection in the mirrored wardrobe, she smacked Alun on the shoulder.

"See how jumpy you've made me?" she hissed.

Whilst Alun tried to work out what he had done wrong, Rhiannon was already rummaging through the dressing table drawers, muttering: "If that diary's anywhere, it'll be in here."

The accountant looked on, as she rooted through the woman's belongings like a frantic bloodhound. After combing through jewellery boxes and piles of clothes, she noticed that her accomplice had not yet moved a muscle.

"Are you going to help me, or just stand there?" she asked.

Alun was framed by the large window behind him and backlit by the streetlights outside. She could not see his eyes through the darkness but knew they could barely look at her.

"It just feels... wrong," he eventually said. "Going through another person's possessions, I mean."

The journalist looked at him as if he were a soldier running away from battle.

"Oh, I see," she said. "You have an attack of conscience now that we've come this far, but you were quite happy to comb through her personal finances."

"That's different —"

"No, it's not! You did your job; now I'm doing mine. If you can't get your hands dirty, then don't bother trying to help. I'll get to the bottom of this mystery myself."

Just as Alun was about to give in, he was startled by a flashing blue light. He turned around to see the police car parking up outside and went diving towards the floor.

"It's the police!" he cried. "Someone's called the police! I *knew* someone saw us!"

Rhiannon crawled over to silence him.

"Quiet!" she whispered. "Nobody could have seen us. Let me hear what's going on!"

They both listened out for the sound of a car door opening. Once they had heard it slam shut, the sound of the doorbell sent them twirling into a panicked frenzy.

"Come on, let's get out of here," Rhiannon said, as she bolted towards the landing.

Alun called after her: "Rhiannon! Turn off your torch!!"

It was too late; Rhiannon had made it to the ground floor before he could even reach the banister.

"Open up!" called the deep voice. "This is *North Wales Police*!"

Alun's worst nightmare was finally coming true: he was about to go down for attempted burglary.

The knocking continued, as he snuck down the stairs and tried to feel his way towards the kitchen. He felt a burst of cold air coming from the back door and went running across the hard tiles. Unaware of the small object blocking his path, his legs became tangled around a metallic stool, and he went flying to the floor with a hard *smack*.

Lying in the darkness, he felt a hand grab him by the arm.

"Keep moving!" Rhiannon whispered and began dragging the dazed man towards the nearest exit.

The sound of a giant boot colliding with a solid door echoed around the entire house. Lights were switched on in the room next door and both trespassers knew this was their last chance to escape.

Alun had just managed to reach the back door, when he was tackled to the ground by a man twice his size. The intense struggle was shortened by the flashing torch across the police officer's face. The man was blinded for a moment, before he realised who was holding the light source.

"What the hell are you two doing here?!"

A very hot and flustered Mel tried to catch his breath. He seemed more relieved to find a familiar face than they were.

Alun was still being crushed by the enormous weight lying on top of him. It reminded him of their little "wrestlemania" sessions as children, an activity that was purely Mel's idea and one that usually involved Alun being choked and squeezed.

"I thought someone was robbing the place," said Mel, climbing to his feet as he picked up a relieved Alun. "Mrs Roden from across the street reported seeing a flashing torch from her bedroom window."

Rhiannon received a stern look from her accomplice which said: "I *told* you someone saw us."

"We're not here to *rob the place*," she said. "We're here to look for a clue."

Her last sentence helped the police officer calm down from his rush of adrenaline. He couldn't help but look amused.

"A clue?" he asked. "Think you're playing detective now, do you?"

"Not as much as *you've* been, Constable," she replied, knowing full well that the mention of his previous job title would touch a nerve.

"This is a missing person case," Mel snapped. "And it's been assigned to *me*. This isn't some murder mystery game for everyone to join in on."

"That's lucky." The journalist folded up her arms in a sulk. "If there has been a murder, the killer's getting away scot-free with Mr North-Wales-Police on the case."

Alun jumped in between them, just as Mel's face looked like it was going to explode.

"Alright, alright," he said, doing his best to break up the tension. "We're all on the same side here, remember?"

"Are we?" asked Mel. "I've got a right mind to arrest both of you."

"But there's no need on this occasion," Alun assured him. "There was no harm done."

"Tell that to my pulled thigh muscle." The large man rubbed his leg and groaned.

"He wouldn't know how to use a pair of handcuffs if his wife strapped him to the bed with them," said Rhiannon.

It was now her turn for Alun's assertive hand-on-the-shoulder.

"We're just going to put back that spare key and all go home," the accountant said to her.

The journalist struggled to contain her frustration.

"Can't we at least finish looking for that diary? Like the number cruncher said: we've all got the same goal."

"What diary?" Mel asked. "There's no diary in there. I've searched that house from top to bottom myself." He took a look at the spotless kitchen. "Not that there's much to search. She was hardly a hoarder."

Alun stumbled as he found himself pushed out of the way whilst the other two locked horns.

"I've been told by a reliable source that Mari kept — *keeps* a diary," Rhiannon said, her saliva sprinkling across the police officer's large nose.

"If she does, then it's not anywhere in *this* vicinity," replied Mel. "I suggest you improve your sources."

She studied his eyes for a sign of doubt but found nothing. With a sigh, she gave up the staring competition and backed off.

"Then I'm clearly wasting the rest of my evening," she said. "I'm all done here."

The police officer watched her storm off across the back garden and called out: "I'm the one that decides when we're all done! Unless you fancy making a quick detour to the station?"

Rhiannon stopped before she reached the wooden gate and turned around.

"How is Sandra, by the way?" she asked. "Does she know you used to go streaking around the girls changing rooms, even in secondary school? She was a lucky woman marrying you."

She left Mel gobsmacked, his mouth almost touching the patio.

"Goodnight, gentlemen!"

Her final words lingered with them, before they drifted off into the nighttime air.

Alun and Mel looked at each other, not quite knowing what to say.

"What the hell are you doing hanging out with *that* woman?" asked Mel.

Alun scratched his head and had to think about the answer. "To be honest with you, I don't quite know."

CHAPTER 12

The aqueduct loomed high above like a towering giant. Its great arches created a series of enormous windows that peered out into the next valley. The impressive piece of nineteenth century engineering had stood there for many lifetimes.

Even though it was only half a mile outside the town of Pengower, Alun had not looked up at the old structure in many years. His new morning routine of walks with Peg had reintroduced him to many of the local sights. They were reminding him of just how beautiful his homeland really was, and how it was a part of the world that he had very much taken for granted for all these years.

With the Border Collie tugging away by his side, he breathed in the fresh morning air and continued to climb his way up the steep banks. Soon, he was standing beside the same canal water that flowed across the great aqueduct. The man-made river was even more peaceful than the valley below, and it was just as Alun had reached an almost meditative state that he saw something that made him want to hide.

Coming towards him down the canal path was a familiar

figure that sent his adrenaline levels to an all time high. This person was not alone, and the accountant was just debating the idea of jumping into the water to get away, when they started to approach him.

"Alun?"

The sound of the person's voice sent a jolt through his entire body. He thought he had long shaken these emotions away, but it was clear they had been lying dormant inside of him.

"Meg?"

His ex-girlfriend stood in front of him like a ghost from another lifetime. Her hair was a different shade of colour and it was no longer straightened, as it had been, everyday, for ten years. Her face gave off a radiant glow, and her right hand was clasped around another.

"What are you doing up this way?" she asked, her voice a higher pitch than it normally was.

Alun stuttered in his response: "I — uh, thought I would — you know —" He pointed down at the impatient Border Collie, who had chosen the perfect time to tangle her lead around his legs. "Taking Peg for a walk."

"Aw, she's beautiful!" Megan knelt down and embraced the excited dog in a tight squeeze.

Alun watched them both and could feel a slight hint of jealousy towards his new pet. If only he could have held Megan in such a way, just for that moment.

The pause in conversation felt like it was going to last forever, until Alun couldn't help but notice the awkward young man standing opposite him.

"Oh, I'm so sorry," Megan said, standing up again so that the two men weren't left to stare at each other. "This is Gareth. Gareth — Alun."

The tall, athletic man reached out his giant paw and shook her ex-boyfriend's hand.

"Nice to meet you, Alun," he said with a charming smile.

His demeanour was so polite that it disarmed the accountant to the point of embarrassment. Alun hated him for it.

"Thought we'd take a walk too," Megan said, and then she laughed uncontrollably. "You're taking Peg for a walk; I'm taking Gareth for a walk!" Another laugh.

Alun did his best to appear amused. "Ha, ha! Yes! How funny."

He saw their hands linking up again and wanted to run away again.

"How are you doing, anyway?" she asked him, in a tone a social worker might ask someone.

"Great, yeah," Alun replied. Apart from having my girlfriend dump me over the telephone, he thought.

"Oh, good. That's good. Well, you look well, anyway." Now he knew she was just being nice. In the time since he had first spotted her walking down the canal, he had just aged thirty years. Gareth's chiselled jaw was now distracting him, and he couldn't help but wonder whether there was such a thing as dumbbells for your face.

"We're just heading to my mam's," Megan added.

At least his morning could have been worse, Alun thought.

"Oh, how is your mam?" he asked.

"Really well, actually." Shame, the man in front of her was now thinking. "She's cooking Gareth and me her special stew."

The worst possible scenario had suddenly been confirmed. Alun remembered the special stew. It had been cooked for him when he and Megan had first started dating. A relationship was never official until the new boyfriend had been offered up a bowl of the special stew.

"Ah, yes, the special stew," he said between his teeth. "Lucky Gareth."

It was during this moment that Peg had decided to relieve

herself in the middle of the path. Soon, all three of them were staring at a large, brown mound.

"Oh," said Megan. "I think we better let you go."

You let me go, alright, were the words circling around Alun's head. And he pulled out a roll of dog waste bags.

"Uh, yes. I should probably sort this mess out," he said, secretly referring to his life.

"THAT'S a right kick in the teeth, that is, mate."

Mel was already on his second pint of lager when he finished hearing about Alun's earlier encounter over at the canal. He had been badgering his old friend for a beer for months, and the accountant had decided that it would provide yet another perfect opportunity to drown his sorrows.

It wasn't that Alun despised his friend's company, it was that they seemed to have less in common now than they had done when they were children. Their mothers, on the other hand, had been very close, and it was this relationship that had spawned years of playdates, sleepovers and uncomfortable holiday trips. You would have thought having a bigger and stronger child on your side at school would have been a blessing. Instead, it had only made him the nearest target for ridicule, dead-arms and the occasional trouser-dropping. Alun had never been very good at making new friends, and so his association with Mel had been more of an act of survival rather than pleasure. It was only years later that he realised the majority of his physical injuries had actually come at the hands of his old friend (a silverback gorilla never knows his own strength).

Mel had always been the most dominant member of his pack of schoolboys. As time went on, he discovered that those same people had never really liked him very much and were only his friend for the same reason as Alun. It was a dog-eat-dog world out there on the playground, and it was hard to bully an abnormally large teenager who was captain of the rugby team.

When it came time for Mel to navigate the less tribal realities of his adult life, it was only Alun who had remained loyal. The accountant had likened Mel to the brother he had never had, and the brother he had never asked for.

"So she's found a new man, has she?" Mel asked him, before he swallowed another mouthful of beer. "That's a great shame. Must have stung you a bit to see her so happy."

His drinking buddy stared into his pint glass and was beginning to have second thoughts about his choice of company that evening.

Mel gave him a large slap on the shoulder and prepared to offer up some of his infinite wisdom: "You know what you need? A new woman."

The other man waited for him to elaborate but heard nothing but a large fist thumping against the table (Mel often liked to hit tables when he was drinking).

The Old Bull's Head was quiet for a Friday night. A game of pool was in full swing down in the corner of the bar, and a group of middle-aged women were getting rowdy over by the jukebox.

"So why are you so interested in this Mari Doyle?" asked Mel, as he came back to the table with a fresh round of drinks.

"Isn't everyone?" Alun asked back. He could feel the off-duty policeman studying him like an all-too-familiar book.

"Not enough to go off galavanting in the night with some annoying journalist." The man moved forward, until his large, purple nose was almost touching Alun's. "It's very suspicious, Alun. Should I be putting you on the top of my suspect list?"

The accountant was slightly taken aback by the man's accusatory glare. A few seconds later, Mel was in fits of laughter.

"Calm down!" he roared. "I'm only messing with you!" The

policeman pulled out his packet of tobacco and began rolling himself a new cigarette. "*Your* face, though! I think we all know that a pen-pusher like you would never have the guts to commit murder."

Alun could have sworn the whole pub had gone quiet for a moment, even though there was no sign of any disturbance after looking around.

"So you really think she was... murdered?" he asked, with a whisper that made his friend chuckle.

"Course she was!" said Mel. "And the whole town knows it. An old millionaire with a family like hers? It was only a matter of time, if you ask me."

His vocal opinion made the accountant nervous. He knew that Mel could have a large mouth when he was drunk. It was a dangerous trait for a local policeman.

"I don't think we should be talking about this here."

"Why? Everyone else in this pub probably is." Mel looked around the room before leaning in so that only Alun could hear. "And I'll tell you another thing: if she *has* been murdered, it'll be the most exciting thing to have ever happened in this town."

He sat back in his chair and saw that he had inadvertently soaked his new cigarette with beer.

"It's not easy being a copper in a place where your most common call-out is a stolen sheep. I'm bored to tears at the moment."

Alun knew that his friend didn't really mean the things he said, or at least, he hoped not. The man always had a habit of spouting out offensive remarks in the hope of making him uncomfortable, and they always worked.

"Hey! Is that fresh bacon I can smell, Dylan?"

A short, stocky man in a local football shirt walked over to the table. His friend Dylan was an equally formidable human being and possessed a permanently sly grin.

"I didn't know they served bacon in here," the short man continued, flaring out his nostrils.

The sight of Danny Doyle made Mel groan with contempt.

"Oh, here we go," said the drunken police officer. "Aren't you supposed to be barred?"

Danny smirked, almost gloating, as he added chalk to the end of his pool cue.

"Not from this pub, I'm not," he replied. "I've got as much right to be in here as you have — even more, probably. Nobody wants a copper around when you're trying to enjoy a drink."

Mel scoffed. "Why? Got something to hide?"

The question appeared to ruffle the man, who had clearly been drinking for many hours.

"Shouldn't you be out there looking for my Mam?" Danny asked him.

"It's my night off, as it happens," replied Mel "And we *have* been looking for your Mam."

It was now Danny's turn to look smug.

"Have you?" he asked, knowing he didn't need an answer. "You could have fooled me. It's been five days."

"It's six actually."

Danny shot his attention towards the scrawnier gentleman sitting next to Mel.

"You what?"

"She's been gone for six days," Alun repeated. "Not five."

The short man, with a lot of pent-up energy, went from angry to amused.

"Well of course *you'd* know, Numbers Man," Danny said, before smiling at the question he was about to deliver next. "How's Megan doing these days?"

The sound of his ex-girlfriend's name caused a nastier cut than Alun would have expected.

Mel placed his large hand against the accountant's

chest, as if Alun were about to leap up into a frenzy of flying fists. He wasn't, of course (as much as he really wanted to), but was glad that the idea of someone like *him* engaging in physical altercation had at least been entertained.

"Leave it, Danny," the police officer said.

"What's he going to do?" asked Danny, pointing at the disgruntled accountant. "Hit me with a calculator?" His friend burst out laughing. "Come on, Dylan. Let's leave Laurel and Hardy over here to enjoy their big night out."

The two men swaggered off towards the pool table on the other side of the bar. Mel's disgusted eyes followed after him and he shook his head.

"He's been a nightmare this year, he has," said the police officer. "I've had him cuffed in the back of my car twice since Christmas."

"I can't possibly imagine why," said Alun, trying hard to ignore Danny's cocky chants on the other side of the room.

Mel relaxed back into his chair and stuck his enormous feet up on a nearby bar stool. "Wait until I arrive at his front door tomorrow morning for a spot of questioning about his mother. He's not so cocky when he's sober."

"I take it our Mr Danny Doyle is yet another person featured on the suspect list?" Alun asked.

"All of Mari's offspring are. Can't rule anyone out in a case like this. You need to eliminate every suspect — and there's plenty of them to get through."

Alun was impressed to hear such a professional approach for a change. His friend must have been watching *Midsomer Murders* again, he thought.

"Any evidence yet?" asked Alun,

Mel shook his head in disappointment "Nothing concrete. But if there is, I'll find it — mark my words."

A sudden thought rushed into the man's head. He leaned forward to keep his next words confidential.

"Hey," he said, keeping his voice down. "Managed to get hold of some interesting old police reports yesterday."

Alun was all ears.

"You remember the old Doyle family farm?" Mel asked.

"I remember people used to say it was haunted," said Alun, the memories flooding back.

"Yeah, that's right! I remember Evan Edwards dared me to go down there once and knock on their door."

The man let out a wicked chuckle, before returning to his more serious tone.

"There's definitely a few skeletons in that place," he said. "Found a few reports of some domestic abuse. Then there's the death of Mari's old husband."

"Tony Doyle?" asked Alun. He only vaguely remembered the Doyle father, but his name had lived on. "He fell off a tree house, didn't he?"

"Nobody ever believed that one. You remember the rumours at school? We all used to think one of the Doyle kids pushed him. That was a rumour for ages."

Alun nodded. Yes, he did recall such a rumour.

"What were the domestic abuse reports about?" he asked, still curious.

"Just some anonymous calls that they reckon were made by one of the kids," said Mel. "One report described the sound of Mari screaming in the kitchen, followed by the smashing of pots and pans. The parents denied it when the police arrived, of course, but it was noted that Tony stank of booze and seemed very agitated. Word on the street was that he liked a drink."

"Must run in the family," said Alun, turning their attention to a rowdy Danny, who was now lying across the pool table and pretending to hump it.

"Hey," said Mel, giving his friend a playful nudge. "I just saw Bev Griffiths looking at you."

They both looked over at the three women still huddled by the jukebox. They certainly appeared to be having a good time.

"No, she wasn't," said Alun.

"Oh, yes, she was," said Mel. "Go over there and talk to her. See if she wants a game of pool."

"You know I can't play pool."

"Who cares? It's all just angles and geometry. You're good at that stuff."

"You mean trigonometry..."

Alun's cynical stare was met with a hard slap on the back.

"See," said Mel. "You'll be a natural!"

It took Alun at least another two pints before he had the courage to make that long, daunting walk over to the jukebox. On his way across the bar, he went through all the potential opening lines. Despite his lofty ambition of capturing this woman's heart in just a few short words, he had forgotten that he was also heavily intoxicated.

As he approached the unsuspecting party, who were all dressed up for a night at the disco, he discovered that the muscles in his mouth were not quite functioning as well as he'd hoped. Instead of a smooth, articulate sentence, he let out a barrage of slurred noises: "Argh — Bev! You'll never guess who I saw yesterday at the dentist!"

The woman in heavy makeup turned around to see Alun stumbling towards her like a hungry zombie. He had certainly grabbed her attention.

"It was your Auntie Nesta!" Alun said.

Bev nodded to her friends, who were equally amused, and pulled out her best surprised-face.

"Did you really?! Wow!" She stepped forward with her cheap looking cocktail and raised her voice so that the others could hear. "Well, maybe you should try chatting up my Auntie Nesta, instead!"

Her words were followed by a cackle of laughter from her surrounding entourage. One of them peered over her shoulder and shouted out: "Bet you love a good ride in the dentist chair, Alun!"

Alun stood there, the world around him descending into slow motion. He tried hard to work out what had gone wrong. It was true: he *did* enjoy visiting the dentist and found the whole procedure quite efficient. Still, he very much doubted that Bev's friend had been referring to the wonders of modern dentistry.

"Do you like... pool?" The question trickled out of him like a mouthful of excess beer.

Bev's expression had become one of great confusion, and she had been left with little choice but to consult with her friends. "Did he just ask me if I like pool?"

The laughter that followed was even worse than the one before.

"He'll be asking if I like pork scratchings next!" Bev cried, trying not to stumble over in her high heels.

Just as the situation could not get any worse, Alun turned to discover that Danny Doyle had been standing within earshot, and he seemed to be as entertained by the whole scene as the group of women.

"I think you're punching above your weight there, tax man!" he called out, twirling around his pool cue.

Alun felt a rush of anger; it was a sensation that was quite alien to him but one he was beginning to fully embrace.

"I'm not a *tax man*, actually," he snapped. "That's someone who works for the government. You'd know that if you ever paid yours."

Danny looked stunned. Not only had he been corrected, but there was now a group of drunken women laughing their socks off at him. Even his friend Dylan had enjoyed a snigger at his own expense.

Alun braced himself as the embarrassed man marched straight up to him, his chest puffed out like an angry pigeon.

"Think you're clever, do you?" Danny asked him. "Stood there in your fancy shoes. I reckon they need a good clean."

The attention had moved straight down towards the accountant's feet, which were sitting in footwear that would be more suitable for an elegant dinner ball. They did not, however, blend their way into the sticky floors of the *Old Bull's Head*.

Danny lifted up his pint glass and poured the last of his beer straight over the other man's well-polished shoes. "There we are," he said. "Much better."

He stared Alun down with an antagonising smirk.

"Ooooh," he said. "Do I detect a glimmer of anger in those eyes of yours, Alun? Is there something you want to say?"

Alun could feel his bottom lip trembling from the pent-up rage. Any dislike of confrontation had been completely overwhelmed by humiliation and alcohol.

"Danny! Leave it!"

The local thug could hear the police officer's warnings from the other side of the room, however, they only fuelled his thirst for cruelty even more.

"I heard Megan has a new boyfriend," Danny said, knowing that his piece of local gossip would touch a nerve. "That's such a shame. I was going to have a crack at her myself."

As the man got right up into the last inches of his personal space, Alun felt his right hand scrunch up into a closed fist. Almost as though it had grown a life of its own, the hand went flying towards Danny Doyle's unsuspecting face.

When his knuckles collided with the other man's large nose, the accountant was surprised how much punching someone in the face actually hurt. The bones in his hand made a loud *crunch,* as if they were striking the bark of a solid oak tree. The feeling afterwards was not of deep satisfaction; it was the dreaded terror of the impending consequences of his foolish actions.

His punch had felt like it had happened in slow motion, but the punch that followed took place at breakneck speed. A few seconds later and Alun was lying on his back in a puddle of beer. His first pub fight had ended quicker than it had started. Now the proud owner of a painful blackeye and a bruised ego, he was starting to doubt whether it had all been worth it.

CHAPTER 13

Rhiannon's eyes followed the bottle of vintage Cabernet Sauvignon as it was placed on the table in front of her. The journalist didn't even really like red wine that much, but it had been the most expensive bottle on the menu and she was quite happy to add it to Barry Doyle's bill.

The Amore Italiano, a warm and inviting establishment, was tucked away in one of Pengower's narrow side streets. On a Saturday night, the Italian restaurant was fully booked and was a popular nightspot for those partial to something a little more adventurous than fish and chips or a takeaway pizza.

The journalist glanced at her watch and took her first gulp of red wine. She had been fifteen minutes early and Barry was half an hour late, meaning her patience and wine levels would soon be at opposite ends of the scale. With a second bottle of red on the horizon, Barry's poor timekeeping was certainly going to cost him.

Lying beneath her elbows on the chequered table cloth was an open property brochure. She studied the photographs of *Derwen Farm* for what must have been the tenth time that evening. Looking at the house's deteriorating roof and dilapidated outside walls, she wondered how the seemingly house-proud Mari of eighty-five, Pandy Lane could have lived in such a place. Something about its isolated location gave her the chills. Perhaps she had truly become a city person, after all.

Sipping away on her glass, she observed some of the other diners and caught sight of a middle-aged couple enjoying their night out. A feeling of loneliness washed over her, and, for a brief moment, she imagined she was waiting for a hot date to arrive (preferably in the form of a lead doctor from her favourite television serial). Instead, she would have to make do with a portly salesman with a hideous personality. She couldn't wait.

Lost in her fantasy of good-looking doctors, she almost missed her man's arrival.

"Sorry I'm late," said a beaming Barry Doyle, who seemed to be wearing the same creased, sweaty shirt as last time. He stared at the younger woman with his beady eyes and couldn't believe his luck. "Busy day at the office."

Rhiannon checked her watch. "You must be quite the workaholic."

The business owner almost seemed out-of-breath after his short walk down the high street, and he plonked himself down with an exhausted grunt. He wiped off the excess perspiration from his moustache and pulled his shirt down over a protruding belly.

"You have to be in this line of work," he said. "We're not the only property sellers in town. Only the ruthless will survive."

He winked at her before pouring himself a glass of wine.

"I hear it's quite the seller's market at the moment," said Rhiannon.

"It certainly is," said Barry, raising up his glass for a toast. "*Make hay*, and all that! Last year was abysmal. May the gold rush long continue."

"Well, I appreciate you making the time to fit me in, Mr

Doyle." She raised a glass in return and pretended to look sincere.

"Please — call me Barry. And who says this all has to be about work?"

He unleashed a seedy laugh that made Rhiannon want to heave.

"A lot of people don't know this, but I'm quite the social animal at heart," he continued. "All work and no play..."

He certainly liked to dish out the proverbs, Rhiannon thought. She imagined he had a whole bank of them stored up to make himself appear more interesting. Typical salesman, really.

"Oh, I'm sure you're a barrel of laughs, Barry," she said with a forced grin.

The man grunted like a restless badger and noticed a copy of his own brochure laid out on the table.

"Ah, I see you've been doing your homework," he said. "So, is *Derwen Farm* still tickling your fancy?"

"It's definitely still of interest," said Rhiannon. "Seems like the perfect place to start a family."

"Family, eh?" The man's good cheer was briefly dashed by the thought of his own relatives. "I've definitely got my own fair share of that. You can choose your friends —"

"But you can't choose your family..."

"Exactly!"

She watched him summon the nearest waiter with the air of an impatient king. He clicked his fingers and waved the menu around like a starving monkey. It had been at least a few hours since his last meal, and he did not do well on an empty stomach.

Rhiannon ordered her own main course and waited. She watched her new dinner date reeling off half the menu to a stressed restaurant worker, who was struggling to keep up.

It wasn't long before they were left alone again, and, in an attempt to no longer have to suffer anymore of Barry's unrelenting banter, Rhiannon tried to keep the focus of their conversation on the Doyle family farm.

"Is there a reason it's been on the market so long?" she asked him.

"Well, it's a bit dated, I suppose," Barry answered, disappointed at not having the opportunity to try and impress her with his previous year's golfing statistics.

"A year is quite a long time."

The man finished off a piece of garlic bread and paused for a moment, having left a permanent shine on his chin from the grease.

"You're quite resourceful in your research, Miss Gallagher."

"I like to know the full story." Rhiannon had genuinely enjoyed the compliment and tried not to show it. She had always considered herself resourceful but not many people had taken notice.

The businessman nodded with a sincere understanding. He'd have done the same.

"Well," he said. "The farm was owned by a local family for a number of generations." Barry's mouth formed a crooked smile and revealed a line of stained teeth. "But something tells me you probably already know all that."

"I'd heard something along those lines," Rhiannon agreed. She felt him studying her like a cold predator. Her instincts told her that he was growing suspicious.

"Tell me, Miss Gallagher," he said. "What exactly is it that you do for a living, if you don't mind me asking?"

The clinking noises of their fellow diners became heightened for a moment.

"I work in transport," Rhiannon answered.

"Transport? Really?" He seemed pleasantly surprised. "That was also my line of work, once upon a time."

Great, Rhiannon thought. She felt like kicking herself for not looking *that* piece of background up.

"I even managed my own fleet of lorry drivers," he added with pride. "Which company do you work for?"

A thousand names swept through the journalist's mind.

"*O'Donnells Haulage*."

The pair of beady eyes opposite her narrowed.

"Never heard of them."

Rhiannon took the time to swallow a mouthful of her drink.

"They're an Irish company."

She found the long pause afterward unbearable.

"Ah, well, that explains it," said Barry, his Cheshire Cat grin returning, once again. He raised his glass. "Sláinte!"

After a short lull in conversation, Rhiannon quickly tried to change the subject.

"I'd very much like a tour of the place," she said, lifting up the brochure. "It's hard to get a feeling for somewhere with just a few photos."

Her body relaxed at the sight of their food arriving. The waiter placed a plate on her side and the rest of the tray on Barry's. The man rubbed his hands together and began tucking into his own private buffet.

"Oh, I agree," he said, with a mouthful of food. "It's the same with people — you never truly get to know a person until you're looking them directly in the whites of their eyes. Don't you agree?"

She did. As she listened to the loud chewing coming from the other side of the table, she decided to take advantage of the man's good mood.

"I hear the landlord of this farm is currently missing," she said, trying to sound casual.

"Ah, yes, " muttered Barry. "The millionaire who disappeared. I'm sure you've heard all about *her*." He took another mouthful of tagliatelle and let half of it hang out around the edges of his mouth. "Isn't it funny how a few numbers on a ticket can turn someone into a local celebrity? Some people get very lucky in life. And others... well, they'll always get dealt a bad hand."

Rhiannon poked at her own meal, finding it hard to attempt the first bite.

"Were you and the owner regularly in touch before she disappeared?" she asked.

"You mean, my *mother*?"

His directness surprised her. She had been prepared to lure it out of him.

"Let's not play games," he said. "If you've done your research on the landlord, you'll have recognised the surname. It's no secret. Only my mother doesn't own that farm anymore — I do. She gifted the deed to me."

"Did your mother clear out the farm before she moved out?"

"My sister had that privilege. I personally have no interest in personal belongings. I'm not really the sentimental type."

What a great surprise, Rhiannon thought, reeling in disappointment. She felt his suspicious glances and tried to pretend it was all in her head. Her impatience to get to the interesting details had ruined the flow of conversation.

"Now tell me," said Barry. "What area of transportation do you work in?"

Not this topic again, she thought. Why couldn't she have chosen a profession that sparked less questions — like accounting.

"I'd rather not talk about work, if that's okay. It's been a long day."

"We'll keep it personal, then."

Her face screamed the words: "No! Anything but that!"

"Tell me about *you*," Barry said, trying to appear friendly, only coming across more sinister. "What are your hobbies? Your passions?"

The woman opposite him kept her gaze firmly on her untouched meal. She struggled enough to talk about her own private life, let alone a fictional character called Miss Gallagher.

"I'd rather not —"

"No?" Barry leant forward, lowering his knife and fork, before he demanded her full attention. "You seem pretty interested in *my* life. It seems you journalists don't like being questioned yourselves, do you, Miss Gallagher? Or should I say — *Rhiannon Williams.*"

Now he had her full attention. She looked up at his hostile stare and smug grin.

"You think I'm a fool?" he asked. "There's not much that gets past me in this town. You're playing a dangerous game poking your nose around my business, young lady."

Rhiannon quivered with rage at his use of the words "young lady". She could have quite easily picked up her salad fork and lodged it straight through his filthy moustache.

"Now, if it's just information you're here for," the man continued, forcing his large stomach against the table to lean himself forward. "I'm more than happy to give it to you for the right price..."

His thick fingers wrapped themselves around the woman's hand like a hungry sea creature. A second later, Barry groaned as a long heel went firing into his knee.

"Don't ever touch me again!" Rhiannon hissed, whilst jumping to her feet.

The wounded man pulled back his hands, rubbed his leg and let out an amused laugh.

"I can see you're a feisty one," he said, with a jiggle of excitement. She hated that he was enjoying this. "What else did you expect, coming here tonight? If you're foraging for dirt, you need to get those hands dirty."

They both looked around to see that the whole restaurant was staring at them. Rhiannon reluctantly sat herself back down and lowered her voice. "I'm trying to get to the bottom of your mother's disappearance."

"Don't go playing the hero with me," said Barry, taking the opportunity to munch on some bread. "Ultimately, we are all out for ourselves in the end. And that includes my salt-of-the-earth mother."

"Really? You're the first person *I've* heard to say a bad word about her."

"Oh, I'm sure I am," he said with a scoff. "It makes me sick hearing how wonderful and selfless she is. Now that she's gone it's even worse. I suppose everybody loves a martyr."

"Shame her eldest son has the reputation of a vile snake."

Barry slammed his plate and threw away his napkin. "You think I give a damn what the people of this town think?"

His shell of smugness had slowly begun to break away. Rhiannon could feel the anger in his voice. People had a tendency to forget themselves when they were angry. It was during these emotional outbursts that the truth would often reveal itself. At this moment in time, the man before her had overindulged in both his food and wine. His irritable mood was out in the open.

"I'm a businessman," said Barry. "I do whatever it takes to succeed. It's dog-eat-dog in this world. Not all of us get to strike it rich off the back of a few lottery numbers."

"You sound bitter," said Rhiannon. He caught her smile and realised she had somehow got a rise out of him. The kick to the knee had done nothing, but her persistent talking had worked like a charm.

"I've had to scrape and claw for everything I have," he said, thumping his chunky index finger against the middle of the table. "You seem like a tenacious enough person. We probably have a lot more in common than you think."

It was now Rhiannon's turn to laugh. "Hardly."

"I like people with a bit of fight in them." Barry sat back in his chair. He was exhausted now from both the food and their heated conversation. "You should give up that local rag of yours and come work for me. You'd go far in our line of work."

"I didn't come here for a job offer, Mr Doyle."

"No? Then what *did* you come here for?"

She hesitated in her answer.

"You wanted to learn more about me?" he asked, reaching out his arms as if he were welcoming someone in. "Well, here I am — an open book."

The journalist nodded. She was tired of dancing around the real questions.

"When did you last see your mother?"

"Oh, I don't know. A week ago? Maybe two? I was never much of a mummy's boy."

"You said she gifted you the deed to a house."

"I took the old dump off her hands, you mean. I had to find *some* way of squeezing some money out of her."

She admired his lack of shame. It took a monstrous human being to be that cold.

"Why now?" Rhiannon asked. "After all these years living on a family farm — why does she move out now?"

"She was convinced that moving closer to town was the best decision for her," Barry replied, chewing on his toothpick. "She didn't want to cycle anymore, not after that nasty accident she had. It was me she asked to help her find somewhere. I saw the perfect place come up, right near the church. The rent was so reasonable that even an old, tight-fisted bat like her couldn't say no."

Rhiannon thought about the house on Pandy Lane. It *had* been close to the church, but she had not given it any consideration.

"What's so special about the church?" she asked.

"You tell me," said Barry. "The woman's obsessed with that place. I'll never know why." The man's face went dark for a moment. "I'll just be glad to finally get rid of that farm. I'd happily tear the place down — too many ghosts in that rotten place."

He caught himself getting lost in a trail of painful memories and had to shake himself back into the present.

"Look at that," he said, picking up a napkin and wiping away the sweat from his forehead. "You've got me all emotional just thinking about it."

"Let me go fetch the violin," said the cynical reporter.

Barry saw her cold expression and couldn't help but laugh. "I like you, Rhiannon. You're alright, for a nosey journalist."

He leant forward and attempted (what was intended to be) a friendly pat on the arm. What he received in return was a faceful of vintage red wine.

The entire room gasped as a furious Rhiannon rose to her feet with her empty glass.

"I told you not to touch me!" she snapped.

Barry shook his head, like a dog shaking himself dry, before he smiled.

He looked around at the gawking spectators and shrugged. "Such a waste!"

"Shame you'll have to pay for it," the journalist hissed. She grabbed her belongings and stormed past him. "Don't worry — I made sure it was the most expensive one on the menu."

"I wasn't talking about the wine." The smug businessman sniggered to himself before raising his own glass. "Sláinte!"

The doors of the *Amore Italiano* flew open. Rhiannon

stomped her way out into the street and tried to calm herself down. She was disappointed that she had let such a sleazy oaf like Barry Doyle get underneath her skin. You're stronger than that, she said to herself. Emotional outbursts in a public place were not her style. It was in that moment she realised how the tenacious journalist — the master interrogator of London's lowest of the low — was now a shadow of her former self.

It appeared that the collapse of her failed marriage was taking a greater toll on her than she had realised. At that moment, she wanted to burst into tears. But she would not waste them on *him*.

As she stumbled across the cobbles of Pengower's main high street, Rhiannon's head began to throb. The vast quantities of red wine was raging through her system, and she struggled to navigate herself along a road she once knew like the back of her hand.

In the distance, she saw a figure crouched down against a red letterbox. The man was groaning into his hands, and, in the glowing light of the overhead lamp post, she tried to make out his face.

"*Alun*?!"

Her question startled the man, who looked up at her with a humongous black eye.

"Rhiannon?"

Alun dragged himself up from the pavement and held up his nose to stop the excess blood.

"So how was *your* night?" he asked, straightening up his crooked glasses.

"I've had better," said Rhiannon.

"Fancy grabbing some fish and chips?"

CHAPTER 14

The neon lights of *The Crispy Cod* burned their way through the tired eyes of its hungry customers. Business was always booming at this time on a Saturday night, and the drunken punters of Pengower were now celebrating their last hurrah with trays full of deep-fried chips and mushy peas.

"The portions seem bigger than they used to be," Rhiannon said, as she tucked into her large fish cake.

"You're probably just getting smaller," said Alun, who couldn't quite make sense of his own answer.

The two unlikely drunks sat beside each other in the seated windowsill, munching away on their trays of food.

"*Argh*! Why does red wine always give me a headache?" Rhiannon groaned. She turned to her friend and offered him a napkin. "Here — your lip's bleeding again."

She began dabbing away at his sore mouth. The accountant, who felt very sorry for himself by this point, was quite happy to allow her hands-on gesture.

His eye looked much worse in the harsh light than it had

done in the street. She winced and attempted to lighten the mood: "So, should I be more worried about the other guy?"

"Not when the other guy is Danny Doyle," Alun muttered. He was in no mood to rescue his pride. It was clear which one of the two had come off worse in *that* fight.

"Danny Doyle?" Rhiannon tried not to sound too excited. The thought of Alun engaging in a physical confrontation gave her a tingle of goosebumps. Regardless of whether he had won or lost, she did like a man who could stand up for himself when the time came. The thought disturbed her, but it might even have been a little sexy. Once she had realised the preposterousness of her drunken musings, she shook them away, immediately. "You're kidding! How on earth did that come about?"

Alun sighed. "Same way it always does, probably. People like him never really grow up."

The woman beside him smiled to herself. "I never had you down as a brawler, Alun Hughes."

"Neither did I," said Alun. "It's amazing what you're capable of when you've had a bad day."

"Well, you're not the only one to have locked horns with a Doyle tonight," she said. Her good mood drifted away at the thought of the repulsive Barry and his bushy moustache.

"You had your dinner with Barry tonight?" It was Alun's turn to perk up now. "How did that go?"

"We won't be making it a regular thing, put it that way." She looked down at her pile of chips and had a sudden loss of appetite. "The man certainly fits the exact profile I had him down for. I think the medical term is *slime ball*."

"Did you get anything from him? Surely there must have been *something*."

"I seem to remember asking you the same thing about Reverend Owen," Rhiannon snapped. "People in Mari's circle don't seem to be very keen on dishing out the details. He barely had a good word to say about her — so at least *that* was refreshing. I was beginning to think she was the Mother Teresa."

"I'm sure even *that* woman had her bad days," Alun said with a smirk.

"Old Barry saw me coming a mile off. I think he did it all just to watch me suffer."

"Well, he's not known for his big heart."

Alun turned to see that she was quite serious. He had never been a fan of the fellow businessman, a man who was rumoured to be on a downward trajectory after a few too many bad deals. If he ever wanted to buy a house himself, he would have much rather approached the local competitor down the road.

"The man's heart is rotten to the core," Rhiannon continued. "He'd sell his own mother if he had the chance — and probably a lot worse. Put him straight to the top of that suspect list."

Alun looked at her as if he'd been told to pick another fight with Danny Doyle. "*Suspect list*? What suspect list?"

He was met with a tired frown.

"Oh, come on," she said. "Don't tell me that little, mechanical brain of yours hasn't put together a list of possible murderers. Knowing you, it's probably a ledger — a *murder ledger*, even!"

The accountant looked around to make sure nobody was listening. "Rhiannon, we don't know for sure if Mari's even been —"

The journalist sighed. "Fine, whatever. I know you've got your suspects."

She chucked the rest of her unfinished meal into a nearby bin, and they both headed outside into the cool nighttime air.

They walked down the quiet high street, as their reflections went passing along a series of darkened shop windows: the last stragglers of a lively Saturday night in Pengower.

"I did get one piece of useful info, though," Rhiannon said eventually. "He said one of his sisters did the clearing out at *Derwen Farm*. If all those diaries are still around, then one of *them* will know. Wish I knew which sister."

Alun worked through the Doyle family tree in his mind.

"Well, there's Ceri..." he began.

"And we all know *Scary Ceri*. Not surprising how weird she turned out to be now that I've met her older brother."

"Then there's Lesley, the older sister."

"What do we know about her?"

"I know she's a single mother. Works at one of the cafés here in town. She pretty much keeps to herself. Quite feisty and unapproachable from what I've heard."

Rhiannon nodded. "Surprise, surprise. The joys of the Doyle family genes." She turned to her walking partner and patted him on the back. "You really are a fountain of local knowledge, aren't you?"

Alun shrugged. "It's not hard when you've been living here your whole life. Clients have always liked to gossip."

Rhiannon began counting the names with her fingers: "Barry, Lesley, Ceri and Danny... Well, they'd certainly give the Osmonds a run for their money."

They turned a corner and were faced with a giant statue of a man holding a large book. Apart from this immortalised historical figure staring down at them, the town square was deserted.

"One of those four knows where Mari is," Rhiannon said, staring up at the pale moon. "I know it."

She sat herself down against the man in stone's feet and ran through her own version of the family tree.

"How many grandchildren are there again?" she asked.

Alun decided to respect the statute and remain standing. "Four, I think."

Rhiannon thought back to their encounter in the supermarket car park. "There's Barry's son, Jack, of course, who we've already met."

"Then there's Ruby — Lesley's daughter. She's the oldest of three."

"That's right: the teenager."

"She seems nice enough," said Alun. "Ruby works part-time at Mari's flower shop."

"She'll be out of the job now then." The journalist paused to consider her own employment. "And so will I be at this rate."

Alun sensed her concern and decided that the statue probably wouldn't mind too much if he joined the woman sitting against his feet.

"What makes you say that?" he asked, sitting himself down on the cold stone.

"You're not the only one who had a bad morning," Rhiannon replied. "Turns out my boss wants me to abandon my missing-millionaire story and focus on other things. He's asked me to cover that country show next week. The man wouldn't know a good story if it danced around in his face."

Alun knew the show well. It was a big deal among the local farmers and a highlight for anyone partial to a spot of sheep shearing or flower displays (but he wasn't about to point this out to his ambitious journalist friend).

"I know Mari's story is about to get a whole lot more interesting," she insisted. "I can just *feel* it."

She wasn't the only one who sensed further developments on the horizon. Although murder mysteries were not really the accountant's speciality, he was certain that there was something very sinister going on.

"You know what the worst thing is?" Rhiannon asked. "I keep getting terrified that she's going to just walk back into her life again, any day now, as if nothing has happened. And that would be the end of it all. What kind of person does that make me?"

He didn't dare answer. Alun could think of a few words to describe her, but he didn't think that the adjectives: cold, selfish and heartless would go down very well.

Rhiannon was close to tears again at this point, which made the gentleman sitting beside her very uncomfortable indeed. "I mean — wishing murder on a poor woman — all for a stupid article. Have I finally lost my mind living in this place?"

The answer was a big *yes*, according to Alun's diagnosis, yet he still felt a degree of pity for her.

Just as she let out her first sob, Rhiannon felt a cautious hand trying to pat her on the shoulder.

"You know," said Alun, "if the journalism thing doesn't work out, I've always got plenty of admin work at the office."

The woman couldn't help but chuckle to herself.

"That's very sweet, Alun," she said. "But I think I'd rather an innocent woman were killed in cold blood than do your admin."

She saw the man's look of sheer horror and slapped his arm. "I'm joking! Will you lighten up for just one second?"

Alun nodded in relief. He knew she was just pulling his leg. Yes, of course he knew.

"On a serious note," she added. "I do appreciate the offer."

The two sat in silence for a moment, whilst Alun dwelled on her attempt at thanking him.

After taking in the sights of Pengower's most historical buildings, they both continued their journey through the row of streetlights leading the way.

"Accounts isn't all that bad," Alun reassured her. "It's quiet... it's safe... it's... *predictable*."

"Sounds a lot like you Alun!" Rhiannon's unexpected comment was followed by another hard slap. She chuckled at his playful frown.

"Oh, come on," she said, as they passed the bottom of the hill leading up to the great church. "You can't fool me. You're as deep into this mystery as I am. I bet you've barely looked at a ledger since I turned up at your door."

She was right, Alun thought. His mind had been more than preoccupied since their first encounter at the office. He had thought of nothing else since. As he looked over at her cheeky smile, he struggled to recall who he had thought about the most: Mari Doyle or the woman walking beside him.

"I've been a little intrigued," he admitted. "I'm not going to lie."

Rhiannon scoffed. "Intrigued? You're hooked, Alun Hughes — admit it!"

The silence said it all.

"Well," she continued. "I don't care what my boss says. He can have his little puff pieces on vegetable competitions and sheep shearing. But I'm finishing this story, either way. If *he* doesn't want it, I know people who will."

"I'm happy to help in anyway I can," the accountant said. "We wouldn't want you out of the job or anything."

"You mean, you wouldn't want me messing up your precious filing system everyday?"

Alun nodded; she was bang on the money.

Rhiannon's mood seemed to have lifted at the thought of her next move. Her pace had quickened, and she had that all too familiar fire back in her eyes.

"First thing I'm going to do is have a proper look at that farm," she announced. "If I can't get a guided tour from Barry Doyle and his cronies, then I'll go down there myself."

"Mel says he has some reports down at the police station," said Alun. "If I drop by on him with some pastries he might let me have a look."

His new partner in crime punched the air and threw in

another slap to the shoulder. He was going to be very bruised in the morning, Alun thought.

"Great! You go ahead and work your magic on Columbo, and I'll take care of the farm."

They turned a corner and entered a long residential street full of identical houses. Each one had a nice front garden, and each one was as modern and characterless as the other.

"We make a good team, you and me!" said Rhiannon, as they stopped outside her parent's house. "Thanks for walking me home, tough guy."

She made a strong fist and Alun prayed she wouldn't use it to thump him again.

"Well," he said, puffing out his skinny chest, "nobody would want to mess with *me* tonight. There's nothing left for them to punch!"

The woman in front of him grinned, and they both gazed into each other's bloodshot pupils.

"So this is goodnight then," she said, waiting for him to say something that would wash away the awkwardness.

"Uh, yes," he said. "I suppose it is."

The alcohol levels were still at an all time high in both of their systems. Alun could feel his head pounding, as they faced each other beneath the ever-present moonlight. His head was telling him to go home, but his instincts were willing him to get closer.

Just as he was about to give in to the pressure of his mischievous subconscious, the expression on Rhiannon's face made him stop. Her complexion had gone grey, and her mouth began to twist in a number of different directions.

Right before Alun was beginning to suspect the horrific dangers of a glowing full moon, Rhiannon went diving to her knees in front of her mother's treasured flowerbed.

The accountant winced at the unpleasant heaving noises.

After waiting through the splashes of projectile liquid, he had the sudden urge to make a move.

Trying hard not to look at the carnage beneath his feet, he gave her a well-deserved pat on the back.

His next question offered her little comfort: "Exactly how much red wine did you drink tonight?"

CHAPTER 15

Alun woke up to the feeling of a bristly tongue against his forehead. He opened his eyes to the sight of a big, furry animal in his face, urging him out of bed for a brand new day.

"Morning, Peg," he said with a sigh.

Although the wake-up call had not been requested, he was glad at least *someone* needed him to surface. Sunday mornings had once been a tradition of coffee and pancakes; now they were all about walking off a Border Collie's boundless energy.

The route on that particular morning had taken Alun and Peg to the shores of Pengower's great lake. This tranquil body of water was known as the largest natural lake in Wales and attracted more than its fair share of fishing, boating and paddle-board-enthusiasts during the busier summer months.

At the crack of dawn, there was hardly a single person in sight. The sound of the water splashing against the smooth stones helped to ease the suffering of the hungover accountant's swirling mind. On the other hand, his headache could also have been the result of the previous night's physical altercation at *The Old Bull's Head*. Either way, he was starting to feel a lot better.

Alun released his dog from the burden of her lead. As he watched her charge off to disturb the floating ducks, he heard a female voice coming from behind him.

"Alun!"

He turned around to see, none other than, Bev Griffiths running towards him. Her bright pink gym clothes made her stand out a mile away, and she wore a range of advanced exercising accessories that were more suitable for a championship triathlon. She might as well have stumbled straight out of one of his mother's eighties step-aerobic videos.

"I thought it was you," said Bev, trying to catch her breath whilst checking on her heart rate monitor. "Nothing like a morning run, eh?"

Alun had never gone out for a run in his entire life and found the simple act of walking to be enough of a physical strain.

"Oh, absolutely," he said in agreement, wishing that his dog was ready to leave.

She began stretching on the spot in her heavily-branded sporting clothes.

"That was quite the display you put on last night," she said, twisting her waist and lifting up her legs. "I never knew you had it in you."

The groggy man rubbed the bruise on his sore cheek bone and wanted to look away.

"I like a man who can put up a good fight," she added.

Alun was beginning to wonder whether Bev had witnessed the same confrontation, as he was quite certain he hadn't had much opportunity to fight at all. It was only seconds later, after he had landed the first blow to Danny's hard head, that he had found himself on the receiving end of a very painful assault. Still, he recalled that she had been very drunk and was quite happy to indulge in her faded memory.

"Oh, well," he said, as if a bout of hand-to-hand combat was a regular occurrence in his life. "It was no big deal, really. I don't normally condone violence for the sake of violence."

The woman giggled and began looking him up and down, as though he was a piece of meat from Dai's butcher shop.

"You're a man of action — not words," she said. "I hear you."

Bev took a few steps closer and put a hand on his shoulder. She gazed at him in such a way that he was quivering in his new pair of wellington boots. He wanted so badly to run away, but he knew that the woman would soon catch him, especially with her honed cardio and solid calves.

"I hope I didn't ruin your night out," he said, his body tightening the more she stroked his delicate neck muscles.

"Not at all," Bev assured him. "It spiced things up, actually. There aren't many men at our age who would put their body on the line for me like that."

He was quite certain that her safety and wellbeing had not been his prime concern when the punches had come his way, but, once again, he was happy to keep the illusion.

"I assume you'll be going to *The Pengower Country Show* next week," she said, her voice deep and passionate in his ear.

"Uh, well, actually —"

"I'm looking for someone to go with..."

Less than ten minutes later, the woman in bright pink continued her morning run, leaving Alun dumbfounded by the side of the lake. He had somehow managed to take his dog out for a walk, only to return home again with a date to the country show. The man didn't know whether to feel pleased or utterly perplexed. Had it usually been that easy, he would never have walked over to that jukebox in the first place.

. . .

THE AISLES of Pengower's only supermarket were reaching their maximum capacity. Shoppers flowed from one section to the next, like a colony of busy ants, all keen to finish their weekly shop in record time.

Rhiannon was yet another member of the town's small population to regret their choice of location that morning. Her son, Gwyl, was already on the verge of another meltdown, and it was hard enough shopping on a budget without someone else adding in a string of unnecessary items. The three-year-old hated the food shop as much as she did, and her raging hangover only added to the sheer horror of it all.

Why she had guzzled down that additional glass of wine she would never know. There was a good reason why she normally avoided drinking: three-year-olds were not very understanding when it came to hangovers. The shame and guilt of a self-inflicted headache was only made worse with an energetic child.

By the time Rhiannnon had reached the deli meat section, the tears and tantrums were in full swing (and they were just from her). Just as she was about to abandon her number-one-rule of parenting — which sometimes involved a lot of begging and far too much pleading — she was approached by an unexpected blast from the past.

"Rhiannon?" asked the woman in smart clothes with a trolley-load of the supermarket's finest produce. "Rhiannon Williams? Is that you?"

The voice was somewhat familiar, but the face was as alien as the contents of her shopping list.

"You don't recognise me, do you?" the woman asked again.

Rhiannon stared at the friendly face. A flash of familiarity conjured up the image of a lonely, insecure teenager with a passion for gothic makeup.

"*Ceri*?" she croaked. "Ceri Doyle?"

Her old classmate flicked back her blonde hair and lifted up a hand.

"Well, not quite," she said, showing off the large wedding ring. "I'm Mrs Ceri Thomas, these days."

The tired mother cradled her upset child and took a moment to take in this confident looking woman with her cheerful smile. "I can't believe it. You look so... *different*."

"I'll take different!" said Ceri with a giggle.

Rhiannon realised her poor choice of words and attempted to improve them. She was trying hard not to cause offence, but her wits had long been disposed of across her parent's unlucky flower bed the night before. "No, no — I mean — you look well... You look *really* well!"

Ceri gave the exaggerated blush of a person who had clearly been told this many times before. Fortunately, the compliment had not grown old.

"Why, thanks!" She took notice of Rhiannon's own appearance: the pale complexion, the loose clothes, the years of stress crying out through her raw eyes. "Uh... you look well too!"

Gwyl was getting restless and was now reaching out to be picked up. His mother took one look at his pleading face and gave in. He was the only person who could bring out her softer side.

"Looks like you've got your hands full," said Ceri. "I bet that other half of yours owes you for this one."

"Actually, there is no other half," said Rhiannon, squeezing her son even tighter. "Just me, myself and this little chap. The only two halves I need." An anger descended on her face at the thought of her ex-husband. "And, yes, that other man owes me a lot."

"Oh, I'm sorry to hear that."

"Don't worry — *we're* not. Better off without him, to be honest."

She lifted Gwyl into the trolley basket itself so that he could rummage around.

"So!" said Ceri, hoping to lighten the mood with her cheerful tone. "What brings you back to Pengower? A quick little visit?"

"I wish!" Rhiannon replied, searching her handbag for a sugary snack that she packed for emergencies. "No, we're here for the long haul."

"Well that's great! Home is where the heart is, eh?"

Rhiannon gave her a blank stare. Ceri's newfound, happy-go-lucky attitude was already beginning to irritate her. "Something like that," she said. "Or maybe, home is where the cheap mortgage is. It made more financial sense at the moment."

Ceri nodded, as if the country bumpkin knew it all too well. "Right, yeah. I know exactly what you mean. I was going to live in Sheffield once. Why go anywhere else, when everything you need is right here already!"

"Except maybe a *John Lewis*."

Rhiannon sighed as she saw her comment go straight over Ceri's head and back down again into the raw meats section. "I'm joking."

The confused face burst into life again. "Oh, right! Yes. Haha!"

Ceri noticed her old acquaintance's trolley slowly trying to make its escape towards the next aisle, and she followed along.

"So what is it you're doing with yourself these days?" Rhiannon asked, as manners got the best of her. It seemed Ceri had been waiting in great anticipation for this question.

"Well, here's a funny thing," she said. "You know our old school?"

The other woman nodded. *School*: a place of happier times, or at least, it had been for the former hockey team captain.

"Guess who the Headteacher is?"

Rhiannon could see the excitement bubbling up inside of her. Surely not, was her first thought. "You're kidding..."

Ceri flung out her arms like a giddy child on sour sweets.

"That's right! It's been quite the year, I can tell you. Opportunities like that don't come around very often. Especially around these parts."

"No... I'm sure they don't."

The two trolleys navigated their way through the shop, until Rhiannon's had decided to make a sudden detour towards the checkouts.

"So how about you?" asked Ceri, ignoring the subtle hint.

"Me? Oh, I'm... a writer." Rhiannon had never hesitated so much in her whole career. In her early years, as a junior member of a thriving national newspaper, she would have answered the question in a heartbeat. However, the word *writer* felt like quite a loose term as of late.

Her lack of enthusiasm had done nothing to dampen the enthusiasm of her fellow shopper.

"Oooh! What kind of writer? Are you a novelist? I'd love to meet one of those."

The writer felt another blow to her fragile ego.

"Uh, no. I don't write novels. I'm a journalist."

"Newspapers! How exciting! God, we could do with a decent one of those around here. Right now we're stuck with some tatty, old rag that only seems to be interested in farming."

The finishing blow had been landed. Rhiannon's professional pride was now lying in the middle of the canvas, its mouthpiece lying in a pool of blood.

She tried to seem surprised. "Is that right?"

Her shopping was soon flung across a stained conveyor belt as fast as her hangover shakes would allow.

"Who do you write for?" came the inevitable next question. "Anyone I'd know?"

Rhiannon shook her head. "Probably not." Her hands continued to shovel cheap ready meals to the pile of moving groceries, until a sudden thought crossed her mind. "Actually, my current writing assignment is based around your mother, funnily enough."

The mood changed as if it had been battered with a sledgehammer.

"Oh, I see," said Ceri, her jovial tone a distant memory. "What's so special about *her*?"

"Well, she won eighteen million pounds for a start. Not many people can lay claim to that." A pile of colourful scratch cards caught her eye near the counter, and, for the first time in her life, she considered buying one. "Now she's... missing."

"So you've heard." Ceri couldn't hide her disappointment. She had enjoyed boasting to the most popular girl in school, the one who had previously never given her a second thought. Her intended portrayal of a perfect adult life was fast evaporating. "Obviously, we're all quite worried."

"Yes, I'm sure you all are." Rhiannon could see the life inside of her slowly draining away. She couldn't help but feel a little guilty. "I'm planning to have a look around your old home this afternoon. You didn't happen to be the one who helped clear out all of your mother's belongings, by any chance?"

"No, that was Lesley."

Rhiannon was flooded with disappointment. "Oh, that's a shame."

She reached for her purse and made a swift dash for the cashier.

"Hey!" Ceri called. "Why don't I come with you?"

The journalist was taken aback and even doubted what she had just heard. "Excuse me?"

"*Derwen Farm* — I could tag along. It's Sunday, and my

husband's at rugby this afternoon. I could drive down and show you around."

Rhiannon's natural instinct of suspicion was overwhelmed by the prospect of opportunity. She had no idea why Ceri would even dream of wanting to help, let alone spend time with her, but she wasn't about to argue.

"You'd do that?" Rhiannon asked.

"Of course! Anything I can do to help. I've still got a spare key, actually."

"Have you, now..."

Something did not feel right, but it was hard to deny such a friendly gesture.

Ceri continued to talk to her whilst settling up her bill. "I can even bring some muffins with me that I made this morning. It could be a right girly afternoon! A proper catch-up!"

"Sounds... great."

The two women made their way out of the busy supermarket and into the car park. Rhiannon listened to Ceri's relentless flow of one-sided conversation and was adamant the woman was about to start skipping alongside her.

"You know, I'm not in touch with any of the girls we went to school with anymore. Bethan Roberts, Lowri Jones, Merryl-Ann..."

Rhiannon felt her headache coming back again. "No?"

"Nah. People grow up, don't they? They've got new lives now. It's quite sad actually."

She saw that they were now on the other side of the car park.

"Well, this is me," said Rhiannon, upon reaching her own car. "Now you're sure it's no trouble showing me around your old house?"

"Anything I can do to help find my mother — I'll do it," Ceri replied. She tried interacting with her three-year-old but received nothing but a cold shoulder. "Did this little one want to come?"

"No," said Rhiannon, without the slightest hesitation. "He can stay home with his grandparents."

Ceri was secretly relieved. She had never really gelled with children. "Do your mum and dad still live on Tegid Street?"

"They do, yes. That's actually the same street we're living on now."

"Oh, that's such a lovely street." She clapped her hands in celebration. "Which end are you on?"

"The same end as my parents." Rhiannon cringed. "We're living with them."

"Oh, I see," said Ceri, with a look of pity that made the other person want to slap her. She gave the journalist a patronising rub on the shoulder before heading off on her own way. "You really are looking so well, Rhiannon!"

Ceri's parting words echoed through Rhiannon's sore head for the entire duration of her loading up the car. As she fastened her son into his car seat and walked around to the driver's door, she caught a glimpse of a young man staring at her from the other side of the car park.

The trolley attendant, Jack Doyle, saw her notice him and continued on with his work.

CHAPTER 16

Black clouds hung low over the enormous landscape. The hills were still recovering from the torrential shower that had since eased up into a light drizzle.

A large Range Rover was making its way along a narrow road running alongside the great lake. On the other end of this long stretch of water was a farmhouse that Rhiannon hoped would hold the secrets to Mari Doyle's disappearance.

"It's a nice car you've got," she told her driver, as she sat in the passenger seat, staring out at the scenery she had known all of her life; unlike herself, it had not changed a bit.

"Oh, thank you," said Ceri. "Gethin convinced me to get it at the start of the year. We're both on pretty decent salaries for round here, and the cost of living is pretty low, so we thought: why not? You've got to enjoy yourself, haven't you?"

Rhiannon took notice of the designer handbag on the backseat. "Why not, indeed."

"Ceri Doyle, the headteacher," she said with a shake of her head. "I didn't see that one coming."

"It's mad, isn't it?" Ceri let out an excited jiggle at the thought of a scene from her favourite musical film. "Now I *rule the school*!"

"Lucky you." Rhiannon hated musicals and was oblivious to the reference. She thought about how much money someone would need to pay in order for her to work alongside some of her old teachers (it was a *lot*). "Is Mr Humphreys still teaching maths?"

"Old *Humpy Humphreys*? No, he left years ago — thank God! Couldn't stand the bloke."

"I remember Dewi Dobson letting off a stink bomb in his work bag. I've never seen a grown man get that angry ever since."

Her driver sensed her amusement and it didn't go down well. Ceri knew what it was like to be a target of high school pranks — both as a teacher and a pupil. "Teenagers can do that to a person," she said, squeezing the wheel until her hands went pale. "I've had my own share of meltdowns during my earlier teaching years. But it only made me stronger." Her dark mood began to brighten. "You see, there's an art to controlling the class: little tricks, little methods of getting right inside those infantile heads of theirs. Once you establish a certain reputation, you can have all of them in the palm of your hand."

Her passenger listened and felt a cold shudder. Rather them than her, she thought.

"Well," she said, eventually, after a tense silence that required a chainsaw to cut through. "I'll take your word for it, Ceri — or should I say: *Mrs Thomas*!" Rhiannon's nervous laugh dragged the other woman out from her gloomy trail of thought and back into the car. "I suppose kids can be a little cruel sometimes."

Ceri agreed. "*You* enjoyed your school years, though, I'm sure,"

"They were alright, I suppose."

"Oh, come on!" Ceri's attention shifted away from the road for a moment, something that concerned her passenger. "You were a right little-miss-popular back then. If we had one of those American-style proms, you would have been Prom Queen by a mile off."

Rhiannon inhaled a deep breath as the woman's hands returned back to the steering wheel.

"I'll take that as a compliment. Not that it means anything these days." She looked out of the window to see a lonely sailing boat floating in the middle of the lake. "Popular, unpopular... It's all for nothing in the end."

Ceri could hear the words being spoken, but she didn't appear to be listening. "Those memories last a lifetime, don't they?"

The sight of a small farmhouse caught both of their attention. Rhiannon had never realised how visible it was from the main road, although this did not mean that it was easily accessible (as she would soon discover)..

Derwen Farm had been in the Doyle family for three generations. Less than a mile from the shores of the lake, and only a short walk from the village of Llanlyn, the property was now a shell of its former self.

Rhiannon looked down at the state of her muddy boots, as she opened the second of three rusty gates. After crawling its way through deep puddles and vicious potholes, the Range Rover crossed over multiple acres of overgrown fields, all via a single track that was barely fit for a horse and cart.

Their final destination was an empty yard overlooking a large barn and a line of derelict sheds.

"Well, here she is," Ceri announced. "Home, sweet home."

Rhiannon peered out at the hollow surroundings, a place long abandoned by its former owner and in much need of some tender love and care.

"This place must hold a lot of memories for you," she said.

Her driver unfastened her seatbelt. "It certainly does."

On the other side of the great barn was a tired house with a peeling front door and a fragile roof. An old tractor covered in weeds was parked outside, unlikely to ever start again. What was once a front garden was now a haven for wild animals, as they lurked amongst the long grass whilst peaking out at the visiting strangers. A tyre swing dangled from a giant oak tree, swaying in the breeze as it had done for many years.

The infamous tree house had already caught Rhiannon's attention, as she followed her guide around the back exterior of the house. She had heard about the dreaded fall that had taken the life of Tony Doyle, a fatal incident that had been very much open for interpretation as far as the youths of Pengower were concerned. Had he fallen? Or was he pushed? Only the darkened windows of the lonely farmhouse would ever really know for certain.

"Did you want to have a look inside?" Ceri asked, holding up a set of keys.

No, was the honest answer. But Rhiannon knew that she didn't really have a choice; she had come *this* far.

"I don't know how your mother lived here on her own," Rhiannon muttered. She watched Ceri unlock the front door in the manner of a person who had done it many times before.

"It's not much different from when we were living here as children," Ceri said. She had uttered these words with such contempt that it made the other woman curious.

"Really?" It was a sincere question, for the Mari *she* knew kept a spotless townhouse. "I got the impression that she was rather houseproud."

Ceri turned to her with a patronising smile. "You really don't know my mother very well, do you?"

The door swung open, and the journalist didn't even have a

chance to respond. She was led inside the house, across a terracotta floor that had seen far better days before its decades of abuse by muddy shoes. A damp smell hung in the air due to poor ventilation and an absence of heating.

"I've not been back here in a while," Ceri said, as they entered the old dining room, a place where many memories were still held.

Rhiannon watched her stare into the empty space where a large table was once placed. "What was your father like?" she asked.

The question seemed to have caught Ceri off guard. "He seemed like a good man." She pictured him for a moment and smiled. "He might have liked to bend the rules from time to time, but still, his heart was always in the right place."

She caught herself letting out a short sob and tried to stop herself. "I'm sorry," Ceri said. "I wasn't expecting to feel like this. I don't know what's come over me."

Rhiannon walked over and placed a hand on her shoulder. "Visiting an old home can bring back a lot of emotions. It's only natural."

"I just wish there were more happy memories," she said with a nervous laugh.

"Was it really that terrible?"

Ceri looked up at her with a frown. This question had evoked nothing but anger.

"You honestly have no idea, do you?" she snapped. "Nobody does! But you will soon. I'm going to show you *exactly* what was so terrible."

Rhiannon could feel a rush of adrenaline. It was the same kind of feeling a person felt when there was a whiff of danger in the air.

She had not been prepared for such a sudden change in mood. The Ceri she had met back in the supermarket was now gone and had been replaced by a woman who appeared deeply scarred, at least on the inside. It was as if something in that house was engulfing her with a cloud of pure hatred.

"Ceri..." Rhiannon said, in her most calming voice. She forced them both into direct eye contact. It was the same approach she used when her son was on the verge of a tantrum. According to the parental literature, children of that age just wanted to be understood. They were often left with no choice but to express themselves with an emotional outburst. She wasn't comparing Ceri Doyle to a toddler, of course, but she knew that adults were often more similar than they thought. "I can't understand if you don't tell me."

Ceri felt a hand against her trembling arm. She looked up at her, almost embarrassed.

"I'm sorry," she said. "I brought you here because I wanted you to know the kind of person you've chosen to write about. The *real* person."

"I'm all ears," Rhiannon said, feeling slightly better now for her personal safety. Ceri's decision to accompany her had been a strange one, and she was pleased to be nearing a more truthful explanation.

"I don't think my words can quite do the person justice," said Ceri.

"Then whose words am I supposed to hear it from?"

The woman in front of her became nervous. "Perhaps you need to hear it from Mari Doyle, herself."

CHAPTER 17

Alun had been washing his dog when the doorbell rang. His Border Collie had come home with half the contents of Pengower Lake on her coat, and she stank like they'd taken a detour through the town's sewage system.

"I'm coming!" Alun cried, trying to wrestle the canine with his towel before she could attempt the inevitable shake-off — *not this time*, his owner had decided. Unfortunately, his efforts had all been in vain; Peg had not only managed to slip away but was soon showering the white walls with dirty bathwater.

The doorbell rang again. Alun had received a few unexpected visitors over the last few weeks, but the person standing on his doorstep this time was probably the most unexpected of them all.

"*Danny*?"

The sight of an awkward looking Danny Doyle caused the accountant's black eye to throb even more. Flashes of the night before caused him to contemplate the idea of slamming the door shut and hiding under the covers. Despite the sudden onset of PTSD, Alun could tell, just from looking at the man, that he was not the same rowdy drunk he had encountered in the pub. Instead, he found a rather sheepish individual who was trying to hide his nerves.

"Alright, Alun?" the man asked, in his most macho of voices. The cheap bottle of sparkling wine in his hand only ruined his hard image even more. "This is for you."

Alun received the unexpected gift with both confusion and a little apprehension.

The man in the tank top shuffled with his hands in his pockets, like a schoolboy who had been sent to the headmaster's door. He avoided eye contact by looking around to make sure that nobody was watching.

"My girlfriend said it's a nice one," Danny said, nodding at the bottle.

"Oh," Alun replied. He had decided he preferred the barrage of flying fists than suffer anymore of what was happening in that moment. "Uh, thank you very much."

Danny flexed his tattooed arms and scratched his head.

"Mel told me to come say sorry," he mumbled. "You know... about last night."

The accountant nodded; it all made sense now. "Last night? Oh, I see what you mean. No, all that was nothing, really." He could feel the bruise on his cheek wanting to object.

"No! I was bang out of order." Even during an apology, Danny couldn't help his natural thirst for confrontation. "I'd been drinking all day, see. Didn't know what I was doing. I thought I could buy you a pint. To say sorry, like. No hard feelings, yeah?"

There had definitely been plenty of hard feelings, Alun felt like saying. He rubbed his sore back.

"Oh, there's no need to do that," Alun replied.

"I won't take no for an answer," Danny insisted. "The round is on me, come on."

The man in wet pyjamas looked shocked. "You mean, *right now*?"

"Yeah, why not? The pub's open at eleven. I'm heading down there anyway."

He began walking away, as if their drink together was a foregone conclusion. Alun grabbed his coat and slipped on some shoes. Danny did not seem like a man who took no for an answer, and, after witnessing his violent temper, the smaller man was in no mood to re-enact any of the events from the night before.

It seemed Mel had a lot to answer for. He would deal with him later.

STARING at the cold pint of weak lager sitting on the table in front of him, it occurred to Alun that he was still trying to recover from his last indulgence of beer from the night before. "Hair of the dog that bit you," he thought to himself. He had never been fond of those colloquial expressions, and he did not need to be reminded of any more dog hair (his scuffle with Peg was still too soon).

The real dog that had bitten him was now sitting on the chair opposite, his own pint of discounted beer clutched firmly in hand. Danny Doyle sipped at the thin layer of froth and looked around at the empty bar. A cheesy eighties power ballad was the only source of ambient noise, and the two men had barely said a word since they arrived.

"It's a nice beer, this one," Alun said, purely out of desperation to break the silence.

"Any pint that's less than two quid tastes good to me," said Danny. "You could get five of those for less than a tenner."

The accountant raised his glass at the man's impromptu attempt at a financial calculation — finally something he could relate to. "That's a whole night out sorted," he said with a chuckle.

Danny looked at him with confusion. The attempt at some male banter had gone straight over his shaved head. It seemed five pints of beer did not make a night out, at least, not in Danny Doyle's eyes.

"Mel told me you've been trying to help find my mother," the burly man said.

Alun took a large mouthful of beer to hide his surprise. "Well, I wouldn't say I've contributed very much. I'm not a detective."

"You've done more than the police have." Danny cleared his throat as if he were about to spit. "And nobody else in this town has bothered to look for her."

"She seems very well-liked around the community." Alun saw the stern glare coming back at him and realised the man might have thought he was trying to argue. It was time to deflect: "At least, that's what I've heard."

"Doesn't make a difference, though, does it? People always show their true colours in the end. Family are the only people you can really trust."

The other man sipped his drink again. He hoped that Danny was right about his last statement.

"Would you say your family is close?" Alun asked.

His question was followed by a loud snort. "Nah, not really." He stared into his drink, and, for what was probably the first time in public, he gave away a glimmer of sadness. "We used to be, though. Back when we were younger."

Alun observed his rare exposure of sentimental feelings. The hard, macho side of Danny Doyle had momentarily melted away and was replaced by the fragileness and insecurity of a needy younger sibling. He was, after all, the baby of the family.

"I'm sure we'll find her," Alun said.

The man looked up and realised he was being comforted. With a shuffle of his bulky frame, he shook himself back into bloke-mode. "She's probably lying in a ditch for all we know. Or kidnapped by some sick bastard who's holding her to ransom."

Alun wanted to point out that a silent kidnapping was not actually how a ransom situation worked, but he decided to let it go. The man was quickly working himself up (something he seemed to have a habit of doing).

"You know, I did hear a rumour..." Danny continued, looking around to check for prying ears. Alun's ears, on the other hand, were more than ready for what they were about to hear. "I reckon my mother might have been in a relationship with someone. Isn't that nuts?"

"What makes you say that?"

"I hear things. Secrets don't last very long in this town. People talk. People see things." He leaned in, until his breath was steaming up the pint glass underneath his chin. "The woman is a *millionaire*, for crying out loud. I bet you there's a whole load of blokes out there who'd be looking to marry her."

Despite his neanderthal behaviour, the man was not as stupid as he looked, Alun thought. People had married for a lot less than eighteen million. Danny's theory might have been getting warmer by the second. The idea of someone marrying another person for their money seemed like a rather strange financial strategy to the accountant, but he did not know Dai the butcher well enough to assess his true motives. He had bought many a pork chop from him over the years, and the man had seemed nice enough.

"Have you got any ideas on who the man could be?" he asked.

Danny's eyes squinted with suspicion. He sat back in his chair, having expected the accountant would have needed more convincing. Most people had accused him of being paranoid and the rest had moved straight up the man's growing suspect list.

"I've got my thoughts on who it might be," he replied, staring him down like a cautious pitbull. "I hear you were both quite close. You tell me, Alun."

Alun's heart began to race, as he realised what the man might have been implying. "Who — me?" He let out a nervous laugh. "Good grief, no! We got on well, but I would never say that we were close. I was just her accountant."

"*Was*?" Danny began moving closer again, his tattooed forearms slowly inching forward towards Alun's side of the table. For a man who had failed English in school, he was very well-acquainted with the use of the past tense.

"I mean, she's *still* a client — but nothing more than that."

"She used to tell me that you were a lovely young man," Danny said, who was enjoying watching the man sweat. "'*That Alun Hughes is such a gentleman*,' she used to say."

Alun would normally have been flattered, but, in this instance, he was more interested in his personal safety.

"Oh, did she, really?" he asked, his high-pitched voice not helping matters in the slightest. "Well that's nice of her. I wish more women my own age would think that. I only ever seem to impress the mothers." The image of Rhiannon's mum sprang to mind.

"The — what?" came the disgusted response.

The black eye began to throb again, as Alun realised what he had just said. "Oh, no — I didn't mean —"

"Are you telling me you go around getting off with other people's *mams*?" Danny was right back up in his face again, his stale breath reaching up into the other man's nostrils. "Is that what you were doing with mine? I bet you loved counting all her money. You do it for a living. Maybe that's why you went ahead and married her — so you could have it all to yourself!"

Alun quivered in his chair as the thug grabbed hold of his collar. He was now in perfect punching range and awaited his fate with a small prayer.

Danny could smell the fear, and he began laughing hysterically.

"You should have seen your face!" he cried out. "You really thought I had you down as a grave-digging scumbag!" He gave his relieved new drinking buddy a slap on the back. "Loosen up, numbers-man! There's no way you'd have the nerve to pull off a stunt like that."

The man polished off the rest of his pint and wiped away the tears of laughter.

"Fancy another?" he asked. "Come on, I think you need one."

Alun could think of nothing worse than another round with his playful new friend, but, as it turned out, he didn't really have a choice in the matter.

As Danny headed over to the empty bar, he called out for some immediate service. Moments later, he was greeted by a pair of giddy, young lovers, as they stumbled out of the back room in each other's arms. The sixteen-year-old girl took one look at the impatient customer and gasped.

"*Ruby*?!" Danny roared.

The young barman in his early twenties was now equally shocked, especially considering he had just been making out with the man's niece.

Ruby Doyle removed her arms from the young man's neck, as if it was suddenly burning hot. She saw the fury in her uncle's face and let out an embarrassed smile. "Oh, hiya, Uncle Danny..."

ALUN LEFT *The Old Bull's Head* in an even more fragile mood than when he had entered. The aftermath of a young Ruby

Doyle's appearance behind the bar had not been pretty, but it had at least put an end to his boozy lunch with Danny. The outraged man would not be frequenting the pub again anytime soon, not after the drama that had just taken place that morning.

It turned out that the teenager was not as innocent as she had always seemed. It wasn't just Mari's flowers that she enjoyed wrapping her hands around, but it appeared she also had a partialness to older boys — or in this case, a young man. Perhaps her part-time job at the shop had actually been used as a distraction, Alun thought. With the business closed, those idle hands were now free to do whatever they pleased.

He had never seen a barman run so fast in his life — not at *that* pub, anyway — and he wondered how long it had taken for a livid Danny to catch up with him. Either way, he had the afternoon back to himself, and he wished the young man a speedy escape.

The midday sun was nowhere to be found on the streets of Pengower that day. Those same dark clouds that Rhiannon had looked up at over the lake were now hovering over the quiet town square.

Alun strolled through the small town, his long overcoat still covering up the pyjamas that he hadn't even had the opportunity to change. As he made his way past the row of closed shops, he noticed a bustle of commotion outside the butcher shop. Other passersby were gathering to gawk and stare at the cluster of police vehicles and lines of crime scene tape. Amongst the crowd of spectators was a tall police officer trying to keep them all back.

"What's going on?" Alun asked, when he finally reached a flustered looking Mel.

"I've already said: *get back*!" The police officer took a second glance and realised that the person he had just accosted was actually his friend. "Oh, it's you." He removed his hat and wiped off a layer of sweat from his shiny head; it was going to be a long day for the small-town copper. "I can't say too much at this stage."

"How much do you know, *exactly*?" asked Alun, who knew his friend far too well.

"Only what they'll tell me," said Mel, who was far too tired to keep up the pretence of being well-informed. "And it's pretty vague, if I'm really being honest. I only started my shift about an hour ago." He glanced behind him at the group of officials, all gathered underneath the striped, red and white canopy. "Now I've got flaming CID waving their badges about. They seem to forget whose patch they're on right now."

Alun looked over at the shop window and saw, what appeared to be, the flashes of a forensic investigator's camera on the other side of the glass.

"CID?" he asked. "That sounds pretty serious."

"Course it's serious," said the stressed-out police sergeant. "They've only gone and found —" He lowered his voice so that only his friend could hear. "They've only gone and found a *body*."

Alun felt very lightheaded all of a sudden, and it was not from the hangover.

"*Please* no..." he said to himself. The moment he had been dreading for weeks had finally arrived. Despite his sudden attack of nerves, he felt a strange obligation to ask something: "Who found her?"

Mel raised an eyebrow. "I never said it was a woman."

His words began to counteract the other man's growing dread. "It's not?"

"No!" The police officer lent in and decided it was best to whisper the next piece of information: "It's the body of Dai Jones."

CHAPTER 18

Rhiannon tried not to appear shocked. She was hoping the woman would elaborate further, but, instead, she was led up a chewed staircase. Presumably, the family had owned a dog, she prayed. They walked to the end of a narrow hallway full of doors and stopped beside a discarded ladder. "I was hoping this was still here," said Ceri, propping it up against the dead-end wall.

They both looked up to find a square door leading up into the loft.

Ceri turned to her, as though a trip to the attic was normal procedure for entertaining house guests. "The answers you're looking for are up there."

Rhiannon took a deep breath and placed her hands on the ladder. There was no turning back now, and she needed to find out exactly what was hiding beyond the ceilings of *Derwen Farm*.

The solid piece of wood was lifted up to reveal a square hole, and Rhiannon's lungs burned from the explosion of falling dust. Her legs had morphed into jelly, and her senses were heightened to the point of an impending panic attack. She had never been comfortable on a ladder, let alone one as tall as the one she was now climbing. All of this, she thought, at the request of a woman she believed was missing a few marbles.

"There's a switch to your right!" Ceri called from down below.

Rhiannon took her final step into the unknown, and she hauled herself up into the small space. With the help of some illumination, she could see that she was surrounded by piles of boxes from every angle. She crawled her way through them, wheezing and coughing from the excess dust.

Many of the boxes appeared to have been recently opened, their contents exposed — like old wounds from a long time ago. Before she could make out exactly what was inside, another presence beside her leg caused her to yell out in horror.

Her eyes were now squeezed tight from the rush of fear, and when she slowly reopened them again, she saw a flickering tail trying to force its way through a small gap between two of the boxes.

Someone had once told her that rodents were more frightened of humans than she was of them. Why, therefore, every mouse *she* had ever encountered always felt the need to rush out and startle her, she would never understand. *They knew what they were doing.*

Just as she was beginning to pull herself together, the sound of a voice behind her was more startling than the furry animal.

"Jack told me you were looking for a diary."

Rhiannon turned around to see that Ceri had joined her inside the narrow space. She was curled up in the corner, as if frightened by the contents of the boxes.

"I always knew that this was where she kept them all," she said, pointing towards the piles of small notebooks that were spilling out over the floor. "Some habits never change."

The journalist picked up a random notebook and checked the date: *April 2nd, 1981.*

She gazed back up at the mountains of boxes and realised there was a lot more reading ahead of her than she had bargained for. She had been looking for a diary, and now, just like Mari, she had won the jackpot.

"There must be a lifetime of diary entries up here," she said in disbelief. "Did she really write in them *every single day*?"

Ceri nodded. Her mind had become preoccupied with flashes from the past. "Every. Single. Day."

Rhiannon had always found it a sad irony that she — a so-called *journalist* — had never managed to keep her own journal. Like many people, she had started quite a few over the course of her lifetime but had never made it through a whole week. After witnessing the results of her ultimate antithesis, it was clear that she may well have saved herself some valuable floorspace.

"She said it helped her sleep," Ceri said. "I don't think I could sleep with all those crazy thoughts going on in my head, either."

Rhiannon turned around. "*Crazy*?"

The woman nodded and hugged her own body for comfort. "I only fully realised it later on. When you're living with a person as nuts as she was, you never see it until you're far enough away."

"How, exactly, was she... *unhinged*?" Rhiannon asked, dying to read a snippet of a diary. Unfortunately, she had deduced that the person sitting near her would require her full attention for what was about to come.

"Most mothers I know don't raise their kids like it's the eighteen hundreds. We didn't even have electricity or running water! How crazy is that? Then there's all those daft rituals."

"Rituals?"

"Ever since dad died —" Ceri choked on her own sentence and fought hard to hold back the tears. "She was never the same after that."

Silence hit the attic like a gust of wind. Rhiannon had asked her question but was none the wiser.

"She used to give us these sedatives," Ceri continued. "At least, that's what I think they were. We were told it was medicine. Then, as we got older, she started spiking our food and drink. Barry reckons it was a form of antidepressant. Something to numb us into functioning zombies."

The woman now hanging on Ceri's every word felt a bulging lump in her throat. She was a mother herself and could never imagine such a thing.

"Why would she do that?" she asked.

The third-eldest of the Doyle children came out of her trance for a moment and acknowledged her listener. The sadness and fear morphed into anger.

"To control us," she said. "We were apparently quite a handful — or so I'm told. *Unruly* is one word she used to say. But that never gave her the right. Then Danny came along, and he was even worse. Have you met my little brother Danny?"

Rhiannon shook her head. "I have a friend who's quite familiar with him."

Ceri stretched out her legs to improve her circulation; it was fast becoming an uncomfortable environment for everyone present. "My mother once told me that, when *she* was a little girl, she used to dream of marrying some fancy gentleman with a big house. She pictured her perfect children, her perfect family — all living together in some weird, revolting fantasy. And where did she find herself?" She looked up at the low ceiling and smiled. "Stuck here — in this old place. With her rotten children and hopeless husband. God, she hated *him* even more than us. I think it's quite safe to say that Mari Doyle really was living the dream!"

She let out a croaky laugh that was both amused and hysterical.

Rhiannon's own legs were quickly starting to cramp up against the hard floorboards, and she checked her watch with little regard for discreteness.

"Gosh, is that the time?" she said. "It's later than I thought. I should probably be getting back."

Ceri watched her stuffing some of Mari's diaries into her handbag. Her eyes were cold, as if the person in front of her was now transparent. "Of course," she said.

"I only need a couple of these for now," Rhiannon said, admiring the piles of handwritten thoughts and musings for what she hoped would be the very last time. "There's no way one person could get their way through a whole lifetime of these."

Outside, the sky had grown dark. A brand new cluster of black rain clouds had hovered their way over the valley and were now getting ready to unleash their contents over the roofs of *Derwen Farm*.

The two women made their way out of the house and into the yard. Rhiannon looked over at the dangling tyre. It now evoked an entirely different emotion than it had done the first time she saw it. She had previously associated it with the joy of a happy child, swinging back and forth in the warm breeze of summer. Now that happiness had been drowned out by the cruel reality of Ceri's memories.

As they walked alongside the corrugated wall of the rusty barn, she tried to process everything she had just been told; it had been a lot to take in. Around the next corner, she saw an impressive treehouse propped up with four solid wooden beams. It was a far cry from the treehouse a child would have normally cobbled together, like the one she had made with her cousins many years ago. Clearly, a lot of effort and ingenuity had gone into building something that had already stood the test of time. She had never known a child's den to require planning permission before, but this piece of craftsmanship was very much on the edge.

"Is that where —"

Rhiannon did not need to finish her question. Ceri had seen her looking.

"Yes," she said. "He fell, just over there." She pointed towards a patch of grass where her father had taken his great fall. "Let me show you something before we go."

Rhiannon's feet felt glued to the ground, as the woman headed off towards the enormous rope ladder leading up into the top of the tree. Her body was reluctant to follow; it knew, as did she, that it was a very bad idea. In the end, her manners won over (she did need that lift home, after all).

The rope ladder was as unsteady as it had appeared. Each step involved a new set of muscles that were seldom used in day-to-day life. Rhiannon grunted her way up to the giant platform in the treetops and almost lost her footing a few times.

Ceri had made it to the top in half the time, having had years of practice that were still paying dividends.

"I'm beginning to think you're not so keen on heights, Rhiannon," she said, as her guest came belly-flopping onto the damp wood.

"Is anyone?" Rhiannon asked, spitting out a piece of bark. "This is the second ladder you've got me up this afternoon."

"I quite like heights," Ceri said, taking a moment to breathe in the cool air and admire the view she knew so well. "It makes me feel safe."

"You'd be safer down there." The other woman pointed towards the patch of grass at the bottom of the rope ladder, a place very close to her heart at this moment in time.

"Dad spent months building this place. My mother used to hate it. She would rather he spent that time doing up the kitchen or focusing on the bathroom. But he never cared about any of that stuff." Ceri took a quick look over the edge and a darkness descended over her. "It was always a cruel act of fate that this treehouse also became responsible for his death."

Despite her reluctance to be up there, Rhiannon could not fault the stunning view. She saw that they were the exact same level as one of the bedroom windows that overlooked them. "Did anyone see him fall?"

Ceri gave her an angry glance. "None of us did. It was late in the evening, and we were all inside. I remember seeing his body, lying there in the grass, almost peaceful. It was morning by then."

"I'm very sorry," Rhiannon said, regretting that she had even brought up the subject. "It must have been very hard for you."

"Hard?" Her question was spat out with a tone that she had yet to express that day. "You think *you* know what *hard* is?"

The journalist's mouth went very dry, and the ground below her felt like a very long way down.

Ceri's eyes were wild with rage. She took the other woman by the hand and pulled her in towards the base of the tree. Carved out was an unusual marking that Rhiannon felt would be very at home in a *Wicker Man* ritual.

"This is what I wanted to show you," she said. "Do you know what that is?"

The other woman shook her head and was more interested in holding her balance.

"It's definitely not a love heart with two initials," Rhiannon said, trying to lighten the mood. Unfortunately, as she was slowly discovering, it was very hard to light a candle in a gail force wind. "I was expecting to read something like: *Tarzan was here*."

"You won't find it so funny when I tell you," Ceri snapped. "It's called a *hex*. I made it almost twenty-five years ago."

"A hex?" Rhiannon was adamant that the woman must have been joking but chose not to smile — just in case.

"Black magic was something I took very seriously in those days. It was my only safety blanket."

Her fellow secondary school alumna was not overly surprised. Had someone asked her back then, whether Ceri Doyle was prone to practising witchcraft in her spare time, she would have thought nothing of it.

"Oh, did you?" she asked, realising that her wrist was still being held. "Well, it's nice to have a hobby, I suppose."

"I carved out that hex for *you*, Rhiannon Williams."

"Oh, I see." She didn't know whether to be flattered or very, very afraid.

"That was the day you spread those rumours of me being a witch. Something I had to live with until our graduation."

Rhiannon wanted to point out that she hadn't been that far off the mark, but, again, thought it was best not to argue at such a great height.

"You made my life hell when we were younger," Ceri continued. "You, and your hockey-playing minions."

She shoved her former tormentor backwards with a vicious force.

"Now, Ceri, we've been over this — it was a very long time ago."

Ceri pointed towards the carving in the middle of the tree and hissed: "And yet that carving is still as visible as the day I made it. Scars last a lifetime, Rhiannon."

They moved to the edge of the platform and Rhiannon felt her heart racing. "Ceri, please," she said with genuine remorse. "Anything I've done to hurt you in the past — I'm truly sorry. We were all so young and stupid back then. I was probably more stupid and naive than anyone. I didn't have an upbringing like yours, but my home life wasn't a walk in the park either."

Ceri was listening, but very little of the other woman's words appeared to be registering.

Rhiannon raised up her hands and continued to spill her heart out: "Any pain or misery I ever caused in school has been well and truly accounted for — trust me on that one. If life is just one big netball competition, then I won't be coming out as the winner — that's for sure." She took another step backwards. "You wanted me to suffer? I've suffered. I don't know much about black magic, but that hex of yours has probably done its job —"

Just as the woman opposite darted towards her, she felt nothing but empty air beneath her right foot. Ceri Doyle's hysterical face was the last thing Rhiannon saw before there was nothing but sky. There had been nothing to grab hold of or anyone to call for help, and, in a moment of sheer terror, she realised that she was falling.

CHAPTER 19

The fall had gone by slower than an action replay on *Match of the Day*. Rhiannon's world was fading into darkness, as she felt the bottomless void behind her, pulling her down into an early grave. She could feel the air leaving her lungs and the memories of her life whizzing by her in a single heartbeat.

She was just starting to accept the helplessness of her situation, when a cold hand wrapped itself around her wrist. A sharp pain poured across her scalp, as her hair was yanked by yet another hand.

Rhiannon cried out in pain, a type of pain she had not expected from falling out of a treehouse.

Ceri's face was grimacing down at her, and she used all of her remaining strength to pull Rhiannon back up towards the platform.

The rescue had lasted a whole thirty seconds, an amount of time which Rhiannon had discovered was far too long to be dangling by one's hair. Both women sat back into the safety of the treehouse and enjoyed their moment of rest.

"I'm sorry," Ceri eventually said. "I don't know what came over me."

Rhiannon glared at her and resisted the urge to snap with a venomous response. For now, she was just happy to be alive (unlike many of her torn hair follicles).

"Well, thanks for saving me," she replied. "That fall would have been nasty."

The other woman nodded. She sat there, sheepishly. Her recent outburst was still a source of embarrassment.

"We should probably get going now," Ceri said.

Rhiannon rubbed her head and felt more motivated to go home than she had done in a long time. "Yeah. I think we probably should."

~

THE DRIVE back into town was less than three miles, but, for Rhiannon, it had felt like a hundred. Ceri and her passenger had barely said a word since they left the farm. All that could be heard now was the squeaking of two windscreen wipers, as they fought against the torrential rain.

The spire of *St David's Church* peeked into view, still far enough away that it looked like it was built with a handful of matches. Despite the lack of conversation on their return leg of the journey, Rhiannon had decided to break their silence with a question that had been nagging her all afternoon: "Do you think your father really fell?"

Ceri turned her attention away from the road for a moment. She was surprised but not shocked. This was an answer that she didn't even need to think about: "No. I never have."

Silence descended on the Range Rover, and the journalist nodded at her confirmed suspicion.

"Any ideas on who might have pushed him?" Rhiannon

asked. She knew full well that (even if the woman *did* know) it was very unlikely she would tell her.

"Whoever it was," she said, " that person did my mother a favour. She hated that man with all of her heart by that point. I never really understood how a person could despise the person she had chosen to spend the rest of her life with, but, then again, I never really understood my mother. She's always been barking mad." She paused for a second and caught a glimpse of her own reflection in the windscreen. "I often wonder whether it's genetic. My grandmother was even loopier from what I remember."

"Did your grandmother also practise witchcraft?" The mere mention of the word made her feel silly, but, judging by the expression on her driver's face, it was a very serious matter indeed.

"It's supposedly been in the family for generations," said Ceri. "My sister reckons Granny was part of some Satanic coven."

"A — what?"

"It's a cult, I suppose. They do charms and rituals. Many of them worship the Devil."

"Oh..." Rhiannon felt a cold shudder. She was relieved to see that the air conditioner was running full blast.

"None of us really know the history of it all," Ceri insisted. "And to be honest, none of us really care. All I know is that the whole thing is a load of old rubbish, and I'm just glad all four of us managed to get away from it when we did. Its effects have left some deep scars."

Her passenger could not have agreed more. She had met two of the Doyle siblings at this point and could attest from first-hand experience that both had their issues. Still, a mother who preached the dark arts was a factor she would never have seen coming herself.

"I met your brother, Barry, the other day," Rhiannon said.

"Oh really?" The look of contempt in Ceri's face was clear. "And how did you find *him*?"

The other woman considered her answer very carefully and tried to think of some redeeming qualities. "He had a cracking moustache."

FOR THE FIRST time in her life, Rhiannon could not have been more pleased to see her parent's front door. Little did she know it then, but her day was about to get a whole lot stranger.

"How could you go galavanting around with your mates at a time like this, young lady?" her mother said, when she entered the living room.

It was like being a teenager all over again. Many people would have loved the idea of living out their youth for a second time, but Rhiannon was in her mid-thirties. She was a woman, a mother, a working professional — and now she was sharing a house with the same two people that had aggravated her all those years ago. The fountain of youth was not worth it.

The fact that her mother, Morwenna, had referred to Ceri Doyle as one of her "*mates*" was the strangest part of all.

Morwenna Williams had always been prone to exaggerated outbursts. Most of the time, they were completely unjustified. The rest of the time, they were out of pure boredom.

"Your father's a complete mess," Morwenna wailed, pouring herself another glass of rosé and taking a moment to breathe. "What with him being one of his oldest friends, and all."

Her daughter ignored her judgmental stare and gave her attention to the little boy poking his head around the doorway.

"Hey, kiddo!" she said, scooting over to him with one of her monster hugs. "How was your afternoon?"

Morwenna laid herself out across the white sofa and put a

hand over her own temples, as she often did when a migraine was coming on. "Oh, I can't bear it anymore," she groaned, fanning herself with a magazine.

Rhiannon sighed. She decided to ask something that her mother had been wanting her to ask since she first entered the house: "Whatever's the matter, mam?" she asked, making no effort to sound sincere.

All of a sudden, Morwenna's mood lightened, and she soon sat up like an eager vampire.

"Well," she said, "you know they've only gone and found a *body*?"

Her daughter froze. If the woman was trying to get her attention, then she had succeeded magnificently. "*Whose* body — *where*?" The barrel of questions in her head was overflowing.

"Oh, I see," Morwenna said. "*Now* you're interested in what I've got to say. Shame it only took a homicide murder to be heard for once."

"Mam!" Rhiannon snapped. "Just tell me what happened."

Her mother was enjoying every minute. If only she could have always had such power. She imagined it was the same thrill a magician received when people begged them for the secret of a magic trick. Sadly, she also knew that people very quickly lost interest once the method of that trick was finally revealed.

"It'll be all over the papers by this evening, I'm sure," Morwenna said, swilling her wine. "Fancy such a thing happening in a town like ours!"

The younger woman gritted her teeth and tried to resist the urge to throttle her. Her mother had clearly forgotten what she did for a living. She had no idea the amount of torture it was for her – the only reporter in the area — to be the last person in town to hear about the biggest story in decades.

"Listen, if you're not going to tell me, I can just —"

"Dai Jones!" Morwenna cried, her self-manufactured grief

resurfacing, once again. The crocodile tears were back. "Can you believe it? Your father and him used to play five-a-side football together. He was practically family."

"The *butcher*?" The name Rhiannon had heard was far from the one she had expected. As well as being confused, she was also disappointed.

Dai Jones was about as close to her family as the dentist. It seemed that, even in a moment of public tragedy, her mother was still willing to scrape that last, remaining barrel for a noteworthy social connection. Imagine their faces, Morwenna thought to herself, when she would tell all her friends at Zumba class.

"He was more to us than just a butcher," Morwenna corrected. "In many ways, he was like a brother to your father. And that makes him my brother-in-law."

Rhiannon rolled her eyes and tried to ignore the whimpering that followed. She felt something wriggle in her trouser pocket and pulled out her phone. A text message from Alun Hughes read: *Heard the news? Regards, Alun.*

She let out an initial scoff at the unnecessary sign-off. Only Alun would have sent a text with the word *regards*. It was as if the man had forgotten she had his number saved.

"DOES SOMEONE *ACTUALLY* LIVE HERE?" Rhiannon asked, as she sat there, looking around at the plain walls, minimalistic choice of furniture and the complete absence of day-to-day clutter.

Alun entered his living room with a tray of tea and a confused frown. The room appeared perfectly in order to him: no mess, no unnecessary possessions, a generous amount of floor space.

"I mean," she continued, "I get the whole Stoic-single-bachelor thing, but, *really*? Would it kill you to get some ornaments? Something to add a bit of soul?"

"Ornaments just get dusty," came the reply.

He placed two coasters down on the glass coffee table. They were ready for the two, identical plain-white mugs containing tea that was brewed from a loose-leaf tea pot (none of that unpredictable *tea bag* malarkey).

His guest had been in a foul mood ever since she had arrived. The news of Dai Jones' death had caused a ripple around the entire town, and it appeared the big-city reporter had indeed been the last to know.

"*Somebody* must know," she said, disappointed at the absence of a biscuit (too many crumbs, she assumed).

"About his secret marriage to Mari?" Alun asked.

"No, about his secret Cumberland sausage recipe... *Yes* — the marriage!"

She stewed away on his uncomfortable, Swedish-made sofa. Thankfully, her tea was not stewed. Alun would never have allowed *that* to happen.

"There were some rumours floating around," Alun said, thinking about the words he had heard earlier that afternoon with his new drinking buddy.

"What kind of rumours?" She glared at him like someone who was in much need of a good night's sleep.

"Oh, just something Danny Doyle told me over a beer today."

He had been waiting to deliver that news. The unlikely meet-up sounded as daft coming out of his own mouth as it was to experience it.

Rhiannon's mood lifted for a moment. "You went for a beer? With *Danny Doyle*?"

Alun smiled. "Turns out he's a nice guy, after all."

She sensed the cheeky spirit in him and decided she didn't

have the energy for games. "I don't even want to know how that came about. I've got enough on my mind after that little trip to *Salem's Farm* this afternoon."

"You went to the farm?" It really *had* been a big day, he thought.

"Oh, yeah," Rhiannon replied. "I had my own little chauffeur and all. Turns out that whole family are bonkers — broomsticks included."

"Broomsticks?!"

His stunned reaction was one she had been waiting for all afternoon.

"Do you believe in witchcraft, Alun?" Her smile only made the man even more suspicious.

"As in... spells and cauldrons?" he asked in return.

"Now, now," she said, with a waving finger. "You've been watching too many films." He watched her slurping her tea with a cynical frown. "I'm talking about *real* witchcraft here. It turns out our friend Mari had a little passion for the dark arts."

He waited for the laugh, but it never came. "Who told you that?"

Her confidence evaporated quicker than a puff of magic smoke. "Ceri Doyle told me."

Alun nodded; his suspicion at the questionable source had been confirmed.

"I know, I know," Rhiannon insisted. "I didn't believe any of it either, at least, at first." She pulled out her stash of diaries and handed him a copy. "But it doesn't matter what we think. The point is that Mari was as serious about spells as you are about figures."

The accountant, who was as open-minded as the next person (provided that next person was of sound mind and possessed at least somewhat of a logical brain), flicked through the pages as if he'd found them beside a lavatory. There was no doubt it was Mari's handwriting, but the words scribbled in ink did not sound anything like what had come out of her mouth during their financial meetings.

"There's a lot of rambling," Rhiannon pointed out. "But it's all the makings of a mad Satan-worshipper."

Alun knew less about Satan than he did about God, but he could see what she meant. The dates flashed out at him as he flicked through the pages. These journal entries were made over a decade ago but there they still were. The accountant was surprised that someone so enthralled in a world of charms and potions had never chosen to mention it during their quarterly discussions on value added tax.

"This can't really all be true," he said, eventually.

"What?" asked the journalist. "The dark magic? Or the fact she actually believed in spells?"

"Both, I suppose."

"The diaries are just the start," Rhiannon continued. "This woman actually tried to make her children believe it all." She thought about her own childhood. "I mean, I thought Santa was a bit far-fetched. But a reindeer-powered sled now seems quite plausible."

"It just doesn't make any sense," said Alun, scratching his head at the long passages of blasphemous worship that would make a cardinal weep. "I thought she was a regular churchgoer."

"Maybe she was spying on the *other side*?" Rhiannon shrugged. "Guess you never really know someone."

"I don't really know how all this explains her disappearance."

Rhiannon let out a wicked grin. "Maybe she turned into a cat?"

Her host was not nearly as amused.

"It does confirm one thing, though," she continued. "We're now dealing with a rich person who was also a raving lunatic."

"Those two factors usually come hand-in-hand in my experience," Alun said, thinking about some of his clients over the years. He flicked through some more pages, until he came across what he presumed was the extract of a curse. His face lit up, as the melody of a famous tune entered his mind. "You know there's a Fleetwood Mac song about a Welsh witch?"

He paused, trying to contain his amusement.

"Don't you even dare say it."

"It's called —" The threatening glare coming his way was enough to make him retreat. "Never mind."

They both went silent and continued their exploration of Mari Doyle's mind. Their eyes studied the language of a world so alien to their own, a world filled with dark rituals and cryptic meanings.

"I wonder what a coven is?" Alun eventually asked. "It's a word that comes up a lot."

"It means a gathering of witches — like a collective. They meet up in secret." Rhiannon saw him staring at her in surprise. "I used to watch a lot of *Buffy*," she added.

Alun nodded. That made a lot more sense.

"Well, all this is very far from the realms of my knowledge." He scratched his head and closed up the diary. It was like turning off a noisy stereo, and his mind could now relax.

"That's a shame. I thought there might have been at least a hint of darkness in that quiet soul of yours, Alun Hughes." She knew the comment would make him uncomfortable, and it did.

He ignored the flirtatious look on her face and tried to change the subject. "I think whoever killed Dai Jones used a lot more than charms and curses."

His words killed off the playful tone in the room, and they both thought about the butcher who had recently met his grisly end. They thought about him lying there at the back of his shop, like one of his slaughtered pigs.

"Is it frogs or bats?"

Alun shook away the disturbing image in his head and turned to his guest.

"Excuse me?" he asked back.

"Witches," Rhiannon clarified. "Is it a bat they turn into? Or a frog?"

"Uh, I'm not sure. I think one of those might be vampires."

"Ah, okay. Never mind then."

CHAPTER 20

The office of the *Merioneth Press* was not known for its dynamic team and pulsating atmosphere. Unlike your typical newspaper operation, the majority of this team consisted of two volunteers, three part-timers and a cat called Gary.

Morgan Morris, the Editor-in-Chief, had been working at the local press for over a decade. This scruffy looking individual, with his greasy combover and stained teeth, was more interested in pursuing a career in pop music than he was in journalism. His treasured *Gibson Les Paul* took pride of place on top of his desk, as he proof-read the latest article about the recent chaos of a broken-down food lorry.

After blacking out the last of many uninspiring passages with his thick, red marker pen, he chucked the sheet of paper away and saw his newest member of the team making her way towards her desk. She was not only late, but she was determined to avoid any social interaction until she was safely tucked away behind her divider.

"Rhiannon!!" Morgan cried out, leaping out of his chair.

The groggy reporter had barely placed her plastic container

of food down, before she saw her excited boss perched against her desk. She had worked for a range of different editors over her career but never one as hopeless as Morgan Morris. When he wasn't boring her with tales of his band's latest gig, he was sending her on assignments that were barely fit for an apprentice. Worst of all: the man didn't know a good story even if it snuck up behind him and pulled down his baggy trousers.

"Loved the cheese shortage story," he said, gnawing on that same piece of chewing gum; it had been in his mouth since birth, according to the rumours. "That angle on the melted brie was pure genius."

"Glad you enjoyed it," said Rhiannon, making sure to avoid all eye contact in the hope he went away. The man often reminded her of an art teacher she once had — too cool for school and left to fumble his way through a job where nobody would call him out. She knew, as well as Morgan knew, that he was way out of his depth. The editor needed her far more than she needed him, and she had grown tired of humouring the poor man.

"I'm sure you know what story I'll be putting you on today," Morgan said, propping his feet up to highlight that laid-back style of his.

"You mean the one I should have been working on in the first place?"

If there was anything more irritating to her than the sound of her editor's patronising voice, it was his sniggering laugh.

The man announced his reply to a room full of disinterested office staff: "She's a funny girl, this one!" After another congested giggle, he hunched himself over and pulled out his 'serious face'. "No, no," he said to her. "I'm talking about the death of our local butcher. There's no way you could have covered this story a few days ago — unless you got a time machine!"

Rhiannon sighed. She barely had the energy to explain, especially to this moron.

"If we thought the cheese shortage was bad," her boss continued. "Imagine the implications of this to our raw meat? We'll all be vegetarians by the end of the week!"

That unique laugh of his gave another loud performance.

"I'm thinking of making the focus less on meat," she said, "and more on *murder*."

The entire office went quiet.

Morgan was frozen on the desk. He was a deer blinded in the headlights, a deer with receding antlers and a mouth full of chewing gum. He processed that last word of hers. It was a word seldom used within the walls of the *Merioneth Press*.

"Murder?" he asked. His natural instinct was to laugh the idea away, and he did, until he realised she was serious. "We don't get murders here in Pengower. You've been living in that big smoke for too long."

"I'll let the readers be the judge of that," she said. "First, a local millionaire goes missing. Then, her recent husband turns up dead."

"Dai Jones was her *husband*?" The editor hated being ill-informed on a subject, and it was something that happened all too often.

Rhiannon pulled out her phone and showed him a photograph of a certificate taken from the *Registration of Births, Deaths and Marriages*. "The whole relationship was actually kept secret. Although, someone else clearly knows."

"But we don't know for sure if Dai was even murdered," said Morgan, squinting at the small image.

"Not unless he slipped and fell backwards on one of his own knives. Oh, and apparently it *wasn't* one of his own knives."

She waited for the man to register her information (it always took him a while to put two and two together). "But, how do you —"

"I confirmed the cause of death yesterday with my source at the local police station," she interrupted. "He wears a big, tall hat and enjoys fiddling with his handcuffs."

For the first time in his life, the editor was lost for words. "My, my," he muttered. "You *have* been busy."

She watched those rusted cogs of his turning in that small head. The penny would drop eventually, she knew.

"Well, how very exciting!" Morgan cried out, leaping to his feet and clapping his hands. "Ladies and gentleman," he announced. "It appears we have a *murder* on our hands!"

His skeleton crew stared back at him with gormless faces.

The editor in the flamboyant shirt leapt around the office like a galloping gazelle.

"I hired this girl for a reason," he said, clicking his fingers and pointing towards Rhiannon. Oh yes, she thought to herself: make it all about you.

"And now," the editor preached, "my keen eye for strong talent and good journalism is going to give our readers the story of the year." He lifted up his hands to the sky, his loose and unbuttoned shirt exposing a clump of wild chest hair. He envisioned the main headline in giant letters. "I can see that front page now: *Butcher is butchered!*"

Rhiannon shuddered at the choice of title. They would definitely need to work on that.

~

THE STREETS of Pengower had a strange atmosphere for a Wednesday afternoon. It was the day before the annual country show, an event that most of the population had been eagerly awaiting for weeks.

Dai Jones had amassed a great deal of loyal customers since he first opened his shop doors, and the news of his death had come as quite a shock. Not only would they never get to taste one of his homemade sausage rolls again, but they had now discovered that there might be a murderer in their midst.

A copy of the *Merioneth Press* was tucked underneath Alun's arm, as he strolled out of his local cafe after a hearty, late lunch of beef cawl. He had expected to read many of the front-page-story's finer details, but what he hadn't anticipated was the whirlwind of commotion that it was now causing across the local community.

People died all the time in Pengower and from various causes: heart attacks, old age, farming accidents. But not one of them had ever met their untimely death at the hands of a local killer (or, at least, so they thought).

His local greasy-spoon had been a hive of gossip that day. Every customer within earshot could be heard expressing their own theories and opinions (whether he wanted to hear them or not). A small part of him had felt quite sad that his little part-time mystery was now being shared with the entire town. Perhaps Rhiannon's article had been a little premature, or, at the very least, an unnecessary cash-in on everything they had discovered. He knew, deep down, that she was probably feeling the same way. But he also realised that everyone had to pay the bills.

"Alun!" a familiar voice called.

The accountant turned around to see his law-enforcing friend, flagging him down from outside a betting shop. Mel had always loved his gambling ever since they were younger and had lost quite a lot of pocket money on the school playground. All those hours of practising blackjack had still not paid off when it had come time to hit the hopscotch tables.

As a man of fractions and logic, Alun had never seen the appeal to it all, himself. He hated leaving anything to chance.

"Have you seen this?" asked the policeman, waving his own copy of the local newspaper. "That friend of ours really does know how to cause a stir. CID will be livid."

"I thought you hated CID," Alun reminded him.

Mel thought about it for a moment. "Yeah, that's true." He rolled up the paper and patted his friend's shoulder. "What are you up to now?"

"Well, actually I'm —"

"Pop in here for a sec, would you? I could do with your help."

Moments later, Alun found himself staring up at a wall of screens. At least half a dozen horse races unfolded before his very eyes, and, despite his friend's uncontrollable excitement, he felt nothing.

After being presented with the strangest list of names he had ever seen, he pointed to a horse that reminded him of his favourite television programme.

"Come on, *Final Countdown*!" Mel bellowed, as did a small group of elderly regulars.

The horses galloped their way around the circular course, until one of them shot forward into first place on the home stretch. Unfortunately, this same horse was not called Final Countdown, and the outraged policeman had to make do with seventh place.

Scrunched-up betting slips were soon catapulted towards the screen, and the group of punters all groaned in unison.

Having not placed any money down himself, Alun felt very little emotion towards the final outcome. That was, until he saw the face of a furious Mel glaring back at him.

"I thought you were supposed to be good with numbers?" the police officer snapped.

The accountant shrugged. "I told you I wouldn't be of any help. I work in finance, not horses."

"Well you're not helping out *my* finances, that's for sure." The large man let out a deep grunt and checked his newspaper for more races.

Alun looked around at the crowd of regulars, all whispering and foraging for that next hidden gem. Each one had that terrible headline on the front page, with each copy serving as an uncomfortable reminder of death and murder.

"Are they looking at any suspects?"

Mel peered up from his fixtures and saw Alun's eyes locked in on that front page.

"How would I know?" he asked back. "That D.I. on the case barely speaks to me — or anyone else for that matter. He looks old enough to be in school."

The sergeant marked off his next target: a thoroughbred called *Jerry-Ran-Through-Us*.

"These detectives they send over here," he continued, "they haven't got a clue about *real* police work. They think their fancy criminology degrees are enough, when they can't even hold a conversation. The locals of this town will eat that young man alive when he goes knocking around asking questions."

Alun followed him to the nearest counter. Mel reluctantly pulled out his wallet and put his last remaining notes on a horse that he was quite confident would triple his money. Although, he had been wrong before.

"Shouldn't you be out there catching murderers?" asked the man behind the counter. He held up his own copy of the *Merioneth Press* and pressed it against the glass window.

"We're all entitled to a lunch break, Jonno," Mel snapped. "I've seen you take your fair share." The moody cashier took his money and continued the judgmental frown.

"I heard it was one of the Doyle kids," Jonno muttered. "Or maybe they all did it."

Mel snatched his new betting slip. "If I want any suggestions from you, it'll be on the thirteen-ten at Chelmsford." He walked Alun back to the screens and scoffed. "Everyone's a detective."

They watched another race and said very little for most of it. Alun knew his friend well enough to know that the rare silence meant he was deep in thought (or as deep in thought as a man like Mel could go).

"Who do you think it is?"

Mel snapped out of his trail of thought and turned to him. Alun's question had sparked an interest.

"I've got a few theories," the police officer said.

"One for each family member?"

"One for each member of this town." Mel checked over his shoulder to make sure nobody was listening. "Turns out the weapon used is a steak knife from *The Amore Italiano*."

Alun was visibly shocked. "But that must mean —"

"The person who killed Dai Jones has dined at that exact, same restaurant," Mel confirmed. He seemed like he had been dying to share that particular detail.

"Well I know Barry Doyle has for a start," Alun said, thinking about Rhiannon's meal the other night.

"Him and half the people in this town. We've only got one decent restaurant, so at least this person has good taste."

A chorus of groans erupted from behind them, as the last horse galloped over the finishing line. Mel looked down at his betting slip as though he'd been issued with a parking ticket.

"You must be bad luck, Alun Hughes," he said.

"We all get unlucky sometimes." The accountant took one last glance at Dai Jones' photograph on the front page of his friend's newspaper. "Even lottery winners."

CHAPTER 21

Alun had woken up that morning in the best mood since his last accounting audit. He usually found it quite hard to enjoy a good mood, for a good mood was often followed by a very bad one. When it came to the heavy burden of feelings and emotions, the accountant had always preferred to remain on a steady, even keel. Too much excitement would inevitably lead to great disappointment.

Still, it appeared that some things were finally looking up for Alun Hughes. Unlike the failed exploits of his teenage years, he had finally achieved the unthinkable: he had secured a date for the *Pengower Country Show*.

With a single row of identical clothes, Alun's wardrobe was the epitome of efficiency. Having such a narrow selection of colours not only spared him the daily torment of choosing what to wear, but it also freed up his brain power for the deliberation of more important things (like his new gluten-free meal plan). Now he could grab a clean shirt without the slightest deliberation.

Being economical with his cupboard space had proven highly efficient up until this point in time. But today was different. Today, he needed a shirt that screamed "unpredictable". If it didn't convey the aura of danger and rebellion, it had to at least imply the type of person who might sometimes choose to leave a dirty bowl in the sink. According to his latest book on personal development, being unpredictable was the key to having a good time. Although, how a person was expected to derive pleasure from a lack of organisation was still beyond his own understanding.

Faced with a line of immaculate shirts, Alun opted for a shirt he had once bought on a holiday in Barmouth. He hadn't worn it since, but desperate times called for desperate measures.

They may not have had coconuts and palm trees on the North West Coast of Wales, but they did have their fair share of flamboyant shirts. A loud shirt screamed fun, confidence and a big personality (or so Alun had heard). To keep a woman like Bev Griffiths from falling asleep on him, he needed all the help he could get.

After making his way into town, he noticed that the mood on the street was a vast improvement from the previous morning. The locals were preparing themselves for an evening they had been waiting for since the start of spring. It was an occasion of celebration, community and bunting — lots of bunting. If they were really lucky, there was also an opportunity for some good-old-fashioned sporting events that would probably involve a farmyard animal or two.

By the time Alun had reached the end of the high street, he caught sight of Dai's butcher shop, all closed and without life. On the opposite side of the road was another establishment, a place that interested the man even more.

Unlike *Jones Family Butchers*, *Blodwen's Flowers* was alive and well. Its shop window glowed like a beacon of hope with its neat flower arrangements and dainty fairy lights. The spirit of Mari Doyle's business had been miraculously preserved by the undivided loyalty of her teenage shop assistant. Alun was impressed: it can't have been easy maintaining the ongoing illusion of business-as-usual, especially when the owner was nowhere to be found.

Ruby Doyle was buried deep in her magazine when the accountant approached the counter.

The young woman looked up at him with her heartwarming stare and undeniable beauty.

"Alun!" she said, cheerfully, with the enthusiasm of an excited old friend. In that moment, she made him feel like he was a close family member (a family he was quite happy not to be a part of).

"Hello, Ruby," he said.

She blushed at the memory of their last encounter. "Sorry about the other day. I was so embarrassed."

"No need to apologise," Alun said. "We've all been in that situation."

He tried to recall his own experience of snogging behind the bar of a public house, but it must have slipped his mind.

"I knew you would understand," she said, sensing his discomfort. "It's not our fault we fell in love."

"*Love*?" the man asked. It was a word that had become quite alien to him.

"I suppose it sounds a bit silly saying it out loud. But we both feel it. Bryn uses the word all the time. He even bought me a *Pandora* bracelet. Now, if that doesn't say *love* then what does?"

She lifted up her silver-bound wrist. Alun did his best to look impressed. He had always thought Pandora was a character in Greek mythology, but it appeared every day was a school day.

"Who are those for?" Ruby asked.

Alun looked down and remembered he was still holding a bouquet of flowers.

"Oh, just a friend," he said.

"I wish I had friends who bought *me* flowers." Ruby slipped out a knowing wink. She had heard it all before. "Although, if you really want to melt your friend's heart, I would go with your classic red roses over those pink carnations."

She watched her customer exchange his flowers with the uncertainty of a monk in a mobile phone shop. The larger price tag was hard to ignore; it seemed love was indeed expensive.

Alun handed her the roses and tried not to wince at the sound of the large number being punched through the till.

"You're doing a good job of keeping the shop running," he said. "I'm sure your grandmother would appreciate it."

The teenager shrugged. "Gives me something to do over the summer, I suppose. Nana always trusted me to open and close when she wasn't here. Thought I might as well keep my job. There's not many of those around at the moment."

The accountant nodded. He understood the importance of financial income. In fact, he was somewhat of an expert in that field.

"It must have been hard for you, though, I'm sure," he continued. "Your grandmother's disappearance has been a shock for us all."

She handed him back the flowers and chose her reply very carefully. The man was clearly fishing for something, and she had already put up with enough questioning already.

"I don't feel any shame," she said, "if that's what you're getting at."

Her change in tone startled her nosey customer. "Oh, no! I didn't mean anything like that."

"I'm young, but I'm not stupid, Alun. I've seen the way people judge my family. Like we've all got something to hide." She pulled out a chocolate bar and began munching away. "Just because Nana decided to up and leave us one day, it doesn't mean our lives have to stop. Whatever reason she had, it has nothing to do with us."

Spoken like a true Doyle, Alun thought. There was no doubt that the young woman standing there before him was as shrewd as her relatives. Barry Doyle would have been proud.

"Did you know about..." He turned to the window, where the butcher shop across the street was in full view.

"Dai Jones?" Ruby couldn't help but laugh. "Most people round here know that man was nothing but a slimy loverat. Always has been, apparently. But it never seemed to stop the women he chased after — my grandmother included. She seemed to think he was some kind of saint. Never could understand the attraction myself. Maybe you have to be over thirty to fancy him."

Alun had wanted to point out that Dai was easily over sixty, making a person over thirty quite young (just like himself). But this was now just his own age talking.

"So you knew they were in a relationship?" he asked, hoping that he didn't sound too much like a police officer.

"I had my suspicions," she said, chewing away on the last of her snack. "Especially when he kept showing his face in here, flirting away, in that stinking apron. But I never knew how far it had actually gone. Never knew my Nana even wanted herself a bloke, to be honest. She must have been gagging for it. She should have known he was after her money."

He observed her look of disgust, before it melted back into that innocent smile.

"Anyway," she said. "Hope those flowers get you lucky tonight."

Her playful wink made him shrivel up with embarrassment. "Oh, it's nothing like that," he mumbled, clutching his purchase and slowly backing away towards the door.

"Yeah, yeah! You're a proper love machine, Alun Hughes. Go get her, tiger!"

She giggled at his awkward reaction and watched him hobble out of the shop like a lost penguin.

Alun stepped out into the safety of the outside world. As he headed off down the street, he heard a familiar voice crying out to him.

"Alun!"

He turned around to find Rhiannon crossing the road to greet him.

"Did you see the article?" she asked, beaming with pride.

"It's quite hard to miss it, when it's splashed across the front page."

The journalist blushed. "I know, right? Talk about a headline. Shame I have to follow it up with a story on cow manure." She looked down at the impressive bouquet of roses. "Those for Dai, I assume?"

"Uh, no." Alun searched hard for the right words. It was like facing his parents and telling them he had a girlfriend. "They're actually for a woman."

"A woman?" She tried brushing off her surprise with a look of amusement. "Did she die, too?"

The joke did not go down well and was deemed rather inappropriate, considering the circumstances. "You might know her, actually. Her name's Bev Griffiths."

"Bev? As in, Sara Griffiths' older sister?" Rhiannon's amusement was squashed at the thought of Bev Griffiths' athletic figure and smug face. She had seen the woman many times since returning to Pengower. It was hard to miss her during those twice-daily runs of hers, scuttling past everyone in brightly-coloured running clothes. There were surely hundreds of different running trails in the area, but Bev just had to choose the one route with the most prying eyes.

"Turns out, she likes a man who can use his fists," Alun said, followed by a ludicrous attempt at some shadow boxing (it was a good job he was only pretending to punch). His own attempt at some humour had also failed to land.

"I'm sure she does," Rhiannon said with an eye-roll. "I also seem to remember she whacked the hell out of Iwan Emyr with a hockey stick that time she caught him with Rhys Parry."

Alun had forgotten about that incident. He could still visualise that wooden hockey stick smacking against the teenager's jaw. "Well, I suppose she does seem a bit sporty."

"Can't say I've ever been that struck on her, really." She caught sight of her own reflection in the shop window. "Reminds me of the type of person I might have become if I hadn't left this place."

"I'm sure you'll change your mind once you get to know her," he said, checking on the state of his roses. "Do you think she'll like them?"

He held up the bouquet so that she was forced to look into their curling centres. It was only then that she noticed their beauty — that deep red, bursting out at her, like a beating heart. She imagined for a moment that the flowers were actually for her and felt a tingle in her stomach.

"I prefer carnations, personally. Hope she doesn't have hayfever."

Rhiannon's words not only stung but created a feeling of sheer panic.

"I didn't think of that," Alun said. "We're supposed to be going to the show together."

"Well, I guess I better get going," said the reporter, who had a large camera dangling from her neck and was already buckling under the extra weight. "The chief's got me interviewing some hunky farmers later. Or, at least, that's what he told me."

"I'm sure they're a lot less controversial than murdered butchers."

His comment prompted them both to gaze towards the closed shop on the other side of the street.

Rhiannon sighed. "Everyone's a critic."

Just as they were both about to wish each other luck, Alun handed over the flowers. "Here, take these." She looked back at him as though he'd palmed off a newborn baby. "You're right — it's not worth the risk if she gets hayfever. I'll make do with chocolates."

His friend clutched the bouquet with a slight feeling of guilt. She loved the thought of being given flowers, but not in this way. It turned out that she was secretly a hopeless romantic and hadn't even realised it.

"Oh, I meant to tell you," he said. "Congratulations on the front page story. I'm sure it's made you very happy."

She waited for him to walk away before attempting a reply: "Yeah, it's... it's been a blast."

As the reporter stood there, alone on the side of the pavement, she felt a bizarre feeling in the pit of her stomach. It was hard to say for certain, but her instincts pointed towards one terrifying question: was Rhiannon Williams feeling jealous?

CHAPTER 22

The grounds of the *Pengower Country Show* were already buzzing with activity by the time Alun and his date had entered the main gates. Tucked away in its usual venue on the outskirts of town, the show had taken over what was normally a large field full of unassuming sheep. Now, this patch of well-trodden and generously manured grass boasted a whole host of farming-themed attractions, some of which included: sheep dog trials, pedigree cows and even a vintage tractor display. If the *Royal Welsh Show* was *The Grand National* equivalent on an agricultural calendar, then the *Pengower Country Show* was at least a *Kentucky Derby*.

The event held many fond childhood memories for those who were lifelong residents of the small town, and Alun was no exception. He would never forget the first time his father attempted the annual cow-pat-tossing championships, a sport that was rumoured to be a local speciality. In fact, it was the only real time of the year he ever saw his parents letting loose for a few hours (although he had later come to realise that the complimentary rhubarb punch might have had something to do with it).

This year, the newly-single accountant had expected to be attending the show on his own. Instead, he found himself on the arm of a person he considered way beyond his own league of attraction.

Nipping at their heels was a Border Collie that Alun was very pleased to have tagging along for support. He clutched her lead as though it was her own fault that he was stuck in this highly uncomfortable situation in the first place. Social events had never been his cup of tea, and he had hoped that Peg would provide some much needed distraction when the conversation started to run dry (which it inevitably would).

Growing up in a small town had meant that Alun was used to bumping into people he knew everyday, but he was not used to seeing so many of them giving him so much attention. His surprise date had caused quite a stir among those who liked a spot of gossip, and this new and unlikely couple were soon attracting the stares of a certain local reporter.

Rhiannon peered through the lens of her enormous camera, as she lurked beside a wooden stand containing every type of pitchfork known to man. Her long lens allowed her to follow the couple's movements whilst still keeping a safe distance.

Squinting through her viewfinder, she saw them starting to hold hands, a sight that caused her to switch focus towards something less nauseating. Through the crowds of happy people she came upon a whole host of familiar faces, many of which she had spoken to over the course of the last few weeks. People like: Barry Doyle and his team of property minions, Ceri Doyle in full headteacher mode, the young Jack in his voluntary stewarding shirt. There were also a few individuals she was still keen to meet and had not yet had the privilege: Reverend Owen from the church, Danny Doyle and his bulging chest muscles, the teenager, Ruby Doyle, who, unbeknownst to Rhiannon, was actually the person walking around inside the purple dragon costume.

"You could've been a bit more subtle," said a deep voice beside her.

She lowered the camera and found Mel munching on a jacket potato with far too much topping.

"That article you wrote has only gone and scared the living daylights out of people," Mel continued. "There's nothing like the word *murder* to put an entire town on edge."

"Subtlety doesn't sell newspapers," Rhiannon replied. "Besides, I think most people are grateful for the excitement."

"Whatever helps you sleep at night. Personally, I prefer catching criminals rather than glorifying them."

The police officer stuffed in another mouthful, only to have half of it spray out across his jumper. He was glad police uniforms weren't white.

"Sounds like you'll catch this person in no time, then," Rhiannon said, not hiding her cynicism. "Did they find any fingerprints on the knife yet?"

Mel did his best to wipe away the mayonnaise but only managed to create a large stain. "Lab results can take weeks. But it's only a matter of time. I'm more worried about the fact that someone burgled Elfyn Wyn's office last night."

"The solicitor?"

"Not just any solicitor."

Rhiannon felt a shiver. "Let me guess..."

"Mari Doyle's solicitor," the man confirmed. "Nothing was reported stolen. But they'd had a bloody good rummage."

"And the will?"

"Still there, Elfyn says. But that doesn't mean they didn't read it. With Dai out of the picture, somebody in this town now knows the heir to Mari's fortune. They're probably walking among us right now."

They both looked out into the crowds of people, all laughing and having a good time. From what the police officer had told her, Rhiannon knew that one of them would be laughing even more on the inside, but which one, she had no idea.

"Are there any key suspects?" she eventually asked, knowing full well that the man was as shrewd as his jacket potato.

"Pretty much anyone in Mari Doyle's circle of friends and family," he replied.

"Great. So that's half the town, then."

Mel nodded. "Probably even more I would imagine." He thought about that good looking detective and his youthful face. "But that's D.I. Wonderboy's problem, not mine. Right now, my only responsibility is the security of this event."

He stood tall, the stain of mayonnaise still prominent below the *North Wales Police* badge on his chest.

Rhiannon saw him eyeing up another food stand on the other side of the field. "You'd better run along and make sure those Welsh cakes are all nice and secure then."

The policeman laughed and had no shame in admitting it was probably a good idea. He left her in the company of her beloved camera, and she lifted up the lens as if it were an all-seeing eye. Soon she was firing away snapshots, immortalising every corner of the show inside her digital memory card.

Over on the other side of the field, Alun and his date were taking in the sights of this year's offering of food stalls. He enjoyed food as much as the next living person, but he was no self-proclaimed "foodie" as Bev Griffiths had so often described herself.

"Do we really have to have that animal with us?" she whispered, as she was tripped up for the second time since they arrived.

"Sorry," Alun said, "she's just a bit excited with everything. She'll settle down soon."

He had wanted to say that animals were actually quite commonplace in a country farming show, but he was not ready to finish off his first date too early.

They continued along the tables of infinite food samples, until they reached an area of the show that still gave Alun goosebumps.

"Oh, look," he said, pointing towards a cluster of gaming activities that harked all the way back to his childhood. "They've brought Popty-ping-pong back!"

Bev looked over at a selection of timeless games that she considered to be much more at home in a fairground. There were variations on all the classics: the ring toss, hook-a-duck, Jacob's Ladder — all with a brand new theme: farming.

Unlike Alun, his date didn't seem that excited at the prospect of playing Popty-Ping-Pong. A Pengower favourite, Popty-Ping-Pong was an unusual take on the old-fashioned carnival classic: the Milk Can game.

"I don't know how these child magnets are still allowed," Bev sneered. "It's daylight robbery in my experience. Half the stuff is glued down."

The accountant sensed his chance at cementing his heroic moment of the evening (an important component of any perfect date). If there was one thing he knew about, it was holding his own at a game of Popty-Ping-Pong. His father had also been a fan, and, in an effort to get some practice in before the next show rolled around, they would line up their drinking mugs on the kitchen counter and battle it out to the sound of a boiling kettle. Dealing with the poor aerodynamics of a projectile tea bag was far more difficult than getting a ping-pong ball into a coloured jar, making them both fiendishly skilled when it came to the big day.

"I'll take three balls, please," Alun said, much to the disapproval of his embarrassed date.

The man behind the counter handed him his ammunition, and the accountant could not have looked more excited. It was like stepping up for the very first time when he was seven years old: the nerves, the pressure. He had never felt more alive.

What followed was the sweet sound of polymer on glass, as each of the three balls were potted into brightly-painted jars; the old dog still had it.

Bev was less excited and felt a burst of terror in her knees at the sight of an enormous stuffed unicorn making its way towards her. Alun presented his furry winnings to her like a proud hunter with a mounted moose. The woman cringed, until the sight of another person approaching them left her no choice but to force out an excited smile.

"Sorry to interrupt," Rhiannon said to them. It was hard not to be distracted by the couple's new third wheel: a furry creature with a pink coat and long horn.

Bev recognised the journalist's face and folded up her arms. "We're not interested in being part of any more click-bait articles, if *that's* what you're after."

"Uh, no," the other woman said. She was slightly surprised that Bev could even read a newspaper. "I'm looking to have a word with Alun, actually."

Both women turned to look at the accountant. He was quite right to be nervous, and the answer he gave next was vital in keeping the peace.

"We're a little busy, actually, Rhiannon," he said, with a look that begged her to leave them to it.

His words only fuelled Bev's smugness even more. She liked a partner who could back her up and Alun had done well to tick that box. It seemed her pub brawler really was a man's man, after all.

"There you go," she said. "Run along and bother someone else."

Rhiannon felt a flash of anger burning up inside of her. She wanted to stick that unicorn somewhere extremely tight. Instead, she ignored the evil glare and turned to face Alun.

"It's something you'll want to hear," she said. "Some confidential new information."

The word confidential had always come in useful. Everyone was always intrigued by something only a few people were allowed to know. Bev, on the other hand, was not a fan of the word at all.

Alun looked to his date for a sign he could be excused but only received a stern stare.

"I'll just be a second," he said to her, shattering his previous brownie point.

The two associates stepped away to find some privacy and turned their back on a fuming Bev.

"She seems nice," Rhiannon said, as they both huddled like teammates in a sporting match.

"Don't even start," Alun snapped. "What's this important news about?"

"Well, I've heard from a very reliable source..." The accountant rolled his eyes at her; he knew who that was supposed to be. "Mari's solicitor had a break-in last night."

Her words had the same impact on him as they had done on her. "Surely not..."

"Surely — *yes*! Someone wanted to see that will. And now they know what it says."

"But that means it would have to be someone who stands to inherit, someone who was hoping to find their own name."

The reporter's eyes lit up with excitement. She could feel his growing interest.

"But if the name they found was someone else..."

"God help them," Alun said, with a shudder. He went through a list of possible faces that included all of Mari's next-of-kin, as well as anyone else who may have made an impression on her. "But it all depends on when this will of hers was drafted. If she wrote a will after her marriage to Dai, then why bother knocking him out of the picture? If someone writes a new will after getting married then it voids the marriage agreement."

"If someone murdered Dai to get their inheritance, then they must have known about the will."

Alun continued searching his brain for possible solutions. He had often likened it to a giant database or search engine, only with more glitches. "You know, there is still a very important person we haven't yet factored into that murder. A suspect we haven't even considered."

"Like who?"

To Rhiannon's great frustration, he failed to answer. He seemed more interested in the woman behind them, the one still clutching her stuffed toy.

"Listen, I'm kind of in the middle of something right here," he said. "Couldn't this conversation have waited?"

His irritable tone took Rhiannon by surprise. He had never been keen to leave her company before. Normally, it was him chasing *her* for a conversation, something she had taken great pleasure in making very difficult. "I thought you'd be interested."

"No, you assumed I'm as obsessed as you are." His words stung, deeper than he would ever have realised. She had heard the word "obsessed" before and it hadn't been used with much affection. Alun saw the pain in her face and gave a deep sigh. He placed a concerned hand on her shoulder; it made the woman want to break his fingers with a single snap. "It's the *Pengower Country Show*, Rhiannon. It comes around once a year. Can't you just switch off for one day?"

It was like reliving a forgotten nightmare. The conversation had been exactly the same last time, except they had come from the mouth of a man she had once loved with all her heart. She had ignored the words back then and was trying to ignore them now. It was this same, obsessive nature that her husband had also despised, and the same, exact trait that made Rhiannon who she was. She just wasn't able to help it.

"Fine. Sorry to interrupt."

They both turned to see an impatient Bev. Her enormous hair had managed to force its way into their private conversation. "Would you mind taking a quick photo for us?"

She pointed to the camera. Rhiannon had forgotten she was even carrying it and turned to see Alun's pleading face.

The journalist sighed. "Sure. I'd love to."

Bev grabbed her date by the collar and forced him into an intimate pose. She pulled out her favourite smile, the same one she had used in countless social media posts.

The camera was lifted up and managed to cover the photographer's disapproving frown. Rhiannon moved her finger to the trigger, before it hesitated at the sight of something leaping up and down in the corner of the frame.

"Let go!" Bev hissed. "Get down — right now!"

Her shrieks fell on a pair of pointed, hairy ears.

"Peg! Drop! *Drop*!" The Border Collie continued to leap up and down, oblivious to her master's cries of protest, until her long snout took a great bite out of the unicorn's pink backside.

Rhiannon giggled under her breath, as half of the cuddly toy was yanked away in a cloud of white stuffing. The timing could not have been more perfect: she pressed the button and captured the moment in one single frame.

Just as the reporter was starting to feel better about the evening, her personal space was suddenly invaded by a large woman with facial features that mirrored an angry bulldog.

"Excuse me," said the woman carrying an enormous bowl of

trifle. "Is it true that you wrote that front page story in the *Merioneth Press*?"

The journalist sensed the confrontational energy coming her way but was passed caring. Criticism was the nature of her job. "You mean, that one with the awful title? Yes, that was me."

Rhiannon stood tall, and she stood proud. Unfortunately, she was not prepared for the entire bowl of jelly, cream and custard. The onlookers gasped, as the entire pudding was tossed all over her.

The trifle's creator put on her best shocked-face. "Oh! I'm so sorry! How clumsy of me." She shook Rhiannon's hand and gave her a serious scowl. "I'm Lesley Doyle, by the way. Pleasure to meet you."

Alun looked on in horror at his helpless friend, who was now dripping from head to toe in soggy pudding. The sound of the pink unicorn being mauled and shaken only made it worse.

"Would you all excuse me for a moment?" he asked. "I'm just nipping to the toilets."

He left the scene as fast as he could without coming across as rude. His desire to escape the unbearable tension created an urgency in his step, and he looked forward to the confined safety of a portaloo.

Once he had re-emerged from his plastic cocoon, Alun took a quick detour around a wall of brightly-coloured tents. He was in no rush to get back and hoped that Bev wasn't too upset about the ravaged unicorn.

As he passed the last of the stripy marquees, he heard a sound that made his body freeze and his blood curdle; it was the sound of a loud scream.

CHAPTER 23

The scream was enough to glue the accountant's shoes deep into the patch of long grass. He knew he had heard it, and he knew he had to act. But *wanting* to act was a whole other matter. The prospect of getting in between a murderer and his victim was not tempting, but he decided to dash inside the tent anyway (before his logical side had a chance to take over).

His appearance on the other side of the zipped door only seemed to ignite a second scream.

Rather than having the unpleasant responsibility of rudely interrupting a bloody assault, Alun was instead presented with the startled faces of Ruby Doyle and her bartender boyfriend. The young couple released each other quicker than if they had been drenched by a freezing shower.

Ruby shook the hay out of her hair and straightened out her purple dragon costume. Her lipstick was smudged, with most of it having been transferred to the face of the young man in her arms.

Alun cowered in the open doorway. He didn't know which way to look. "Oh! I'm sorry to interrupt. I thought..."

"*Jesus*, Alun," said Ruby. "You scared the hell out of us."

The barman seemed quite happy to keep his sordid intentions very much out in the open and began fastening up the belt of his trousers.

"I thought something terrible was happening," Alun said.

"Oh, *something* was happening alright," the barman confirmed. His comment prompted a playful slap from Ruby.

"Please don't tell anyone," she said. "You saw how my uncle reacted."

Alun thought long and hard about his next move and tried his best to convey at least *some* air of mature authority. "It's none of my business who you spend your time with."

The teenager gave him a seductive wink. "I really appreciate that, Alun."

The accountant's awkward reaction caused the two lovers to howl with laughter.

"Bye, bye, Alun!" the barman called, in a mocking voice.

Alun looked down at Ruby's purple dragon head lying on the floor. Its face grinned at him, almost as though it had been privy to everything that had gone on inside that tent. The accountant shook his head in disapproval and made his escape.

He marched himself back outside and across the field. By the time he had returned to Bev's side, he was as hot and flustered as the two people he had just left.

"Oh, here you are!" she said, grabbing him by the hand and tugging him towards another couple. "Alun, I'd like you to meet Erin and Celyn."

The two people he was faced with would have been far more at home on the cover of a fashion magazine than strolling around a country fair. Celyn, a strapping man with shoulders the size of a barn, shook his hand.

"Nice to meet you, Alun," he said. The grin on his face

exposed a perfect set of sparkling white teeth. He pointed towards Bev. "You're a lucky man!"

Bev blushed and gave him a shove. "Enough of that, Celyn!"

Alun tried to ignore their playful chemistry.

"You know, Celyn here is taking part in the big shearing contest," said Bev. "Aren't you, Celyn?"

The proud man thumped his chest. "Wouldn't miss it for the world! It's good exercise."

"Sheep shearing?" Alun's question caused an awkward pause. His tone had been more judgmental than he had intended, but it was genuine. Manhandling a creature covered in wool would not have been his first choice of exercise. Fortunately, he never put himself in a position where he even had to choose any.

"No, it's camel shearing!" Bev snapped. "Course it's sheep!"

"You fancy it then, Alun?" asked Celyn, knowing full well the likely answer. He had sized up the man in front of him from the moment they had first met. This peculiar fellow appeared to be far more familiar with the layout of a keyboard than he was with the anatomy of a sheep.

"I don't think Alun is really a hands-on kind of person," Bev assured him.

"Well, that's not *quite* true." Alun had not known exactly why he had said such a sentence. He had just been offered a way out and had let his sheer disdain for the smug farmer get in the way.

"It's settled then!" Celyn slapped him on the back with a force that would crush a small animal. "Time to show off those big guns, cowboy!"

"Oh, leave him alone, Celyn," his girlfriend chimed in. "The man's only small."

Once again, Alun decided to let his pride dictate his fate. "I don't think it's really a matter of size..."

The farmer sensed his dismissive tone and revelled in the

prospect of competition. He had always been competitive, and the accountant beside him was asking for a right good thrashing.

"If I didn't know any better," he said, " I'd say that was a challenge!" Alun's horrified expression only excited him even more, and he couldn't resist another slap on the back. "See you out there, Big-Man."

Alun watched him strut off across the field, his dashing good looks a magnet for anyone that he passed. "Uh, yes. I suppose you will," the accountant muttered.

"Are you sure about this, Alun?" asked Bev. The prospect of her date looking an absolute fool in front of the entire town was not an appealing one. "Celyn's a full-time farmer. Have you ever even sheared a sheep before?"

"It's a sheep, Bev. It can't be *that* hard."

Half an hour later, his famous last words echoed inside his mind, as he stared into the daunting abyss of a closed gate. He knew that behind those bars was an animal who was not prepared to go down without a fight. Clutched in his hand was a giant pair of electric clippers that felt powerful enough to rebel against him and cut off his own hair.

The contestants of the prestigious sheep shearing competition were all lined up in front of an eager crowd. Alun appeared to be the palest out of all of them, having spent far too much time indoors, where he belonged. The cries of his supportive date only seemed to increase his nerves even more.

A portly man with a tartan flat cap and a long walking stick signalled for everyone to prepare. With a sharp blow of his whistle, the gates flew open and unleashed a line of charging sheep.

The more experienced competitors of the group grabbed their animal into a firm hold and began shearing away at the layers of wool. Somehow, Alun had also managed to catch his sheep, but it was a short-lived victory.

Whilst Celyn was already well on his way to producing an

entire rug's worth of wool, his newfound rival was being kicked and shaken in the most bizarre rodeo display the audience had ever seen.

Bev cringed, as she watched her supposed hero being dominated by a creature only half his height.

"Steady... Steady!"

Alun's words of reassurance were having little effect, and the sheep had long discovered which of the two was really in charge.

His dog barked out from the sidelines. She watched her master wrestle with his opponent, until he found himself dangling with his back to the ground and hanging on for dear life.

The hysterical Border Collie yanked at the lead with such great force, it sent an unprepared Bev stumbling forwards like a helpless puppet. Released from her ball and chain, the dog set her sights on something very round and very fluffy.

Alun looked down to see that he was now shearing nothing but thin air. His sheep had made a desperate getaway in the opposite direction — away from the advances of a salivating creature with pointed ears and a wagging tail.

"Peg — no!" Alun cried.

The sight of his potential new girlfriend, who was now lying in the grass with an empty dog lead, had told him everything he needed to know.

He turned his attention back to the great chase and witnessed the entire contents of a children's activity table splash into the air from the sudden impact.

Over at the burger van on the other side of the field, Rhiannon had her own problems. Armed with half a packet of napkins, she continued scrubbing away at the vast amounts of excess trifle.

"I see you've met my sister, then," said a familiar voice.

Rhiannon looked up to see Ceri Doyle.

"She's absolutely delightful," Rhiannon muttered, the paper towels proving to be useless against the generous amounts of custard and fruit sauce.

"I wouldn't take it personally," said Ceri, her gaze falling on a busy Lesley over by the bakery display.

Rhiannon continued her attempt at cleaning down her blouse, only to realise that it would probably never look the same again. "*She's* the one taking things personally. I bet she doesn't have a problem reading all the other rubbish articles out there. She doesn't exactly strike me as a *Financial Times* reader."

"What makes you say that?"

The journalist sighed. "She reads the *Merioneth Press* for a start."

Ceri raised up her arms and was handed a chunky lamb burger. "I'm surprised she has the time to read anything. I don't know how you raise three kids on your own and have time for anything else."

"She's a single mother?" Rhiannon asked, thinking about how hard it had been raising her own child. She respected anyone with enough bravery to have more.

"Her ex-husband was a right piece of work. They lived in Corwen until she managed to get out of there. Figured she and the kids were better off without him."

Rhiannon nodded and watched the woman's ketchup go splattering over her burger. "I know that feeling," she said.

"You probably just got off on the wrong foot," Ceri said with a mouthful of lamb. "She works three jobs at the moment. I don't blame her for being grumpy. Her youngest has autism and her eldest son, Craig, is in prison. Then there's Ruby, and she can be a right handful."

"What's the son in prison for?"

"Armed burglary."

"Every mother's dream," said Rhiannon. "She must be so proud."

They both caught a glimpse of Lesley Doyle over in the distance. She looked to be helping out behind a cake stand (a cake stand with one less trifle).

"Luckily, Jack got off lightly," said Ceri.

The other woman turned to face her. "Jack — as in Barry's son? *He* was involved?"

"His cousin Craig was always a bad influence. He's a good lad really, Jack. Very weak-minded, though. And weak-minded people are very easily influenced."

Rhiannon pictured his face again, staring at her in the car park. She knew that the young man was hiding something. "He seemed very close to his grandmother."

"You can say that again," said Ceri, with a look of disgust. "He was like the son she never had, the child she'd always wanted — someone she could control and brainwash. I'd dread to think of the poison she put through that boy's brain." She was struck by a cold chill, and it made her shudder. "Jack never really knew his mother. And as for his father, well... you met him, didn't you?"

Rhiannon nodded. He was hard to forget. "I'm sure he's been a huge bundle of love."

"Lesley tried to keep her kids close, but they only ever pushed away. Feel a bit sorry for her, really."

The journalist and the woman behind the cake stall made eye contact. Lesley wanted her to know that she had not forgotten. Rhiannon had no doubt that she *had* and broke off the staring competition.

"Never thought me and her would have something in common," she said. "I know all about the joys of single-parenting. Maybe all we need is a good chat — mam-to-mam."

"I would wait a bit until the dust settles," Ceri warned.

Rhiannon spotted another stain, this time on her trousers. "I think my clothes agree with you."

The two women looked over to their right and saw something white and fluffy heading towards them.

Ceri squinted at it in disbelief "Is that a *sheep*?"

Seconds later, and the animal went shooting past them. A Border Collie covered in wet paint followed closely behind.

"Peg!!" came the cries of a desperate Alun, who was now giving chase after his lost battle on the shearing stage.

The dog saw her furious owner trailing behind her, panting and wheezing, as if he had just done twelve rounds with a heavyweight boxer. She abandoned her quest for the sheep and made a sharp diversion back towards the crowd.

Alun stopped to catch his breath and looked on in horror, as his troublesome pet made an unexpected detour back towards Bev. He couldn't bear to look and was forced to wait for the inevitable outcome that only a dripping wet dog could provide.

Bev's cry could be heard from all sides of the field. Rhiannon struggled to contain her amusement at the sight of the woman being drenched from head to foot with colourful paint. Peg continued her enormous shake-off, and her owner witnessed the final moment of his doomed relationship. It would never recover from this, he thought.

Once Bev's public soaking had finally come to an end, there came another scream — a more piercing and chilling one.

All eyes turned to a tent on the far corner of the field. People began running towards it, until the nearest steward grabbed the edges of the marquee and ripped away the outer polythene wall.

The onlookers gasped at the sight of a distraught Ruby, as she laid across the body of her secret lover. Dressed in a purple dragon costume, the young barman appeared to be dead behind the eyes and surrounded by an assortment of medieval gaming equipment.

"It should have been me!" Ruby screamed. "It should have been *me*!"

Her mother, Lesley, pushed through the gawking crowd and rolled the man over. What she discovered by her foot was a bloodied shot put that appeared to have dented the back of Bryn's head. The blood from his scalp had already begun staining the purple fur and was causing many a wobbly knee from the disturbed audience.

"Somebody call an ambulance!" Lesley cried.

Her daughter continued to sob. "He was only trying on my costume as a joke," she said. "Whoever did this thought it was me."

She received a giant squeeze from her mother, who buried her away from the grizzly sight beneath them.

Mel was the next to barge his way through the wall of people and was his usual flustered-self in the face of a crisis.

"Get back!" he called out. "Everyone stand back!".

Alun watched the policeman crouch down over the young man and place two fingers against his neck. Everyone waited for a verdict, but Mel's grim expression said it all.

"I'm sorry to say this," he announced. "But it's too late for an ambulance."

His words caused Ruby to let out another wail of protest.

The accountant looked over to see Rhiannon peeping around the corner of the tent to catch a glimpse. They made eye contact for a moment, both of them as concerned as the other about what the prospect of another death might have meant. It appeared that the little town of Pengower had amassed its second murder in one month. Unfortunately, there seemed to be little sign of it being the last.

CHAPTER 24

Lesley Doyle had looked at the clock five times already that morning. It was her seventh shift in a row and the longest one so far.

The events of the previous day were still very raw, and she had seen that barman's face a multitude of times during a restless night of broken sleep. She knew that the purple dragon would haunt her dreams for many weeks to come.

She had left Ruby in floods of tears when she set off for work and was keen to make sure that her teenage daughter stayed exactly where she was until she got back. Teenagers were like a cold sore (you never knew where they'd next appear).

Hoffi Coffi was quieter than normal. The smell of coffee and toast was not enough to lure the awakening residents of Pengower that morning, especially when rumours of a serial murderer were already circulating.

Lesley didn't have time to be worried about serial killers. Not only were they a member of staff down that morning, but she had four cooked breakfasts to churn out. Her regulars didn't care about ground coffee beans, stylish decor or dainty plates of avocado on toast; they wanted proper, hearty portions and artery-clogging fried bread.

As she prepared a fresh batch of bacon, the busy cook spotted a familiar figure entering through the front door. Lesley was not famous for her chatty nature and witty small talk (the regulars at *Hoffi Coffi* didn't keep coming back for that), and she certainly didn't have time to be talking to *her*, of all people.

To the woman's great surprise, her latest customer (the person she least wanted to see that morning) was also accompanied by a small boy dressed in a cape.

"You're brave coming in here after what's just happened," Lesley warned, her hands pre-occupied by the busy stove.

Rhiannon casually leant herself against the counter overlooking the limited cooking space. She liked being able to see the kitchen in an eating establishment but not so close that she could feel the heat.

"There's not much that scares me anymore," she said, looking over at her son, Gwyl, who had chosen a table by the window. "Not after a natural birth."

She turned back towards the woman on the other side of the divider. Lesley gave her a stare that could pierce through stone. The woman was as intimidating as her reputation, but Rhiannon could sense a softer side beneath that hardened exterior. Years of reluctant interviewees had made her a good judge of character.

Lesley's willingness for such a long, silent pause was an admirable one. This was a person who couldn't care less what people thought of her, and she was quite happy to take her time.

"If you've come for an apology," she said. "You won't be getting one."

Lesley finished off her deep dive into the depths of the other woman's pupils and continued with her fry-up.

"I've come to issue you an apology, actually," Rhiannon said, waiting for the glance of surprise. It never came.

"And if you're scavenging around for more details on yesterday, you won't be getting any of those, either. I know what you people are like."

Lesley wiped the sweat from her forehead and pushed back the unwashed grey hairs that were protruding over her puffy cheeks.

"I'm sorry about your daughter's boyfriend," Rhiannon added. "And I'm sorry if my article offended you."

"He wasn't her boyfriend," Lesley said, keeping her attention firmly on the food in front of her. "And I don't give a damn about your stupid article. I've got enough on my plate at the moment."

"Believe it or not, but I like to write stories to enlighten people — not upset them."

The reporter jumped at the sound of a saucepan being thrown into the sink. That stare was all over her again.

"You think people even read your dreadful muck?" Lesley asked. She also revealed the first hint of a smile, although it was a wicked one. "I think you need a wake-up call, love. You're not Jeremy Paxman."

Rhiannon sighed. The words stung like they always did when a person attacked her writing. It didn't matter whether it came from an acclaimed critic or an opinionated cafe worker: negative criticism always hurt.

"I'm not here to cause another scene," she said, with a tired sigh. "I'm just a mother trying to kill the morning with her son."

They both looked towards the three-year-old keeping himself amused on the other side of the cafe. It appeared the salt and pepper shakers were a winning source of entertainment. His mother was always surprised how the most mundane items could still fire up a child's imagination. If there was a way she could regain some of that youthful curiosity herself, she would have done so in an instant.

"How old is he?" asked Lesley.

Rhiannon turned around to see that she was distracted by the innocent figure playing in the window. That softer side was finally starting to rear its small head.

"Three and a half," she replied.

The older woman marched around the counter and pulled open a drawer. She grabbed a handful of colouring pencils and a stack of paper, before heading over to the smallest customer in the room. Gwyl's eyes lit up at the sight of the unexpected activity making its way over to him. Lesley ruffled his hair with her strong hands and gave him an exclusive smile.

Rhiannon watched the whole exchange with great fascination.

"I'm not as frightening as people think, you know," Lesley said to her. The cook had finally returned to her post in front of a hot stove. She plated up another order and signalled for her colleague to take it away.

"People say you're a hard worker," Rhiannon said.

"Do they now?" It was hard not to be flattered, especially for a person who prided themselves on keeping busy.

"Your sister tells me this is just one of three jobs."

The mention of her sibling made the complement null and void. "Yeah, well. You have to keep your options open in this town." She wiped down the counter and glanced up with suspicion. "What else has my sister been telling you?"

"Oh, don't worry. Nothing too juicy. Mainly that I was a cow to her in school." Rhiannon thought about it and nodded. "And she was quite right about that."

The mention of her background intrigued the cafe worker. "So, you're a local girl?"

Rhiannon had to think about it for a moment. She hated the

word local and would never have dreamt of using it to describe herself. But it was starting to dawn on her recently that, one day, she was going to have to accept the truth. "Uh, yeah. I guess I am."

Lesley put down her cloth for a moment and leant herself forward so that the two women were practically side by side.

"Then here's a bit of free advice from one local person to another," she said, looking over at Gwyl. "Stop wishing your life away. You should be savouring this time — not killing it. Before you know it, that child of yours will be gone. And he'll be rushing his time with *you*."

Her words of advice had taken the fellow mother by complete surprise. "Oh, I didn't mean —"

"It's tiring, I know — exhausting, even, most of the time. But it doesn't last forever. Then you spend the rest of your life wishing you could go back."

Rhiannon felt a giant lump in her throat. She had heard these words many times before, and from a variety of different parents, but this was the first time she had heard them uttered with such sadness. Deep down, even at her lowest moment, she knew she would miss these days. The young mother was always grateful for any small reminders of this fact, and she hadn't expected one to come from Lesley Doyle, of all people.

"Is your daughter okay?" she asked, breaking what was fast becoming an unbearable silence. "You know, after..."

"She'll be alright," said Lesley.

Rhiannon took that as a "no" and couldn't help but wonder who would batter a man dressed in a mythical animal costume. Or, if the heavy blow had been intended for Ruby, why choose somewhere as public as the *Pengower Country Show*?

"I'm sure it's a lot to take in," she said. "Your mother disappearing, Dai Jones, now this..."

She had chosen her words very carefully, however, judging

by the tightening of Lesley's neck muscles, she hadn't chosen them carefully enough.

"You just can't take off that precious, little press hat of yours, can you?" The woman's gentle tone had switched into one of uncontrollable anger. "You know the real reason why I hated that article? I had to read about my own mother's secret marriage — in a public paper."

"You really didn't already know?" Rhiannon asked. She preferred sentimental-Lesley over angry-scary-Lesley any day.

"That's beside the point," Lesley snapped. "You should have come to us first — her own children — before splashing it around the papers. Now everyone in Pengower thinks we're all a bunch of murdering psychopaths."

"Well, I think it's fair to say there's at least one murdering psychopath out there. If that article helps flush them out into the open, then surely that's a good thing."

The cook shook her head in disgust. "Whatever helps you sleep at night."

Rhiannon watched her return to the stove, just in time to rescue a saucepan of burning baked beans.

"Do you have any idea who could be behind these killings?" she asked, being careful not to stand within reach of the steel pan. At least the trifle hadn't scolded her.

"For all I know," Lesley muttered, "it's probably my mother's ghost. She's come back to haunt us all."

"We don't know for certain if Mari's even —"

"If she's not, she will be soon. You know why? Because that woman was dying long before any of this ever happened."

Her words echoed over the sound of sizzling bacon. Rhiannon needed a moment to respond.

"How do you mean?"

"My mother was terminally ill."

The journalist's mind was becoming more scrambled than the eggs cooking in Lesley's pan.

"That's right," said Lesley. "Not much of a story that one, is it? No death threats, no murders... Just boring, old real life."

"But why would anyone try to kill a person who's already dying?"

"Whoever said she was dead? She's probably living out the rest of her days in the sun. Lord knows, she can afford it. She's probably a thousand miles away, and we're all here dealing with her mess."

Rhiannon thought about the idea of Mari overlooking the deep blue sea, sipping on cocktails in the evening sun. How different that was to the cold ditch she had envisioned before. "I hope you're right."

"I had to accept a long time ago that she'd never be leaving us a penny." Lesley spoke as if her skin was as hard as rock, although the force at which she flung around her pots and pans implied otherwise. "She's probably giving all her money to that precious church of hers. One splash of holy water and she's some born-again Christian, all of a sudden."

"You're talking about *St David's*?"

Lesley didn't confirm, but she didn't really have to. "That vicar saw her coming a mile off. His type always do."

Rhiannon thought about the Reverend Owen and his brief meeting with Alun. She had been meaning to have a word herself. It was, after all, the last place Mari had been spotted before her disappearance.

"Mari sounds pretty strong-minded," she said. "You really think she converted that quickly?"

"She dedicated her life to one belief. I'm sure she'd have no trouble following another."

The cook grabbed two more plates of food and walked off to deliver them herself. A perplexed Rhiannon headed over to the table beside the window and spent the rest of her visit eating food and chatting with her son.

Gwyl was barely four years old, but she had been told his drawing was quite advanced for his age. Rhiannon was certain that he took after his mother, who had spent many of her maths lessons doodling on those hideous grid papers. As her fingers wrapped around one of the colouring pencils, she began drawing out a recurring shape from the pages of Mari's diary entries.

Beneath her son's unorthodox rendition of a human head, she created a cluster of jagged lines that looked more at home on one of Ceri Doyle's trees. The image had stuck in her mind from the moment she first saw it.

By the time Lesley came to clear up their plates, the table was scattered with doodles of a dozen happy faces, all with their own unique shapes.

"They're very good," she said, admiring the head with a generous amount of hair. "Who's that one?"

"Daddy," Gwyl replied.

The woman sensed his mother's pain at the mere mention of her ex-husband and decided not to dwell on it any further.

Rhiannon looked up to see that Lesley's gaze had fallen on her sketch of Mari's symbol. It was clear the image had made an impression.

"Does it mean anything to you?" she asked.

The woman's grave expression was enough. "You're messing with some dark forces there, love." She cleared up the plates and refused to look her customer in the eye. "If you want to learn more about the fires of hell, you should speak to that Reverend."

They both exchanged an understanding nod.

"Thanks. I just might."

The two customers packed up their belongings and were soon heading for the door. Just as she was about to leave the everlasting smell of bacon, Rhiannon could feel someone staring at her from behind the counter.

"You're a smart girl," Lesley called out. "Be careful where you go poking your nose."

The journalist was struggling to work out whether her advice was friendly or hostile. Her suspicion was eased by the tone of the woman's final sentence.

"Oh, and sorry about the trifle."

CHAPTER 25

Pengower Lake was so still that Alun feared smashing it into tiny pieces. He threw his smooth, circular stone and watched it skim across the reflective surface. His personal best was eighteen bounces, a record that remained unbroken on this particular morning.

Peg went chasing after her target, bouncing through the water more times than the stone. Thanks to a long scrub in Alun's bathroom, her black and white coat was back to its old self, and the accountant wondered if the same could have been said for Bev Griffiths' hair.

There had been no replies to any of his text messages since their eventful first date, and Alun had begun to accept that his new relationship was dead in the water. To overcome his great disappointment, he had focused his mind on two recent killings that were now hurling the town into a whirlwind of panic. In an area where the average mortality rate was historically very low, news of the second suspicious death had even attracted the attention of regional television broadcasters. Their coverage would provide some much-needed publicity to the town's annual country show (although the risk of murder might prove to be a slight turn-off).

Although the most probable motive behind Dai's murder was quite clear, the reason why someone had wanted to rid this world of Ruby Doyle was as murky as the waters beneath Alun's wellington boots. Perhaps the two incidents were not linked at all, he hypothesised. The accountant knew from his own line of work that it was easier to approach a problem systematically. Locating errors on a trial balance required a gradual process of elimination, and any preconceived theories were often just a distraction from the real solution.

His morning walks with Peg had become the perfect opportunity to clear his brain. As he pondered the various scenarios of this growing mystery, he became distracted by the sight of a figure in the distance.

Standing at the end of a stone jetty was a tall man in dark clothing. He recognised that hunched posture anywhere, and the sight of a police car parked up near the sailing boats confirmed that it was indeed his friend Mel.

The police officer seemed to be frozen in place, his eyes staring into the lake, almost hypnotised by a supernatural force. He took one last swig from the glass bottle in his hand and let himself fall.

"Mel!" Alun cried out, running along the shore in a rush of panic.

His friend's fear of the water had been a well-known fact since their school days. It had always struck him as strange that such a naturally gifted athlete like Mel had never learnt to swim. On land, he had been an impressive specimen of physical genetics; in the water, he was a helpless creature who could barely keep himself afloat.

Peg had also spotted the falling man and was now paddling her way towards him. Her owner went sprinting along the jetty, his arms flailing in the air like a mad, inflatable stick figure. After a poorly-executed dive, he went flying into the water with a heavy *splash*.

The cold shock was like a slap to the face. His lungs cried out for air, as he began crawling towards the large shape bobbing up and down.

Mel's sinking body did very little to help him from being submerged. The lake offered even less assistance and was quite happy to allow its helpless victim to sink to the bottom — never to be seen again.

Just as he could feel the numbness in his limbs begin to spread, the police officer felt a bony arm wrapping itself around his neck.

Alun had grabbed the first piece of Mel he could reach and was now choking him faster than the freezing water. After re-adjusting his grip, he lay back and turned his legs into a pair of whirling propellers.

Peg slipped up beside him and did her own bit to help tug this large man to safety. They kicked and paddled, coughed and spluttered, until their hands and paws could feel the comforting sensation of earth and stone.

Mel went crashing to the shore like an overloaded fishing net. He gasped for oxygen, as did the exhausted lifeguard and his panting assistant. All three of them lay there in silence for a moment until the first person could catch their breath.

"What were you thinking?" Alun spluttered out. "You know you can't swim!"

His friend seemed rather disgruntled for a person who had just been rescued.

"I should have known it was you," he grumbled, reaching into his coat in search of a small whiskey bottle. Amazingly, although dripping in lake water, it was still there. "You should have just left me out there with the fish."

Alun had smelt the alcohol from the moment he had first embraced him in the lake. The combination of alcohol and open water was never a sensible mix. He could also tell the man's fall was more than just a reckless error of judgement.

"Have you completely lost your mind?" he asked.

"Maybe I have," muttered Mel, still sulking. "I should have tried the aqueduct again. Much better chance of success up there."

The other man hesitated in his response. It was hard seeing someone who was normally so confident and energetic look so lost. The man appeared to be deep in a heavy bout of loneliness and self-loathing.

"You wanted to jump off the aqueduct?" he eventually asked.

Mel turned to face him, his expression desperate for a glimmer of understanding.

"I've been such an idiot, Alun. Got myself in a right mess, I have."

Alun squirmed in the wet gravel. He had never been comfortable with emotional conversations, especially when they required him to offer sympathy. There had been the odd occasion when even his father (the most stoic man he had ever known) had broken down after the death of his mother. Seeing his grieving parent descend into floods of tears had made him want to melt away into the nearby wallpaper, until he was safe inside the wall cavities. Negative feelings were for bottling up deep inside where they could no longer do any harm (only for them to later re-emerge after years of fermentation — like a sour wine that was better off left uncorked).

"It can't be *that* bad, surely..." Alun had decided to say.

The look on Mel's face said otherwise. "Sandra and the kids would be so ashamed if they knew the truth."

Alun felt a chill run through him, and it wasn't from the cold water.

"What's happened, Mel?" he asked, bracing himself for the worst.

"I've lost everything," said Mel. "All of it." The police officer took a sip of what was left in his whiskey bottle and wallowed in his grief. "It was just tiny amounts to start with: a few bob on the machines, a tenner on the horses, the odd poker game online. After a while, you start to lose track."

His friend listened with a strange sense of relief. The confession he thought he was about to hear was heading in a very different direction indeed.

"But you've always enjoyed a few bets," Alun reminded him. "Lots of people do."

Mel shook his head. "We're not talking a few bets here, Alun."

The accountant took a large gulp. If there was one thing that truly scared him, it was the prospect of a financial crisis.

"How much, Mel?"

His friend could barely look him in the eye.

"All of it. Our savings, the mortgage — everything."

The silence that followed was the longest they had ever shared. Mel usually had no problem filling in moments of empty air with his booming voice. Instead, he continued to numb his senses with another swig of whiskey. All that could be heard was Peg's heavy breathing as she began burrowing in the wet gravel.

"It wasn't meant to go like this," Mel eventually said. "They said I'd play for Wales."

The shivering man looked down at his knee, the same knee that had robbed him of an opportunity to become a rugby player. It had been all he ever wanted. Without his big dream of turning professional, he had been left with few prospects but a handful of mediocre qualifications and a limited list of local jobs. Had it not been for the police force, he would have lost his mind a long time ago.

"It still hurts sometimes," he said, rubbing the middle of his leg. "Sandra reckons it's psychological, but I know it's taunting me."

"Have you thought about telling her?" asked Alun. "You know — about the gambling?"

Mel clutched hold of his own sweaty, red forehead as though he were trying to rip away the skin. The reminder of his heavy debts sent him hurling back into a sorry mess.

"How can I, eh?" he snapped. "When she's asking about that trip to Florida every day? Or what about the extension? Oh, God, the extension..." He sobbed into his large hands, and Alun started to feel that all too familiar discomfort. It was difficult to know quite what to do when a man as large as Mel broke down in tears. He debated whether to hold him, but he dreaded the thought of that awkward moment afterwards.

The last time Alun had seen his old friend cry was during their fifth year in primary school. Mel had been big for his age and was very tall, even then. But the size had been no match for the cruelty of an icy playground. The boy had even managed to chip a tooth and was blubbering almost as much as he was now on the wet stones.

"She would never understand: the buzz, the excitement... the way it keeps sucking you in, even when you're on the biggest losing streak of your entire life. Putting a few bets on used to be the only thing that cheered me up. Now it's ruined me."

Alun nodded. Even though he was as perplexed as the man's wife on what all the fuss was about, he was not surprised that a person could cripple their bank balance. Investing money into an activity where the odds were openly stacked against you would have made for a very strange business plan. Still, there were enough betting shops in the country to prove that people were more than willing.

The accountant tried hard to sound sympathetic. "Well, if you need to borrow anything, just —"

"Thanks, but keep your money where it's safe," Mel insisted. "I've maxed out every credit card I could get my hands on. I'm not about to do the same to my mates."

He gave Alun an appreciative wink. His friend was secretly quite relieved. Whatever financial deficit Mel was in, it was unlikely he could have done very much to help. He was a little strapped for cash himself at the moment.

"Still, if you need any help," he added, "you know where to find me."

His words seemed to have cheered the police officer up a little, even if it had been just an empty gesture. The man gave him a cheeky grin, and the Mel that he knew was back with a vengeance.

"And where's that?" he bellowed. "Sitting at home crying because you're still single?"

Alun smiled. There he was: that big, annoying, overgrown teenager.

The two men dragged themselves up from the wet stones and began making their way past the parked police car near the side of the road.

"I think I'd better walk home," said the police officer. His alcoholic breath could be seen clouding up the cold air.

"I think you better had," said Alun.

Once the two had parted ways, the accountant and his dog strolled the quiet high street. At the far end was a local bookshop that Alun often found himself perusing every once in a while. Unfortunately, the selection of reading material on offer was more to the taste of its antisocial owner than its paying customers. If a person was very lucky, there was still a chance to come across the occasional hidden gem (or, in Alun's case, a riveting historical fiction novel set during the Napoleonic Wars).

As Alun approached the large window, a peculiar image jumped out at him from behind the glass. It was the cover of a book he would normally have dismissed as "fairytale nonsense". Now, it was reeling him in, begging to be read.

Below the title *Local Legends* was an illustration of a woman with long, white hair and a wildness in her eyes that could tame a wild boar. There was no doubt that this person was a controversial figure in any time period.

Alun stared into the gaze of what he presumed to be a grinning Welsh witch. The grinning Welsh witch stared right back.

CHAPTER 26

The large card with an image of a skeleton loomed over Rhiannon's keyboard. The words *"Happy Birthday!"* were typed in large, obnoxious lettering, and the inside was marked with the phrase: *You're only as old as you feel.*

The card had been her boss' idea. Although her editor had found his joke absolutely hilarious, Rhiannon had actually managed to see a degree of truth behind the image. She was, after all, wasting away, in a job her younger-self would have found quite demeaning.

"Cheer up, Rhiannon!" Morgan Morris cried, as he passed by with his fifth cupcake (they had supposedly been brought in for her). "The grim reaper's not coming for you just yet!"

He lifted up a colourful party horn and blew it towards her miserable face. His laughter lingered around her desk long after he had swaggered back to his office.

She had hoped that a day in work was going to provide a much needed distraction. She didn't need a further reminder of her increased mortality, and the fact that her parents had arranged a family dinner party only infuriated her further.

It seemed nowhere was safe, and the sudden appearance of a new cake landing on her desk made her want to cry.

"I hope I got the right number of candles."

Rhiannon looked up to find Alun towering above her with a proud look on his face. She had expected to find yet another colleague who had received their cold, automated calendar reminder. Her editor had made sure all of his employees received a similar treatment on their birthdays (any excuse for him to inject some obligatory "fun" into the work year).

"How did you know?" she asked.

Alun shrugged. "I called in to see if you were at home and your mam told me you were at work. She also said it was your birthday."

Rhiannon sighed. She was a little disappointed by the response but was glad to see him.

"You know you can just text me?" She pulled the cake towards her and scraped off some icing with her finger. "You didn't have to waste your money on me."

"I made it at home," he said. "Barely cost me a penny."

She gave him a suspicious glare. "*You* baked this?"

"I find it quite relaxing, actually. Baking is very precise. I like precise."

"Course you do," said Rhiannon, rolling her eyes. "Well, are you going to sit down or what?"

Alun looked around the quiet office.

"If you're not too busy," he said, grabbing himself a chair.

This was his first visit to the headquarters of a newspaper. He had imagined a lot more shouting and energy. But this was the *Merioneth Press*.

"How have you been after the...?"

Rhiannon looked up from her computer with a frown. "You mean — after witnessing a battered man in a dragon costume? Or do you mean the trifle?"

Alun stuttered his way through a response: "Oh, uh — well, uh — both, I suppose."

"I'll get over the dead body," she said. "The trifle's a whole other matter."

"Fair enough."

He observed the piles of paperwork scattered across Rhiannon's desk. The very sight of such a messy workspace filled the man with anxiety. How she could work in such chaos he would never understand.

"I spoke to my new friend," she said. "Lesley Doyle."

"You did?" Alun was genuinely surprised. Lesley was not known for being very social. "Was that before the trifle or afterwards?"

The angry glare that came his way made him regret the last question.

"They're a strange bunch, these Doyles," said Rhiannon. "One minute they're punching you in the face, the next minute they're pouring out their hearts." She smirked at the thought of Alun's pint with Danny. "How is the bruised head, by the way?"

Alun frowned. Now they were even.

"So she opened up to you?" he asked.

"Not really. But she did have a few strong words to say about that vicar."

"Reverend Owen?"

Rhiannon nodded. "I think I need a word with him."

"Well, he's very approachable."

"Vicars usually are."

She spotted the small paperback underneath his arm.

"What's that?" she asked. "A bit of light reading?"

Alun lifted up the book and revealed the cover. That same witch he had seen in the shop window was now grinning at Rhiannon.

"Did you know that Devil's Cove is actually a grave?" he asked.

"Devil's — what?" Rhiannon took the book from him and read the blurb.

"It's a corner of Pengower Lake." He lifted up his smartphone to reveal a map of the local area. "My dad took me fishing there once. Quiet little spot. No fish, though."

"If you're here to recommend local fishing spots, then I'd better get back to work." The journalist shook her mouse to wake up the computer.

"Look it up," he insisted. "You won't be disappointed."

She looked back at his beaming smile. He had found something, she was quite certain of that, but she wished he would just come out with it.

Her fingers reluctantly began typing the words: Devil's Cove, Pengower. She hit the enter key and was presented with a long list of articles that spanned multiple decades. The first one was a post from a historical site called *Echoes of Snowdonia,* featuring a list of various place names in and around North Wales. When she finally reached the heading Devil's Cove, a woman's name jumped out at her from the body of the text.

"Branwen..." her lips muttered.

Alun scooted his chair forward and joined her at the computer.

"It turns out Pengower was a hotspot for witch trials back in the eighteenth century," he said, failing to contain his excitement. "Apparently, a string of accused witches were put on trial out there in the lake. Every single one of them drowned in the process."

"Branwen..." Rhiannon mumbled again. "Where have I heard that name?"

Alun gave her a knowing smile and pointed to the diary on her desk.

"Oh, *yes*!" she cried, scrambling for the book and flicking through the pages. "She mentions Branwen in here — several times. I thought it was a family member we hadn't met yet."

"Well, it's funny you should say that..."

She watched him lift up his paperback. Alun had acquired her full attention quicker than a dark spell.

"Branwen was the most famous witch of all," he continued. "Most of her legacy is pure fiction, but a woman called Branwen *did* exist, and she was drowned in Pengower Lake."

He pulled out some papers from his bag. One of them contained a hand-drawn illustration of a woman being dragged through a crowd of people. Below the image was a short caption: "*The central figure in this 1858 depiction is usually identified as Branwen Llewelyn.*"

On another piece of paper was a list of names. Alun placed his finger on the name at the top: Branwen Llewelyn.

"With a little help from the *General Register Office* and the parish records, I managed to put together a family tree."

Rhiannon scanned the long list. She was impressed and struggled to hide it.

"Wow," she said. "*You've* been busy."

Alun was flattered; he made no effort to hide his feelings, either. "Yes, well, I have a lot of time on my hands these days." He began running his finger down the list of relatives, until he reached a familiar name at the bottom: Mari Doyle.

"She's related?" Rhiannon asked.

"Her great, great, great..." He continued to reel off the same word, until the woman opposite felt like punching him in the face. "...great, great granddaughter."

She could feel the smugness radiating off him. "I'll take your word for it."

The journalist continued to read the article on her computer. "So, Mari must have known all this," she said. "Why else would she keep referring to the name, Branwen, in those crazy witch diaries?"

Alun caught sight of an old road atlas buried under a pile of clutter. He pulled it out and opened up a page with Pengower Lake in the middle.

"Devil's Cove was a popular location for trialling these accused women."

"No *male* witches, then?" Rhiannon interrupted. "How convenient."

"The accused were taken to the edge of the lake, bound at the hands and feet, and then thrown into the water," he continued. "If they floated, it was confirmed they were a witch; if they sank, well... it was clear they weren't."

"So they were dead, either way? Who came up with that ridiculous process?"

Alun shrugged. "People who were accused of practicing witchcraft were not generally very popular in the community. They certainly wouldn't be missed."

Rhiannon sat back in her chair and wiped her tired eyes. Gwyl had been up all night with the most violent stomach bug. She prayed it wasn't contagious.

"Well, people still love a good witch-hunt," she concluded. "Nothing's changed there. Except the drowning. So what was so special about this Branwen?"

He thought she would never ask.

"Branwen had been quite vocal about her practices," Alun said. "Normally, when a person was accused and trialled, they denied everything. Branwen, on the other hand, went to that lake willingly. She made a grand speech about cursing the entire town and that her death would someday be avenged. She described herself as the leader of a secret coven known as the *Diafa*."

Rhiannon shuddered. "Branwen sounds as bonkers as her future family."

"Her name lived on, and the Branwen mythology was born. According to legend, her body was buried underneath a giant rock they call the Devil's Tombstone. I used to climb on it as a child."

The journalist yawned and reached for a slice of cake. She had no energy for far-fetched tales about witchcraft and satanic rituals. The only dark force she was interested in was the generous helping of rich cocoa in her hand.

"Talking of witch-hunts," she said, with a mouthful of chocolate, "Who do we reckon is responsible for this murder epidemic we've been having?"

A disappointed Alun began pushing back his chair. He had found his research on local witch trials fascinating, even if she hadn't.

"I probably have less of an idea now than I did with one murder," he said.

"I think it's fair to say that, whoever the killer is, they *must* be one of the beneficiaries of Mari's will — or at least they think they are. Otherwise, why bother?"

"Who says it's even one person?" asked Alun, still sulking about the abrupt end to their brief history discussion.

Rhiannon waved her pen at him, a glimmer of excitement returning to her worn-out face.

"I like what you're getting at," she said. "You think they all did it!"

Her theory confused her weary assistant (unbeknownst to Alun, she had secretly labelled him her trusty *assistant* — a job title he might have taken a slight issue with).

"What? *All of them*? No!"

She ignored his protest and continued to indulge in her theory. "All of Mari's children are in it together — like *Murder on the Orient Express* but with a rubbish moustache. What a great story that would be!"

"Forgive me," Alun chimed in, "but don't you work for a newspaper? They're normally focused on fact — not fiction."

"You'd be surprised," said the journalist.

The accountant pulled out his favourite fountain pen and placed down a clean sheet of paper.

"We need to look at this systematically," he said.

Rhiannon folded up her arms. "Let me guess: it's just like *accounting*," she groaned.

"Well, yes, I suppose it is." He ignored the second groan and wrote down the names Dai Jones and Bryn Vaughn: a dead butcher and a dead barman. "We have two deaths — none of them the result of natural causes, and both of them, we can safely presume, were murdered in cold blood. There aren't many who would take their own lives with a dagger or a shot-put."

"Three deaths."

Alun looked up. "Excuse me?"

"*Three* deaths," Rhiannon repeated. "There are currently three victims — not two."

"You're referring to Mari?"

"No, I'm talking about the purple dragon."

It took a moment for her sarcasm to wash over him. He had always despised sarcasm. The art of conversation was hard enough without even more confusion.

"We don't know for certain if Mari is even dead," he said with gritted teeth.

"Oh, come on," Rhiannon said. "I think we all know by now that the lady isn't going to just walk back into town one day as if she's just been on holiday."

"We can't rule anything out at this stage."

She was losing her patience again and Alun could tell. He tried not to show fear, but it was hard when you could see a person's veins rising up to the surface of their skin. Her twitching neck muscles were another red flag.

"Well, here's one thing for certain," she said, leaning in so far towards him that she could smell his aftershave (a brand that Rhiannon was adamant all the boys at school used to wear). "Nobody's getting their hands on that fortune until she *does* turn up — dead or otherwise."

"Which begs another question," said Alun. He spoke with the confidence of a person who had played out every possible scenario in his mind, and, to some extent, he almost had. "If the person who killed our butcher and barman stood to benefit from Mari's inheritance, and, if they did indeed kill Mari — why not leave her body where someone can find it? Why not murder her at home?"

Rhiannon sat there, listening and eating. The man made a good point, which was why she enjoyed having him around.

"Maybe she was murdered in the woods somewhere," she suggested. "She could have been hiking or something."

"The body would have turned up by now, surely." He inspected the local map and saw the vast areas of uninhabited land. "If there *is* a body out there, whoever knows about it doesn't want it found."

Rhiannon reached over, grabbed his pen and crossed out the name Bryn Vaughn. Then, she replaced it with the name Ruby Doyle.

"The murderer was trying to kill Ruby," she said. "Not Bryn."

"But the person who is actually dead is *Bryn*," said Alun, writing the name back down again. "This is what I mean with facts. You start throwing in personal theories and you end up lost again."

"We're not doing spreadsheets right now, Alun," the journalist snapped. "Solving mysteries is about thinking *outside* the box. You need to get creative."

"A mystery is a puzzle. It involves the left-hand side of the brain — not that sporadic right side."

"Maybe it needs *both*."

Rhiannon gave him a cheeky smile whilst he shook his head. "That's why we make such a good team," she said. "I'm the right side; you're the left side."

The woman could tell Alun enjoyed the analogy, even if he would never admit it.

"So where do we go from here, *Lefty*?"

Alun stared at his sheet of paper, which was now all messy with Rhiannon's amendments.

"We go back to the beginning," he said, drawing a full circle. "The location of Mari's last sighting."

"*St David's Church*," Rhiannon agreed. "What a surprise."

"You said it yourself that the Reverend is worthy of another chat."

Rhiannon smiled. "I bet you that man has a few skeletons in his graveyard..."

Her comment was met with a blank expression. She gave him more time, and, eventually, the penny dropped.

"Oh," said Alun. "You're just joking."

The woman opposite him let out the loudest groan yet and chucked a handful of chocolate cake in his direction. It landed with a *splat*.

CHAPTER 27

The stained glass windows of *St David's Church* were glowing in the morning sun. It was still another hour before the first service, but the Reverend Owen had already lit the candles and layed out all his notes.

He had always been an early riser, and he much preferred to be overly-prepared and in a calm state of mind. Nobody wanted a rambling, incoherent vicar (and he had known a few in his time)

His new organ player, however, did not share the same philosophy. It wasn't easy finding a decent organist in a town as small as Pengower, and they had already been through two players in the space of a month. There was nothing like a clash of bad notes during a hymn like "Guide me, o thou great redeemer" to give a clergyman a headache.

After the shambles of his first service, the new organist had agreed to come in extra early for a rehearsal. The reverend checked his watch: still no sign of him.

Just as the man was about to give up all hope, he heard the heavy creak of the main door opening. His heart began to race but it was soon flattened by a stomp of disappointment.

The two people standing in his doorway were not there to play the organ, and they were not early members of the congregation.

"Oh," said the reverend. "It's you, Alun."

He stepped away from the altar and walked over to greet the two unexpected guests.

"I hope we're not interrupting," said Alun.

"Heavens, no!" said the reverend. "My door is always open."

He looked over at the accountant's friend, who, as most strangers to the church often did, was gawking up at the grand architecture.

"I don't believe we've met," he said to her.

Rhiannon took her attention away from the mesmerising colours and turned it to the charming man with the dog collar.

"Rhiannon," she said and shook his hand. The man's fingers were as cold as ice. She presumed that a lifetime of working in an old building made a person utterly immune to such cold temperatures.

She was not religious, but it was hard not to be overwhelmed by the spiritual allure of such a place.

"Your first visit to *St David's*?" the reverend asked, in a tone that reminded her of a teacher addressing a child.

"I wouldn't get too excited, Father," she said. "I'm not really the 'praise-hallelujah' type. Although, I do like red wine. And I eat a lot of bread."

Alun tried not to look embarrassed.

The vicar chuckled in amusement. "I'm not Catholic, Rhiannon. You don't need to call me *Father*. Tom will do just fine."

She nodded in approval. The name, Tom, worked well for her.

The vicar glanced at his watch again, and it didn't go unnoticed.

"Are you sure we're not keeping you from anything?" Rhiannon asked.

"Not all," he replied. "I'm just waiting for my new organist to arrive. Let's just hope his timekeeping is better on the ivories."

"Wasn't Mari Doyle your organist?"

The reverend's jovial demeanour sizzled out for a moment. He had not been prepared for such a question, not from a stranger.

Alun gave his acquaintance a small nudge in protest. He preferred a more subtle approach, and Rhiannon always seemed to have a habit of running in with guns blazing.

"Why, yes," said the reverend. "She was for a while."

"I'm afraid the nature of our visit is very similar to my last one," said Alun, after clearing his throat to break the awkwardness.

"Oh, I see." The reverend offered them both a pew, which, after sitting down, had turned out to be the most uncomfortable seat Rhiannon had ever come across. "Yes, I remember now. You were concerned about her disappearance."

"She was last spotted outside your church," Rhiannon declared. She could see him trying to avoid her judgmental stare and enjoyed every minute of it.

"Well, I'm afraid not much has changed on that front," said the reverend. "Unless someone else has seen her since then."

"Nope, just you." She felt another nudge.

Reverend Owen removed his glasses and wiped them against the white cloth adorning his body.

"She was the best organist I ever had," he said. "A real talent. All that horrible business with her husband — it's just awful. Having to read that dreadful story in the newspaper was a huge shock. How someone could ever come up with such an insensitive headline is beyond me."

"Guilty!" Rhiannon said, raising up her hand.

Alun could see the confusion on the vicar's face and decided to interject: "Did you already know they were married?"

"Why, yes," said the reverend. "I was the person who conducted the ceremony."

The silence that followed was so long, it caused him to lose his stable composure.

"They didn't want anybody to know, of course," he continued. "It was just the three of us." His mind reflected back on their intimate moment together. "She was so happy that day. I haven't seen such love in a person's face in all my life — and I've done a lot of weddings in my time."

"Do you think that love was reciprocated?" asked Rhiannon.

The reverend shook his head. "It's so hard to tell what another person is really feeling."

"That sounds like a no."

"Uh, well — I wouldn't go that far."

"But you do have some doubt."

"What my friend is trying to get at, Reverend," Alun interrupted, "is whether you think Dai might have married the woman for her wealth?"

"What a dreadful thing to suggest," he said.

"I think it's very much the general consensus among her relatives," said Rhiannon. "You have to admit, it was a little out of the blue."

"Not if you'd have known them like I did."

The reverend had been trained to have the patience of a saint, but his patience was now being thoroughly tested. He knelt down on one of the cushions beneath his pew.

"I've known Dai longer than I've known Mari," he said. "The man was a regular member of this congregation. It was him who introduced me to Mari in the first place."

"Rumour has it that he was a bit of a ladies man," said Rhiannon.

"Yes, well... I got that impression myself, actually. He often had a new woman on his arm. You could say he certainly wore his heart on his sleeve."

"Or down his trousers, more like!" Rhiannon saw that her remark had not gone down well with Alun.

"But Mari was different?" he asked.

"Oh, yes. Very much so. He even persuaded her to get baptised for the first time. That was a first! He hadn't done that with any of the other women."

Rhiannon rolled her eyes. "Lucky her."

The vicar climbed to his feet and gazed towards the stone baptismal font.

"She took to our Christian ways like a duck to water."

"As opposed to her *other* ways?"

Rhiannon's question sent out a shockwave. She knew there was more to this story. She could see it in his horrified face.

"I don't know what you mean," he said, his complexion growing pale.

"Oh, I think you do, *Tom*," she said with a stern frown. "Are you familiar with the word *Diafa*?"

She thought the man's face was about to explode. "How dare you mention such a word," he whispered. The vicar stormed off towards the altar. "I think it's time you both left. I need to prepare for my service."

Rhiannon followed after him, much to Alun's protest.

"You seem to act like there's some truth in it," she called. "I thought all that black magic and satanic ritual stuff was supposed to be made-up."

He kept his back to her as she approached.

"Anything that worships a horned God is far from *made-up*," he said, turning around to face her. He had become flustered and hot to the point his forehead was now red-raw. "The Diafa is a form of pagan religion that was believed to have died out a long time ago. Its name is another word for Satan... or Lucifer."

"You seem quite knowledgeable for a man who specialises in the *other guy*," said Rhiannon.

"Mari was quite open about it," he said. "She took it all very seriously. Sacrificed a lot of happiness for it, as her mother did before her. It was Dai who introduced her to a different God — a more rewarding and forgiving one."

A sculpture of Jesus Christ hung directly above him. He looked up at it and smiled.

"Her love for Dai was so strong," he continued. "He convinced the woman that her lottery win was an act of God — a small miracle. Who knows, perhaps it was. Either way, Mari believed it."

"So she effectively converted religions?" asked Alun.

The vicar smiled. "It was the proudest moment of my career, baptising that woman. Here was a person with so much darkness inside of her, so much hate. It felt like shining a light on the devil himself. Good had literally prevailed over evil, and it was happening in *my* church."

"Why do I sense a 'but' coming?" Rhiannon muttered.

The Reverend Owen lowered his head in dismay.

"She was genuinely a changed woman," he said. "It's as if she had been craving it her entire life: a chance to escape the darkness. She had found a fresh start, a chance to become an active member of the community. She became involved in charity events and bible readings. Many thought she should have run for town councillor, something I know she'd been considering."

"So where did it all go wrong?" asked Alun.

The vicar stared into the flame rising up from one of the candles. Its burning glow sent him into a trance for a moment.

"She got cancer." His cold words echoed throughout the enormous ceilings. "A cruel twist of fate for anyone, of course.

But Mari saw it as more than a stroke of bad luck. She became obsessed it was the Diafa punishing her. She said she could hear her ancestor screaming at her late at night."

Rhiannon nodded. "Branwen..."

The very mention of the witch's name caused the vicar to gasp. "How do you —"

"I read a lot of Welsh fairy tales," she assured.

A confused Reverend Owen tried to ignore the comment and return to his thoughts on Mari. "The cancer was just the start. As time went on, there were even more problems. A month after she was diagnosed with her illness, a fire broke out in her shop — not a huge one, but it was enough for Mari to see it as another sign. Next came the greatest pain of all..."

His two audience members listened with concerned faces.

"I was closing up the church for the day," he continued. "She came bursting in, her eyes flooded with tears. I had never seen her so distressed."

Alun swallowed a large gulp, and he waited for the man to elaborate.

"She told me she had caught Dai with another woman," said the reverend.

"Surprise, surprise," Rhiannon muttered.

"That man had been her rock from the moment they began their new relationship. Like you say, Dai had quite the wild heart."

Rhiannon scoffed. "If that's what you want to call it."

"We all thought he was a changed man." The vicar shook his head in despair. "He broke that woman's heart beyond repair."

Alun listened with great sympathy. He knew what a broken heart felt like and wouldn't wish it upon anyone (even a satanic-worshipping witch).

Rhiannon couldn't help but be enamoured by the man's eloquence. She could certainly tell that he preached for a living, and his ability to deliver a good story was second to none. It was a shame he would not be able to give them an ending.

"Is that when you last saw her?" Alun asked.

The vicar shook his head. "No, she visited me again a few days later. Her mood was a lot less erratic that time. She'd come to tell me she had made her decision: she was going to abandon her Christian faith." He seemed on the verge of tears by this point, and his glasses were steaming to the point they concealed his eyes. "I pleaded with her, of course. But she said she didn't have a choice. The Diafa would never leave her until the day she died. I saw the pain in her eyes — the darkness."

"Forgive me, Fath — I mean, Tom," Rhiannon said. "But you don't really believe in all that dark magic stuff, do you?"

The silence that followed made Alun want to cast his own spell and vanish in a puff of smoke.

"The most important thing is that Mari believed it," said the reverend. "And she did, with all of her heart. You can't hide your true beliefs, even if they might seem extreme to others."

"So she just said goodbye and that was it?" asked Rhiannon.

"She told me about her grandson. Unlike her own children, he had taken a keen interest in this so-called Diafa."

"You mean, Jack?" Alun asked.

"It had all started with a few dark rituals, then it progressed into something of an obsession with the old literature — if there even is such a thing. She had seen his desire to continue this dark faith so that it can live on, as *she* had done with her own grandmother. She mentioned about wanting to help save him."

Alun and Rhiannon looked at each other. They said nothing, but it was clear that the same thoughts were circling in both of their heads.

"Did she say anything else about Jack?" the journalist asked. "Anything at all?"

The reverend tried to think. "Not really. She was not herself at all that day. Her voice was cold and hollow. She'd just mentioned about going to see him later that day."

His last sentence caused a surge of panic.

"She did *what*?" Rhiannon asked.

The vicar considered what he had just said and began to look worried. "My account of the whole thing was all reported to the police, I can assure you."

"Are you sure?" she asked again. "Are you sure you mentioned the part about going to visit Jack?"

The reverend scratched his head and began to stutter. "Uh, w-well, I *must* have. They seemed quite interested in her visit here to the church, so I told them all about that. But as for the part about Jack... Gosh, I can't be sure. If I'm being quite honest, it didn't seem that important at the time. He seems like a nice enough lad. I didn't want to cause him any unnecessary trouble or anything. He was already quite upset at his grandmother's disappearance."

His two guests began swiftly grabbing their belongings. He didn't need to say anything further. The doubt in his voice was enough.

"Uh, hello!" a voice cried out.

All three of them turned around to see a frail man with a nervous face and quivering hands. He was standing in the open doorway. "I'm here to play the organ!"

CHAPTER 28

Barry Doyle was admiring his giant window of properties like a proud father admiring his children. Whether he was posting one up or taking one down, the process of updating his precious advertising board had become something of a ritual.

That week he had sold a property that had been plaguing him for quite some time. The old farmhouse at the edge of the lake had finally attracted a new owner, and he would never have to see that ugly, old building ever again.

He took one last look at the extortionate price tag and licked his lips with anticipation. Just as he was about to pull down the advertisement, he caught a glimpse of a face on the other side of the window. The woman glared at him, and the very sight of her made him crave the taste of a large glass of Cabernet Sauvignon.

“Like a dog with a bone,” Barry muttered to himself, as he headed to his front door and swung it open.

Rhiannon was standing on the pavement outside with Alun by her side. They seemed to be catching their breath and were relieved to have found the man so quickly (normally, for Barry Doyle, the opposite was true).

"We meet again, my love," Barry said to her, his moustache twitching with excitement.

"Where's Jack?" Rhiannon asked.

The property manager didn't know whether to laugh or be offended.

"What on earth do you want with *him*?" asked Barry.

"We need to speak with him — urgently," said Alun.

Barry looked the accountant up and down, as if sizing him up. There was nothing to be concerned about there, he had decided.

"Found yourself a little boyfriend, have you?" he asked. "Could have done worse, I suppose. At least he can count."

Rhiannon stepped forward and grabbed him by the tie. "Listen here, you pathetic little man," she hissed. "Your son is nowhere to be found and there's a psychopathic killer on the loose. Either you know where he is or you don't."

The man coughed and sputtered as she began pulling on his neck tie, until his face changed colour.

Alun tried to hold her back. "He can't talk if he can't breathe," he said.

Rhiannon sighed and let him go.

Barry yanked off the tie and began gasping for air. He looked over at Alun in disgust.

"Good job you've got *her* to fight your battles," he said. After taking a moment to recover from the unexpected strangling, he was soon back to his smarmy, old self. "My son is *always* nowhere to be found. He disappeared for a whole weekend recently."

"Has he been acting strange?" asked Rhiannon.

"He's always strange," Barry snapped. "Takes after his mother. Glad I got shot of her all those years ago. Never understood the boy from the very beginning. The fact he can push trolleys is a miracle."

"And what about taking after *your* mother?"

"Well, uh, yes. I suppose *she* was barking mad too."

"Is Jack working today?" asked Alun.

"How the hell should I know?" Barry roared. "The boy comes and goes as he pleases — always has. I tell you one thing: he won't be living rent-free for much longer if I have my way. He can start learning to pay his own bills."

He stood tall and straightened his creased shirt.

"Now, if you don't mind," he said. "I've got work to do!"

Before he could return to the sanctuary of his office, Barry was pulled aside by one of his estate agents.

"There's some people here to see you, Barry," said the frantic young man.

Barry wanted to throw him through the nearest window. He was in no mood to waste more time.

"What are you on about, lad?" he spat out.

The estate agent was so worked up he didn't even notice the shower of saliva spreading out across his face.

Beads of sweat began bursting out of Barry's large pores, as he was struck by the appearance of three police cars outside his business.

"Barry Doyle!" announced a younger man in plain clothes. He waved his identification and was accompanied by two other policemen. "I'm arresting you for the murder of Dai Jones."

Barry was so shell-shocked, he could barely hear the man reading him his rights. The words had become muffled in his mind, whilst his hands were handcuffed by a familiar figure.

Dressed in full uniform with a grave expression on his face, was Mel. He looked over at Alun and Rhiannon, who were both gobsmacked at the scene now taking place.

"This is absurd!" Barry cried, his cheap shoes dragging along the pavement on their way to the back of the nearest police car.

A young man in a fluorescent work jacket was standing

behind the crowd of spectators. He watched his father's arrest with a face that was devoid of all emotion.

Mel shut the car door and took a short detour past his friend.

"The steak knife came back from forensics," he whispered to him. "His prints were an exact match."

The group of onlookers all gossiped amongst themselves, as the police officers jumped into their cars and drove away.

The vehicles had cleared the street as quickly as they had arrived, and the groups of nosey locals quickly lost interest. As the crowds dispersed, Rhiannon looked over towards the man in the bright coat. Her heart jumped. Jack saw her staring and went running off in the opposite direction. She gave Alun a nudge.

"Come on," she said and began tugging him along the street until he cooperated.

Jack went sprinting down a side street, until it brought him to the supermarket car park where he spent most of his days lugging trolleys.

Over near the main building was a small shelter with a mountain bike chained to the pole. The young man was soon wrestling with the lock and yanking at the chain in a fit of panic.

Little did he know it, but a blue Beetle car was slowly poking its bonnet around the corner over in the far distance. Inside the vehicle, two people sat watching his every move.

"Where do you think he's going?" asked Alun.

"I don't know," said Rhiannon. "But we'd probably better find out."

Jack's mountain bike went speeding out of the car park and into the nearest alley.

"Go!" Rhiannon cried. Her frazzled driver fired up the engine with an urgency he had never previously displayed. "He's heading towards the high street!"

The blue Beetle screeched its way into an awkward u-turn. Alun could hear his car wailing out in protest; the Beetle was not used to being rushed, and it certainly had never tried to break the thirty-mile-per-hour speed limit before. The very notion of going faster than the law recommended made the accountant sick to his stomach.

When they came back out into the high street, Jack was nowhere to be seen.

"There he is!"

Rhiannon pointed to the cyclist now speeding off into the far distance. Her driver placed his foot down hard against the accelerator and received a roar of protest from the car.

Jack Doyle's mountain bike went flying along the pavement, its pedals rotating like a pair of angry pistons. Once he had passed the last row of shops, he joined up with the main road leading out towards Pengower Lake. Cars whizzed past him, as he crossed over to the narrow dirt track running along the water's edge.

Crawling along, less than a hundred metres behind him, was the blue Beetle. Its driver was keeping his speed way below the recommended limit and had caused a long line of angry motorists in the process.

"I can't keep going at this speed," he said to his passenger. "This is a main road."

"Any faster and he'll see us," Rhiannon snapped. "You maintain your speed, and I'll keep an eye on Jack."

Alun cringed at the sound of furious car horns wailing behind him. What had started off as a hot pursuit had descended into the slowest car chase known to man.

Jack continued his journey along the lake's edge, his thick tyres skidding through the grass and mud. He had made the same excursion hundreds of times before but never with such urgency and speed. His lungs burned and his heart raced.

The blue Beetle kept its distance — not that their target was ever going to look back.

Rhiannon kept her eyes on the bright red hoodie bobbing about in the distance. She was glad he hadn't worn green or brown that day, as the surrounding trees and bushes would have camouflaged him instantly. A couple of miles later, and she had already grown impatient.

"Where on earth is he going?"

Alun glanced over at the lake to see that they were nearing a familiar section.

"He's heading to Devil's Cove," he said.

Rhiannon watched her red dot slip away into the green and brown wilderness of the surrounding woodland.

"Are you sure?" she asked, adamant that they were losing him.

Her driver nodded and flicked down his signalling lever. They turned off into a small layby at the side of the main road, and the blue Beetle rolled its way into a parking spot. The sudden absence of engine noise made for an eerie moment of silence.

"What are you doing?" Rhiannon watched Alun open up his door. "You're not seriously thinking about *walking*?!"

"It's not that far," said Alun. "It's the only way to get down there."

He knew the route to Devil's Cove like the back of his hand. A part of him was curious to see if the same picnic table that he and his father used to eat their fish on was still around. Sadly, the fish on offer was usually of the battered variety and never anything they had actually caught. Fortunately, the local fish and chip shop were very good at what they did.

Rhiannon made a reluctant climb into the fresh air. Her footwear was far from appropriate for the muddy terrain to come, but, if her partner in crime was indeed correct, she didn't have much of a choice.

Alun saw the reluctance in her face. It was the same feeling that plagued the bottom of his own stomach.

"Maybe this isn't such a good idea," he said. "We should really be leaving this to the police."

His words of concern reignited the woman's fire. The journalist inside of her was used to drowning out those more inconvenient emotions, particularly the gut-jittering ones, like worry or fear. "You think I'm going to let the police take all the credit?"

"I was thinking more about backup."

"He's just a kid, Alun." She marched off towards the woods (not that she knew where she was going). "Are you coming or what?"

The accountant sighed. He knew it was useless to resist.

They entered the wall of trees like two weary explorers about to enter the dragon's cave. Something told them that there was a secret lurking deep inside, and it was up to them to uncover the truth.

The ground was still wet from the morning shower, and Rhiannon had started to regret the decision of treating herself to that new pair of boots. Her footwear was very much style over comfort and any aesthetically pleasing qualities were now caked in a layer of thick mud.

Alun's situation was not much better, having opted to wear his favourite pair of leather shoes.

"I thought you said it wasn't far," Rhiannon said, after what had felt like a mile of steady walking.

Apart from the sound of squelching footsteps, the woodland possessed a tranquil ambience that Alun was finding rather peaceful. Had he not been chasing down the son of a man who had just been arrested for murder, he would have found the whole experience quite pleasant.

As they traipsed their way through the leaves and dirt, the accountant and the journalist said very little to each other, and it wasn't until the sound of a hollow *clang* that one of them decided to speak.

"What was that?" asked Rhiannon. She turned around to see that Alun had stopped in his tracks and was now typing away on his mobile phone. "Who are you messaging?"

"That extra backup I was telling you about," said Alun.

Rhiannon gave him a confused frown, and then she remembered about a certain local police officer.

"Oh, please," she groaned. "Anyone but *him*."

"It's just a precaution."

He looked down at the one bar of signal and fired off his text message.

"Great," Rhiannon muttered. "I feel much better with Captain Moron on our side. Talk about calling in the heavy artillery." She saw him peering off into the distance before readjusting his glasses. "What now?"

"Is that what I think it is?"

They both kept walking, until the large, brown shape became clearer with each step.

"Weird spot to go camping," said Rhiannon.

Alun grabbed her by the shoulders and pulled her behind the nearest tree. She was just about to protest, when a red figure emerged from the tent.

The young man paused. He could have sworn he heard rustling, but there was not a soul in sight.

Jack Doyle lifted up a shovel in one hand and a dagger in the other. It was time to start digging.

CHAPTER 29

The shoreline of Devil's Cove had a visitor. Out of the surrounding trees came a red figure, and he knew this area well.

A large rock overlooked the narrow fringe of stones resting at the water's edge. Known by many as the *Witch's Tombstone*, the great boulder had witnessed a number of strange events over the centuries. That day, it was about to witness yet another.

Jack Doyle made his way behind the ancient stone and began to dig. The gravel churned against the edge of his shovel, and he focused his mind on the list of remaining tasks. Little did the young man know, but at that very moment, he was not alone at Devil's Cove.

Lurking amongst the overgrowth were two pairs of prying eyes. They were far enough away that his digging had been muted into a series of faint crunches.

"What's he looking for?" whispered a voice.

"Who knows, but I doubt it's buried treasure," whispered another.

Rhiannon felt a sickness in her stomach. Over in the distance were the remains of a recent bonfire. The metallic cylinder pointed upwards towards the sky, like a disused chimney rising up from the ground.

"You don't think —"

Alun shushed her, an action that would normally have got him chastised. He held up a finger to his lips, only to receive a frown in return. The journalist pulled out her phone and relished in the opportunity to take some quick snapshots.

"I really think we should head back to the car now," he said.

Rhiannon was about to respond, when she looked over her shoulder to see that he was already walking away.

"Alright," she hissed. "Just two more seconds." There was just time for one last photograph before she scurried after him through the dirt.

Alun's pace was a lot quicker on their return journey, and his mind was a hive of thoughts and emotions. Rhiannon trailed behind him in a sulk. "I still think we should have waited to see what he's digging up,"

"Whatever's buried behind that rock, I'd rather not know," he snapped. "The man has a knife, Rhiannon. This is getting ridiculous."

He kept marching and longed for the sight of his blue Beetle. As far as he was concerned, this had all been a terrible idea. He wanted to be back exactly where he belonged: tucked behind his desk whilst he reconciled some ledgers. The journalist might have found his own line of work dull but at least it came with a lower risk of mortality.

"But we've come so far," she cried. "Are you honestly willing to walk away without knowing?"

"A man has been arrested," he called back. "The police have made their enquiries, and the real murderer has been apprehended."

He felt a hand grabbing him by the shoulder. It squeezed

tight and twisted his entire body around. All of a sudden, he was face-to-face with those disappointed eyes.

"You don't really believe it was Barry Doyle, do you?" Rhiannon asked.

Alun's struggle to look her in the eye was the only sign she needed. They were about to continue on their way, when Rhiannon noticed a peculiar shape that was now blocking their path.

A few feet away was the large tent they had passed only a few moments ago. It was still there, all quiet and alone, in the middle of the woods.

The journalist grabbed the accountant's hand and dragged him towards it.

"Rhiannon, no!" Alun pleaded.

"Just one quick look and we can go straight home."

Alun took a deep breath. Her deal filled him with both relief and dread. "*Quickly*," he said.

She gave him a playful smile.

They approached the tent with the caution of a safari hunter. The lowering of the zip made a loud buzzing noise that reminded Alun of many childhood camping holidays in Aberdaron.

Rhiannon opened up the canvas door and slipped herself inside. Using the torchlight on her phone, she scanned the entire space, hoping for at least a nugget of something useful.

What she found instead was something far beyond her wildest expectations, something that rocked her blood pressure and chilled her to the core.

Gleaming in the blue light was the outline of a human hand. Wrapped around one of the wrinkled fingers was a large ring that Rhiannon had seen before; it had featured in many of the photographs over at number eighty-five, Pandy Lane. It was distinctive enough that she had made a mental note and still deemed it to be the ugliest piece of jewellery she had ever seen. It was certainly not something that she would be gracing her own finger with — no matter how old she became.

The hand was not alone, and the blue light worked its way up the entire arm. The shape of an entire body was very clearly defined, and sitting at the top was a head of white hair.

Rhiannon let out a winded gasp and almost dropped her phone when she darted back towards the outside world. She came crawling out of the tent in a delirious frenzy, her body shaking from head to toe in a state of shock.

"Alun!" she cried. "Alun — *it's her*!"

She went running into his arms, and the accountant gave her a grave stare. He held her tight whilst she sobbed against his chest.

It wasn't until Rhiannon pulled her face away that she realised Alun was distracted by another presence behind her. She turned around to find Jack standing there, only a few feet away. The old, Victorian dagger was clutched in his quivering hand, and he appeared to be more nervous than they were.

"I knew you were following me," he said. "I need you both to leave her in peace."

It was hard to argue with someone holding such a sharp looking blade. It had a strange beauty in its exotic design, despite its deadliness.

"Jack..." Alun said, his voice as gentle as it could be. "Jack, what have you done?"

The young man looked at him with a horrified face, the kind a scolded child would give a parent. He had always looked up to the accountant and hated to see such a disappointed reaction.

"I need your help, Alun," he said with a whimper. "You're the only one I can trust."

The two terrified people opposite him looked at each other.

"Help with what, Jack?" Rhiannon asked. The dagger in the young man's hand was still a grave concern.

"My burial."

The additional voice made both adults leap with fright. Standing there, outside the tent door, was the last person they had ever expected to see. The dishevelled woman gazed at them with a face so pale that Alun was adamant they were witnessing a ghost.

"Mari?" he asked.

"Hello, Alun," said the woman.

Although her demeanour was as calm as the accountant had remembered, her appearance was world's apart from the smartly-dressed client that had frequented his office.

"You're supposed to be resting, Nan," said Jack.

Mari Doyle stretched out her arms and wiped her tired eyes.

"There'll be plenty of time for that soon enough," she said with a smile.

Rhiannon observed the state of her clothes. They were worn and muddy but perfectly suited to the great outdoors. This was a person who seemed to feel quite at home amongst the elements of nature.

"How long have you been out here?" she asked.

"Oh, I couldn't say," replied Mari. "That's half the beauty living out here: no calendars, no phones, no sense of time."

Alun struggled to speak. He was still coming to terms with what had felt like a miraculous resurrection. "But we thought... we thought you were —"

"Oh, I'm sure you probably did," said Mari. "You know, it's quite a rewarding experience getting to walk around whilst the world thinks you're dead. There aren't many people who get to do that."

A drop of water splashed against her nose. She looked up through the treetops to see a sky of black clouds.

"We should probably get down there, Jack," she said to her grandson. "Before it rains."

"Down where?" Rhiannon asked. "I think we should probably be getting you looked over by a doctor."

Mari let out a husky laugh which caused her to cough. "There's nothing they can do for me now. They've had their chance."

She began walking in the direction of the lake.

"We can't just leave you out here," Rhiannon protested. "Jack — tell her!" She turned to the young man who gave her nothing but a cold stare. "And what's that for?"

Jack lifted up the dagger, almost forgetting that it was still in his hand.

"Give me the knife, Jack," said Alun, gently raising his hand and moving towards him.

"Stay back!" Jack screeched and began slicing the air. The accountant took the hint and darted backwards to avoid being cut.

"Come along, Jack," echoed Mari's voice. "The Diafa grows angry."

Alun and Rhiannon both looked on, helpless, as Jack followed his grandmother on her walk to Devil's Cove.

Rhiannon turned to her friend. "I've got a horrible feeling about this."

Alun nodded. He also had a bad feeling. "I'm calling the police."

She watched him pull out his phone and wince at the screen: no signal.

"Come on," he said. "If we head back to the main road I'll get a few more bars."

His arm received a fierce tug, as he moved to walk away.

"We can't just leave them," said Rhiannon. "Did you see the

look in that boy's face? There could be a life at stake if we don't do something."

The accountant put his phone away and looked into her pleading eyes. Deep down, he felt the same way. He knew something had to be done. He didn't quite know what, exactly. But he knew he had to try something.

CHAPTER 30

The heavy clouds above Devil's Cove hung low above the darkening water.

Mari Doyle was perched on one of the grass banks overlooking the lake. She had spent a great deal of her life looking out at this picturesque view. It was therefore quite a fitting location to spend her last moments, or so she thought.

Her grandson was busy preparing an elaborate formation of stones in the middle of the small beach. She had taught him well. They had performed a whole host of dark spells in their time, and this next one would be their greatest.

"Don't forget to sprinkle the soil, Jack," she reminded him.

Mari took great pride in her attention to detail. She had studied the dark arts her entire life and could never understand how a person could not take them as seriously as she did. People were quite happy to be baptised in holy water and wear crosses around their necks, but yet they laughed at the thought of curses and spells. Mari had always loathed the way her ancestors were depicted as cackling old hags with pointed hats and flying broomsticks; popular culture had a lot to answer for. It seemed not much had changed since the days of organised witch-hunts and public drownings. Her ancient practices would always be demonised and her Diafa would forever be the monstrous figure in every story.

She felt a sudden presence behind her but did not turn around.

"What's he doing?" asked Rhiannon, who was watching Jack and his mysterious preparations. Alun was standing next to her and was equally as concerned.

"He's forming the gate of *Uffern*," said Mari. "It's a mortal window into the soul of the Diafa."

Her audience of two winced at the sight of Jack slicing his own palm with the edge of the dagger. His handful of blood was scattered across the growing rock formation.

"It takes great sacrifice for us mortals," Mari added.

The cynical journalist decided it was best to humour her: "Really? And what sacrifice is that, exactly?"

Mari took in a large breath of fresh air and felt more alive than she had done in years. "Why, the greatest sacrifice of all." She picked up a handful of dirt and rubbed it against her fingers. "You know, I've always found it amusing how a religious person turns to the sky in their hour of need. I would much rather put my faith in the ground than anything way up there. We are children of the earth, after all."

Alun was struggling to listen. It was like the woman he used to know was dying before his very eyes, and he wanted so desperately to shake her in the hope it would bring her back to life.

"Mari," he said, kneeling down to her level. "We know everything: the cancer, Dai Jones, about the affair... You've been through a lot, we know. But none of this will help."

She grabbed his hand and held it tight.

"Ah, Alun," she said. "You were always a gentle soul. I will miss our talks. But I'm afraid you know a lot less than you might think. Clever people always do."

The woman grunted, as she stood herself up and began making her way down the short bank.

The two companions watched her stumble across the bed of stones until she reached her tired grandson. Rhiannon shivered with frustration and went marching towards them. She cried out over the strong wind: "Your eldest son has just been arrested for the murder of your husband! Do you know that?"

Mari turned around to face her, almost amused. "My son's punishment is inevitable. He tricked his own mother and took away her rightful home. Jack has indeed informed me of his arrest. It will do him the world of good."

"The Diafa has no boundaries!" Jack cried, in the midst of his rituals. "Not even my father!"

Rhiannon could see the man's terror. She moved closer, slipping as she went over the wet stones. "Jack, you don't really believe in all this, do you?"

"She has been sent to test us, Jack," Mari interrupted. "The angry mob comes in various forms. They drowned our beloved Branwen and they will do the same to us."

The younger woman had made it over to where Jack was standing. Her concerned expression made him pause. "Your grandmother is not well, Jack," she said. "She hasn't been for a very long time. We need to get her some help."

Her words ached his confused mind, and he covered his ears. "*Quiet*!!" he screamed. "Leave us to be free!"

Jack slashed the air in her direction. The reminder of his blade caused Rhiannon to step back.

"Alright, alright," she said. "You've made your point." It appeared her efforts were never going to convince either of them, and her sympathy was quickly draining away. She had never suffered fools gladly and wasn't about to start at Devil's

Cove. "You carry on! Don't let me stop your little devil-worshiping party."

Her words struck a nerve with the older woman. For the first time that day, she seemed angry. "You think this is about *worship*? You have this completely the wrong way around, my dear." She walked up to Rhiannon and grabbed her by the forearms. "We are not here to worship the Diafa — we are here to be free of him!"

The journalist was more confused than ever. She felt the woman's grip loosen as a sudden bout of sadness washed over her.

"My family has suffered from his presence for far too long," she continued. "I come from a long line of people who were all plagued by his influence. But all that will end — today. When that dagger passes through my heart, it will not only relieve me of his services, but every Doyle from here on after."

The young woman facing her wanted to gasp. It was now her turn to hold tight, and she grabbed hold of Mari's arms to get her full attention.

"If that dagger passes through your heart," said Rhiannon, "your grandson is going straight to join his father. Do you realise that?"

Mari nodded. "Like I said, sacrifices have to be made."

In that moment, Rhiannon could see in the woman's cold eyes that she might as well have been trying to reason with a nearby tree.

A rumble of thunder caused them both to look up.

"He grows restless," said Mari, and she walked over towards her grandson.

Jack had worked himself into a nervous wreck and his grandmother knew it. She placed a caring hand on his shoulder and took the dagger from him.

"Be strong, my boy. I know you have the strength."

Her instruction fired him up. The young man did his best to pull himself together and began walking her towards the centre of the rocks.

Mari took a handful of gravel and flung it around the spiral of stones. Jack stood opposite her with his eyes closed, and she rubbed the dirt on both of their foreheads.

Alun and Rhiannon were gathered nearby, looking on, helplessly, at this ceremony of death. They watched the woman slice into her own palm with the bronze-handled dagger.

Mari trickled her blood against the ground beneath her feet and began chanting in a deep voice: "Blood of the receiver, blood of the slayer..."

The grandmother and her grandson both placed their bloodied hands together and cried out a series of incomprehensible words from an ancient language.

Mari opened her eyes and smiled. "It's now time for the blood of the witness. Are you ready, Alun?"

She turned to see her two horrified onlookers.

"You can't be serious!" Rhiannon cried.

"It's the whole reason why your friend is here," Mari said to her. Alun could see she was looking directly at him. "Jack saw your little blue car following him the moment he left town. He knew it was you, Alun. We needed a witness, and he saw our opportunity. You're the only other person we can trust."

The accountant looked over at his former employee who was now glaring at him like a lost puppy. That teenager who had come to him for work experience no longer possessed the innocence of his youth. Now, he was corrupted by his dark beliefs.

"If this is really what you both want," he said. "Then you may have my blood."

Rhiannon turned to him as if his head had morphed into a demon. "Have you lost your mind?!"

Mari ignored the woman's protest and took the man by his hand.

"You're a good lad, Alun," she said. "I am not in the least bit surprised."

Before he joined the two people in their Satanic circle, the accountant turned around to acknowledge his friend.

"You can't be serious, Alun!" she cried.

"They're going through with all this regardless of what we say," he said to her. "If this is what Mari really wants..."

Mari began walking him across the slippery bed of stones. "I knew you could always be trusted to do the right thing. You never once tried to take advantage of my great fortune."

Rhiannon watched them, gobsmacked and shaking her head. "God, this town is strange..."

Alun felt a strong breeze, and he took his place in the middle of the Uffern. He was not a spiritual man, but he did have a tendency to be superstitious. His voluntary participation in a demonic ceremony was wreaking havoc on his insides. This impulsive decision was already feeling like a very bad idea indeed.

The two people standing next to him were engrossed in their mysterious mantras. Together, they formed a small triangle. Alun's forehead was marked with dirt and he saw the gleaming dagger coming his way.

Jack lifted up the instrument and handed it to their new witness. Alun gazed at the sharp blade and realised it was a bad time to start feeling squeamish (he hated the sight of blood and had never liked cuts).

The dagger's handle was still warm from its previous user. He took a large gulp and turned his hand so that the palm was fully exposed. Mari and Jack both waited for him to do the honours.

The accountant felt a surge of adrenaline rise up through his tight chest. He took one last breath and did what was necessary.

Alun tilted his shoulder and threw the knife as hard as he could towards the lake.

Jack's cry of shock pierced his ears: "*Nooooo*!"

Alun had never possessed much strength in his right arm and it turned out that not much had changed.

All four of them looked on, as the dagger went flying through the air. It landed much closer to them than the thrower had intended and struck the stretch of shallow water with a gentle *plop*.

Alun saw the betrayal in Jack's face and knew the battle was far from over; it was now or never.

Both men went charging towards the lake, almost simultaneously. What Alun lacked in strength he could make up with speed. He even managed to take the lead, as they splashed through the shallow water. When he reached the area where his flimsy throw had landed, he dived head-first into a leap of faith.

The lake was colder than it first appeared, and the accountant's chest compressed with every second. The water was shallow enough that his hands and knees were scraping against solid ground. He clawed and grabbed in a desperate attempt to retrieve the weapon, only to have a furious Jack land on top of him.

Alun knew that the dagger could only have been inches away, but his window of opportunity was quickly being narrowed.

Jack locked him into a vicious chokehold, and he felt the air in his lungs begin to evacuate. The force of the younger man on top sent his head plummeting into the water. His relentless attacker increased his grip and caused him to choke and gasp, until his body went numb. After one last hopeless fight for his life, Alun felt the world around him begin to go dark.

CHAPTER 31

Alun felt his lungs fill with water. His head was completely submerged, and the pair of hands shoving him down did not plan on releasing anytime soon.

The thought of drowning in such a shallow part of the lake was even more frustrating than not being able to retrieve the dagger. But as his desperate fingers continued to feel nothing but gravel and dirt, he began to accept the fact that the end had indeed arrived. That was, until, something very strange happened.

The force of Jack's strength had suddenly decreased, and his entire body was hauled out of the water by an incredible force. Whether it had been an act of God or a very large buzzard, Alun didn't really care. He took his opportunity and shot up to the surface like a hungry carp. Once his oxygen levels had started to replenish, the truth behind his miraculous escape was soon made clear.

He could see the young man being dragged away in an all too familiar headlock. Jack kicked and screamed but received little sympathy from the determined police officer now glued to his back. Mel was completely in control and knew he had all the leverage he needed to drag him back to shore.

Alun leapt to his feet and began choking up all the excess water that had almost been the death of him. The sight of his friend had been a reassuring one, and it wasn't long before a tired Jack was restrained in a pair of tight handcuffs.

Rhiannon was knee-high in the water herself and could not have been more relieved at the successful rescue. Mari had not moved a muscle and was observing the whole scene with keen interest.

"It's all over, Mari," the police officer said, as he towered above her grandson and tried to catch his breath.

The woman almost seemed amused and waited for the other two to join them before preparing to speak.

"Fancy seeing you down here, Officer," she said with a smile. "What are the odds of that?"

Alun lifted up his mobile phone which was now soaked through.

"Not all modern technology is bad," he said to her.

Mel gave him a wink. "I think we can all go and warm up with a nice mug of hot chocolate down at the station. How does that sound?"

He forced the young prisoner to his feet.

"Can I at least ask you something, Mari?" Rhiannon asked. She still had so many burning questions, and her mind was still struggling to connect the pieces. "Those two murders — stabbing someone with a dagger and battering a young man — I mean, you can barely walk. How did you do it?"

The police officer looked perplexed.

"What do you mean?" he asked. "The murderer's been caught. I arrested Barry Doyle myself."

Rhiannon moved closer towards the elderly woman.

"But it wasn't Barry, was it, Mari?" she asked. "I had dinner with that man. He could barely chop his way through a piece of steak without getting out of breath. There's no way he was capable of stabbing a man in a butcher shop."

"There are many ways to take a person's life," said Mari.

"Forgive me," said Rhiannon, "but I think we're dealing with a lot more than just *curses* here."

Mari smiled. She clearly knew a lot more than anyone standing on that shoreline did. If knowledge was power, she had now become an all-powerful sorceress.

"You'd be surprised," she said. "I know one curse that's worked pretty well for me in the past. I'm sure Tony would more than agree."

"Your first husband?" Alun asked.

Mari nodded, and her hardened face began to loosen.

"I loved that man since we were in school together. He'd promised me the world, he did." Mari reflected on her string of painful memories. They still cut deep, even after all these years. "We never had any money back then. Didn't even have running water. Tony always hated not having any money. But I didn't care. As long as we had each other. Then, one day, I wrote him out a business plan. I told him we could grow our own flowers and sell them down the market. I thought it would make him happy. Instead, it made him worse. That's when he told me he didn't love me anymore." A small tear worked its way out from the edge of her tired eyelid. It trickled down her cheek and created a small trail through the layer of dirt. "I thought the whole world was going to end. I felt so alone. A big part of me died that day." Her sadness turned to anger. "I remember finding the jar. I'd locked the bathroom door, and his hair was still all over the floor tiles. He'd had a haircut. And the hair was all I needed. I placed every clump inside that big jar and did all the necessary steps. He even heard me chanting and started to laugh. He'd been drinking heavily that night. The next morning,

I found him. He was lying there — dead — at the bottom of the treehouse. The police said he'd taken an awkward fall after too much to drink. But I knew the truth. It's not like you can arrest someone for a curse — not these days, anyway. I felt terrible at first. Then I realised the truth: I was not alone. And I never would be again. The Diafa had answered my cry for help. From then on, I would spend the rest of my life in his service. Well, for the most part."

The police officer listened in complete bewilderment. "You honestly think you killed your husband with a curse?" he asked. "You people really *are* mental."

"By the time I met Dai Jones, I had become weak again," she continued. "What I mistook for another chance at love was nothing more than a test of loyalty. I failed, miserably. I had become seduced by the idea of *belonging*. All of a sudden, I had the opportunity to become part of a community. It was all I ever wanted: the church, my business, friends... But it was all just a lie."

"But it wasn't, Mari!" Rhiannon cried. She held the woman by her shoulders and forced her to listen. "Dai may have let you down, but everything else was all real. And it was all real because of *you* — not because of some black magic!"

Mari's face darkened. She was in no mood to listen, and she had already made up her mind. "You sound as naive as I was, dear. I got what I deserved." Her cold hands tapped Rhiannon's own shoulders in a gesture of appreciation. "But to answer your question: it was not me who planted that knife in my second husband's back. And as for the battering part, well... I'm afraid I have no idea what you're talking about."

The journalist's trembling hands flopped to her side in disappointment. The woman spoke with such conviction in her voice that only a terminally ill person could. She had no reason to lie.

Mari turned away from the group of people and looked out across the lake.

"Dai Jones was no different to the rest of my rotten family," she said. "All he ever wanted was my money. I wanted him to suffer so badly, with every ounce of my being. I was as angry as I had been in my youth. But a curse is like calling in a favour — there are only so many you can make. I have been deep in the Diafa's pocket for most of my life, and I wasn't prepared to go any deeper. Fortunately, I didn't have to."

The small group of listeners sensed a revelation coming, or, at least, the conclusion they had all been waiting for. Their patience was about to be rewarded.

Mari continued to look off into the distance whilst peering inwards towards the secrets of the past. "You know, it's incredible how the solution to all your problems can present itself in the most unlikely of places — even in your lowest moment. That time, my moment came whilst I was walking along the aqueduct."

Alun froze. He had heard mention of the aqueduct very recently.

"The Diafa has no boundaries," Mari continued. "He can find his way into any one of our souls. The man I found sitting on the aqueduct that day was practically inviting him in."

She turned around with a wicked smile.

"Isn't that right, Officer Jones?"

All eyes now turned to the surprised police sergeant.

"I don't know what she's talking about," said Mel "The woman's raving mad, remember!"

"Oh, come now," Mari insisted. "You were about ready to plunge your way into the pit of eternal darkness when I came across *you*. You were a man of desperation. And the Diafa loves *desperation*."

"Of course," Rhiannon muttered. "Jones... It all makes sense now."

Alun jolted his head to look at her. "*Does it*?"

The journalist appeared to be struck by her own, unique epiphany. Whatever it was, the accountant hadn't shared it.

"David Wyn Jones..." she muttered, again. "That's what it had said on the will."

"You *read the will*?"

Alun was more shocked at her sudden admission than anything he had heard so far that day (which was really saying something). Up until that point, the two partners in crime had shared everything.

Rhiannon saw the pain in her friend's face and turned to plead with him: "I had to find out, Alun." She had never seen him so furious.

"You told me someone had broken into the solicitor's office!" he roared. "That was *you*?"

"I wasn't going to steal anything," she assured. "I just knew the answer we needed was written on that bit of paper — or at least, I hoped it would be. So I thought it was worth the risk."

He looked at her as if she had pulled off a mask. "Do you know how serious that is?"

"I'm a journalist, Alun. I've done a lot worse than that — believe me. Sometimes you have to take a chance to get the full story."

Her tone was determined but the guilt had already flooded her nerves. She hated the way he was now looking at her.

"You lied to my face..." Alun said.

"Because I knew you would act like this!" Rhiannon snapped. "Plus I needed *some* bit of news to help get you away from that godawful date!"

They both paused, remembering, all of a sudden, that their private argument was actually being witnessed by three other individuals. A wounded Alun couldn't bear to look at her, and she stepped away from him to continue her theory.

"The name I found on the will just didn't make any sense," she said. "There must be hundreds of Jones' in this county alone, and so I assumed the person was a relative of Dai's." The reporter turned to the police officer, who had become very quiet by this stage. "Is Mel actually your real name?"

"No," Alun interrupted. He had decided to speak on the man's behalf, for he already knew the answer. "Mel is a nick-name his mam gave him. It's also the Welsh word for honey. He has the exact, same name as his father."

Rhiannon nodded. Again, it all made sense to her now. "David Wyn Jones..."

Mel was lost for words. Mari continued to stare at him, which made the man even more uncomfortable than he already was.

"I'm a woman of my word," she said. "That afternoon, up on the aqueduct, I gave this man a proposition. It was something that was going to solve both of our problems."

Alun felt his entire world spinning out of control. The perception of his childhood friend was quickly unravelling before his very eyes. He remembered about the gambling: that old, favourite pastime of his. "Is this true, Mel?" he asked.

The police officer said nothing and began staring at the ground, like a guilty sheep dog beside an empty plate of food. He tried not to listen, as if the woman had opened up a whole box of painful memories. That dark day on the aqueduct, that moment where he had stood on the brink of life and death, was still very raw. He didn't need to be reminded.

"I offered him the opportunity to inherit all of my fortune," said Mari. "All in exchange for something in return. If the man was willing to take his own life, what difference did taking another person's make? I'd already sacrificed one husband. One more couldn't hurt. If the man on the aqueduct was willing to accept my offer, he wouldn't need to worry about money for the rest of his life."

Alun thought about the debt his old friend had mentioned only a few days before. He had indeed been driven to the edge of his sanity. The accountant had seen, on many occasions, the sheer power that a person's finances had over them. He had also seen it destroy people.

Mari moved closer towards Mel's personal space. "I held up my end of the bargain," she said. "The will was changed that very same day."

"Then you disappeared..." Mel muttered through tightened teeth.

"On that note, why exactly *did* you go into hiding?" Rhiannon asked her.

"It was the only way to ensure my new friend followed through. I couldn't risk him choosing to take the life of a frail old woman over a butcher. It would have been a much easier task knocking me out of the picture." She paused and let out a wicked smirk."Then there was still the matter of punishing that ungrateful son of mine. I had suggested pinning the death of the butcher on Barry to teach him a lesson. I didn't care how, but I knew Sergeant Jones would figure something out. When I heard later about the steak knife... that was very clever, especially for you, Officer. Barry does love his Italian. I knew that glutinous eating habit of his would become his downfall."

She was now standing only inches away from the police officer's quivering face. "I miss our little phone calls, don't you? I used to check in on you every day."

"You kept messing with my head, you mean," snapped Mel, pointing to his large forehead. The resentment was clear. There was no doubt that these two very different people shared a history. "You're a manipulative psychopath!"

His composure had broken, and she was ready to take full advantage.

"I was only helping to usher out what was already there," said Mari. "A part of you that had been lying dormant for all these years: the *real* Mel Jones." She turned back to the two onlookers. "All I had to do was remind him how easy it was to have that will changed. It took time for him to come around, I'll give him that. But, eventually, the temptation worked its charm, and the deed was done."

Alun felt the nausea slowly creeping in. His friend had always been ruthless in his pursuits, but never could he have ever imagined the extreme lengths that were being described here. Having said that, he had been wrong about people before (his failed relationship with Megan sprang to mind).

"Please tell me you didn't go through with it," Alun pleaded.

The police officer saw him staring. They had been like brothers. The look of judgement was the same one he had feared coming from his own family had they known the truth. The shame was drowned out by the need to justify his actions — the need for survival.

"I had to do it, Alun," said Mel. "This was the chance of a lifetime. They don't come round very often and I should know. It was like..."

"Winning the lottery?" Rhiannon couldn't resist.

Mel nodded. The man seemed to be feeling very sorry for himself. "Life has dealt me some pretty harsh cards over the years. When else do you get the chance to inherit eighteen million?"

"Glad to know everyone's got their price," Rhiannon muttered.

Her comment was just loud enough for everyone to hear, and it brought out a flash of anger from the police officer's face — that same, bitter anger that Mari had described — the same anger that could drive a person to commit the unthinkable.

"It wasn't *you* in that situation though, was it?" Mel snapped. "It's easy to judge when the offer's on someone else's table. A lot of people would have done the same thing in my position."

The journalist raised a cynical eyebrow. "So where does Ruby fit in with all this?"

"She had nothing to do with it!" Mel's guard had been well and truly lowered. He tried to calm himself down, despite the brewing rage. He had always let his bad temper get the better of him. "That boyfriend of hers saw me leaving Dai's shop in the early hours of the morning. He approached me about it at the *Country Show*. I caught him in the games tent. He was alone and dressed in that stupid costume. Turned out him and Ruby used that flower shop for bonking in private. The smug little git tried to blackmail me. Luckily, he hadn't told anyone yet — not even Ruby. I couldn't let him walk away after that."

"So you *battered* him to death?!" Alun cried out, still in disbelief at the first murder.

"I had to do something," said Mel. "Or it was all for nothing. I grabbed the shot put off the floor and that was it. I didn't even have time to think."

His friend struggled to sympathise.

Mari was no longer in the police officer's personal space but close enough to bother him with her gnawing stare. "Like I said. The Diafa is strong in that man. I could see it in his eyes..."

Mel's blood pressure shot up to boiling point. His fists clenched, and he went storming towards her. "Enough with your flaming Diafa rubbish!"

Alun stepped forward to block his path. Mel grinded to halt, like a steaming freight train faced with an unexpected animal on a railway line. He saw the determined look in his old friend's face.

"I think you've done enough," Alun said. He stood his ground as if he were dealing with a misbehaving canine — a large canine that didn't know his own strength. Fortunately, he'd had plenty of practice over the course of their friendship.

A surprised Mel puffed out his chest. "Whose side are you on?"

They stared each other down.

"It's over, Mel," said Alun.

"You need help!" Rhiannon cried. Her abrupt contribution did nothing to diffuse the situation and only poked the bear even more.

"You think I need help?" Mel roared. He pointed towards Mari. "What about this old hagg, over here? She thinks she's a witch for God's sake!"

"There's still time to do the right thing," Alun insisted.

"I'm getting what's owed to me!" The police officer's cries were accompanied by showers of saliva across the accountant's face. "I've earned that money! The minute she pops her cloggs — I'll be a millionaire!"

His words echoed through the nearby forest. The enraged man looked down to see that his enormous hands were now wrapped around Alun's collar. He released his grip in a rare moment of self-awareness and tried to shake away his anger. The look of remorse was followed by a jolt of panic: he needed a friend now more than ever.

"Nobody has to know," he pleaded. His voice had reduced to a pathetic whimper. "Heck, I'll share the money with both of you — if that's what you want." His puppy dog eyes didn't seem to be working on Alun, and, in his great desperation, he turned to look at the journalist. "How about it, Rhiannon?"

"I bet it killed you not knowing where I was," said Mari, her smile taunting him from behind Alun's back. "They might never have found my body at all. That would have been a very cruel twist of fate."

Once again, the red mist descended and Mel's gentle tone melted away. "Shut up! Shut your mouth! You're not messing with my head no more!"

Mari grinned, his frustration fuelling her, as she uttered the greatest blow of them all: "There's still time. Perhaps I'll just leave all my money to the cat sanctuary..."

Alun braced himself at the sight of his friend's eyeballs bulging out of their sockets.

"Out of my way!" Mel roared, pushing past him with a force that would rival a bulldozer.

He went charging towards the elderly woman, only to feel an additional weight pulling him back. Alun was locked on tight and had himself wrapped around the larger man's body. Mel tried to shake him off, but his determined friend refused to let go.

"Get off me!"

The two grown men were soon embroiled in a scuffle that resembled two boys on a school playground. Mel, the larger, stronger and more skilled of the two, wrestled Alun to the ground with the ease of an older brother playing with his sibling.

After dumping the accountant on his back against the wet stones, the police officer made the grave mistake of assuming the fight was over. He moved forward to find that his legs were now tangled in a pair of weedy arms.

Shaky but stubborn, Alun continued to hold on for dear life, knowing full well that the other man could do very little without the use of his lower body (or so he thought). A furious Mel came crawling towards him with a thirst for revenge.

It had been a long time since their last playfight, but the larger man knew how it played out. He grabbed Alun by the throat and began cranking his neck in a vicious headlock. They rolled around in the dirt, like a crocodile mounting his helpless prey. What Mel hadn't anticipated this time around was the absence of any rules, and he felt a sharp set of teeth go chomping into his right arm.

"*Argh*!" he cried, as the teeth dug deep into his tender flesh.

Although he had no choice but to loosen his grip, the gloves were now well and truly off. In a burst of rage, the fuming police officer scrambled on top of him.

Pinned to the floor and helpless to defend himself, Alun braced himself for the worst. Mel let out a sly grin, as he prepared to inflict his own share of pain. The more experienced grappler knew he had his old friend exactly where he wanted. He knew that a ground fight was all about weight and leverage, and he now possessed an abundance of both.

After a few cheap punches and a couple of elbow strikes for good measure, Mel began wrapping his giant hands around the defeated man's neck.

Alun's vision soon began to blur and (having almost drowned only a few moments ago) he knew the end was fast approaching — again.

"Nothing changes, does it, Alun?" Mel growled. "All those brains of yours, and you never did learn to get your weight on top."

His grip became a deadly vice that tightened with every second.

The accountant was just about to lose consciousness, when he heard a loud *clunk!* After the hollow sound of metal upon bone, the body on top of him suddenly went limp. Alun let out a giant gasp, as his lungs filled back up with air.

Standing above them was a victorious Rhiannon, who looked down at the unconscious police officer with sheer disgust. Jack's shovel was clutched in her shaking hands. She took pleasure in the thought that Mel's thick skull would be very sore when he came around again.

Alun breathed a sigh of relief (which wasn't easy with a sixteen-stone man lying on top of you).

Revelling in her heroic moment, Rhiannon took the opportunity to break the awkward silence with an appropriate remark.

"It's about time that big head of his was put to good use!"

CHAPTER 32

Alun sat in his office chair, staring down at a completed tax return. It was the last submission of the quarter and a moment that was normally a cause for great celebration. On this day, however, the luxury box of clotted cream fudge on his desk brought little excitement.

It had been three weeks since the events at the shores of Devil's Cove. The mysterious case of Mari Doyle was officially closed. Shortly after Mel had been rendered unconscious by a misplaced shovel, Mari had gulped down an entire vial of potassium cyanide (right before finishing off her ceremonial ending with an impromptu chant to her tyrannical Diafa).

Mel's dreams of inheriting his vast fortune were dashed by the harsh reality of a lengthy prison sentence. Rhiannon's trusty audio recording app on her phone had been an important component in bringing their murderer to justice. The incriminating conversation between a vengeful witch and a desperate police officer had been captured in glorious stereo sound for all to hear.

Barry Doyle's favourite restaurant had confirmed Mel's table booking on the night of the missing steak knife and would likely be offering him a large discount on his next meal. Along with some leftover fingerprints on a certain shot put, the evidence was quickly mounting up. As hard as testifying against his life-long friend was going to be, even Alun couldn't deny the man's carelessly sloppy trail.

Mel had never been the sharpest tool in the box, and now his series of recent wrongdoings had resulted in the rare use of the infamous *forfeiture rule*. The legal clause would ensure all of Mari's fortune remained safe in the hands of her beloved family members.

The image of Mari's peaceful smile, as she prepared to face her final curtain, would go on to haunt Alun for the rest of his life. The self-proclaimed master of the dark arts had gone out on her own terms and in the same exact location as her famous ancestor.

Almost a month later, and it was business as usual over at *Hughes & Son*. The accountant had returned to his organised ways, and it seemed the world as he knew it was balanced, once again. He had enjoyed his brief holiday to the topsy-turvy land of mysteries and murder, however, it was now time to return to an existence of strict routine and perfectly filed ledgers.

Rhiannon's latest front page article was still lying on Alun's desk. The journalist had garnered a lot of media attention since its timely release, and, with the offer of a handsome book deal in the works, it seemed that her dwindling career was not in such a bad place after all.

It appeared that all was indeed well again in the little town of Pengower. As for the local accountant, he couldn't help but feel a strange feeling of sadness.

He had not spoken to Rhiannon since the release of her lauded article, and he hoped that he wasn't the only person who was feeling this overwhelming sense of post-mystery blues. He had spent so much of the previous month calling her up at all hours of the day, he was struggling to cope with all the extra free time. The feeling of increased longing was starting to make him think that he might actually quite like the young woman. Despite her sharp tongue and rude nature, he had found her company to be strangely invigorating. Her thirst for a story and the ruthlessness of her approach were, at times, a little infectious.

He was not quite sure what all these confused feelings actually meant, but they had proven to be extremely distracting during the climax of his month-end accounting period. As he filed away the last of his client's paperwork, he wondered whether there might have been some *new* story or article that the journalist needed help with — like, perhaps, a suspicious death or an unsolved crime — or, heck, even a run-of-the-mill local puff piece. He was willing to help with anything. There was only one way to find out, of course, and the solution to his conundrum was sitting right in the corner of his desk.

The accountant sat in his ergonomic chair for what must have been a whole hour. He stared at the intimidating device with its large receiver and numbered buttons. The landline telephone appeared to be calling out to him, taunting him for being such a coward. "*Just call her*," it said.

Alun chuckled at the ridiculousness of his own, pathetic trail of thought. He stood up in protest and walked away. He would not be dictated to by an outdated telephone.

Just as he reached the front door of his office, he felt something vibrating away in the pocket of his coat. He pulled out the mobile phone and gazed down at the familiar number flashing away on the small screen. The name above it made him smile. Without a moment's hesitation, he answered the call.

"Hello, this is Alun Hughes," he said, in his best attempt to sound casual.

"Is it really?" asked the voice on the other end of the line.

"Well that's a big surprise. Especially as it's the name and number I just dialled on my phone."

Alun smiled at the sound of that brash yet comforting voice. "I was just about to call you, actually."

"Oh, were you? Well I'm glad it's a good time. There's something really important I need to ask you."

Alun felt the back of his throat run dry. His heart rate began to accelerate. This was it, he thought: *the big question*. After wiping the sweat from his clammy hands, he waited in anticipation. Finally, he would get to know if she felt the same way.

"You can ask me anything," he said.

The pause afterwards was unbearable.

Rhiannon cleared her throat (she had just eaten an oat bar) and proceeded to ask her big question: "Do you believe in ghosts?"

It was now Alun's turn to pause.

"I beg your pardon?"

"You know — *ghosts*. Spectres, ghouls... floating little heads in white sheets. *Ghosts*!"

"Uh, well. I don't really know. I've not seen one, anyway. Why do you ask?"

"How does a weekend trip to Anglesey sound?"

Alun thought about the prospect for a second.

A holiday in Anglesey? Both of them — together — on a remote island? The beginnings of another mystery?

The accountant smiled. It all sounded pretty good to him.

ABOUT THE AUTHOR

We hope you enjoyed this book. If you'd like to read more books in this new series, you can join the P. L. Handley e-mail newsletter and receive all the latest news on future releases.

Subscribe to the e-mailing list by visiting the official P. L. Handley website at: www.plhandley.com

Reviews are extremely important for new authors, so please feel free to leave a short review on the book's Amazon page. Doing so will be a huge support in helping to introduce other new readers to this book.

Stay tuned for Book Two in the Murder Ledger Mysteries:

Death By Numbers

Coming Soon...

Printed in Great Britain
by Amazon

48005442R00159